Portrait of a Phantom

Portrait of a Phantom

*The Story of Robert Johnson's
Lost Photograph*

Zeke Schein
with Poppy Z. Brite

PELICAN PUBLISHING COMPANY
GRETNA 2017

*The word "Pelican" and the depiction of a pelican are
trademarks of Pelican Publishing Company, Inc., and are
registered in the U.S. Patent and Trademark Office.*

Library of Congress Cataloging-in-Publication Data

Names: Schein, Zeke. | Brite, Poppy Z.
Title: Portrait of a phantom : the story of Robert Johnson's lost photograph
   / Zeke Schein with Poppy Z. Brite.
Description: Gretna : Pelican Publishing Company, 2017. | Includes
   bibliographical references.
Identifiers: LCCN 2017011230| ISBN 9781455622450 (hardcover : alk. paper) |
   ISBN 9781455622467 (e-book)
Subjects: LCSH: Johnson, Robert, 1911-1938. | Blues musicians—United States.
Classification: LCC ML420.J735 S34 2017 | DDC 782.421643092—dc23 LC
record available at https://lccn.loc.gov/2017011230

*Photo on page 66 by Zeke Schein; photo on patch by Annie Leibovitz. Photo
on page 144 by Nick Kushner and Zeke Schein. Photo on page 212 by Cathy
Schein. All other photos by Zeke Schein.*

Printed in the United States of America

Published by Pelican Publishing Company, Inc.
1000 Burmaster Street, Gretna, Louisiana 70053

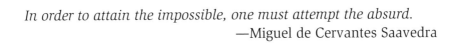

In order to attain the impossible, one must attempt the absurd.
—Miguel de Cervantes Saavedra

Contents

Foreword

In 1961, I was the first rock and roll artist signed to Columbia Records. I hung out with the legendary John Hammond in his office on the second floor of Columbia and he played *Robert Johnson—King of the Delta Blues Singers* for me. John knew I had a flair for the blues—I ate it up, became hung up on Robert Johnson back then.

When I first met Zeke Schein, at the front counter of Matt Umanov Guitars in New York City, we hit it off right away. In the years since then, we have been checking out new guitars, sharing our stories, and playing songs written by Robert Johnson. Zeke plays Robert Johnson riffs like an authentic Mississippi Delta blues surgeon. I shared with him a life-size painting I did, inspired by the two existing photos we had of Robert Johnson. When Zeke found his lost third photo, we were ecstatic. When you love the music and the person behind the music, you want to know more about him. That's what this book is *all* about.

Dion DiMucci

Introduction

Some days I wonder what drives the cosmic bus. Is it chaos interspersed with occasional blind luck, or is there some type of order involved, maybe fate? I don't know, but there are times when one feels a slight shifting of the earth's axis. Things click into place and the stars align, suddenly making sense like the big picture in a game of connect the dots. That's how it felt when I first saw the photo.

Up until that moment, there were only two known photos of Robert Johnson, the King of the Delta Blues, who is said to have sold his soul to the devil at the crossroad in exchange for extraordinary musical talent. Robert Johnson, a guitar virtuoso who influenced Bob Dylan, Eric Clapton, Led Zeppelin, the Rolling Stones, and all who followed in their footsteps. Robert Johnson, whose legend continues to inspire authors, filmmakers, and artists worldwide.

Despite his popularity and the extensive research on his life, Johnson remains a phantom. His history is a house of cards that collapses under close examination, because no matter which way you look at it, there are always a few cards missing.

For fifteen years, I had studied Johnson's music and everything written about him. Then I spotted what I believed to be a lost third photograph of him on an online auction site. If I was right, the photo was priceless in both historical and monetary value.

Call it blind luck or call it fate: when I looked at that photo, I saw the dots of my life begin to connect. Knowledge I had acquired from years of selling records, cameras, and guitars would help guide me. My interactions with well-known musicians, actors, and historians who were Robert Johnson fans now seemed more significant. Each was a dot waiting to be connected. I realized it wouldn't be an easy job, but I also knew that the big picture could be worth the effort. If I bought the photo and connected the dots, I might get a peek inside of the cosmic bus. All I had to do was to pick up the crayon.

Chapter 1

Down by the Highway Side

The crossroad is real. Close your eyes and listen. Robert Johnson is there, down on his knees asking God to save him, alone and afraid as the night approaches. Keep listening and walk side by side with the devil, feel the Hellhound's fiery breath, taste the dust of too many miles spent running. Hear the wind howling through the strings of Johnson's guitar, echoing the heartache of lost love.

Legend has it that Johnson sold his soul to the devil in exchange for supernatural musical talent. His fellow musicians say he could hear a song once and play it back perfectly. He was an outsider, always on the move, traveling under different names—an enigma.

Robert Johnson's music continues to inspire generations far beyond his time. The stories about him are fantastic, but the facts of Johnson's life are bare bones compared to what is known about his contemporaries. Early blues greats Son House, Skip James, Muddy Waters, and Howlin' Wolf all lived to a ripe old age and died of natural causes. Robert Johnson died young, under mysterious circumstances. No one knows exactly what happened, but all accounts agree that he died suddenly and badly.

According to Sonny Boy Williamson II, the jealous husband of a woman Johnson was having an affair with poisoned him at a Mississippi juke joint in August of 1938. Williamson, a harmonica virtuoso, claimed to have witnessed Johnson's murder. He described knocking an open bottle of whiskey out of Johnson's hand when the club owner's wife brought it to him, warning, "Man, don't never take a drink from an open bottle. You don't know what could be in it."

Johnson shook his head and replied, "Man, don't never knock a bottle of whiskey outta my hand." Williamson watched helplessly as Johnson drank from another open bottle that appeared soon after. According to Williamson, Johnson became sick and died in his arms later that night.

As a narrative, the story has a lot going for it: music, murder, sex, revenge, the perfect ending for a blues legend. It circulated through the grapevine and was accepted as history. But there's a problem. Mississippi was a dry state in 1938, and bootleg whiskey was never served in sealed bottles. One must also consider the source. Sonny Boy Williamson II had a reputation for telling far-fetched stories.

Another possible cause for Johnson's death is Marfan syndrome, a connective tissue disorder. Like many people with this condition, Johnson had unusually long, thin fingers and a lazy eye, both visible in his existing photos. People with Marfan syndrome are prone to aortic ruptures and other heart conditions, which frequently kill them in their teens or twenties.

Some historians think that Johnson died of syphilis or pneumonia. Others believe that he was shot or stabbed, based on the testimony of people who claim to have known him. And then there are those who say that Johnson met his early demise because he had made a deal with the devil and the payment was due. Robert Johnson's death certificate simply says "No Doctor."

In his song "Me and the Devil Blues," Johnson sang, "You may bury my body down by the highway side." He followed this line with what might be the most punk rock lyric ever written: "Babe, I don't care where you bury my body when I'm dead and gone." It was a prophetic line, too, as no one knows what became of his body. Even so, burial markers have been placed at three different church cemeteries in his honor. He may not have cared where he was buried, but others did.

The first marker stands in a field of clover beside Mt. Zion Missionary Baptist Church in Morgan City, a North Mississippi wide spot in the road. The pastor of Mt. Zion doesn't know if Johnson is buried at this location but thinks his body might lie nearby in an unmarked grave by the side of the road. The marker, a stubby granite obelisk, is etched with Johnson's famous cigarette photo and a heartfelt epitaph:

> Robert Johnson
> "King of the Delta Blues Singers"
> His music struck a chord that continues to resonate. His blues
> addressed generations he would never know and made poetry of his
> visions and fears.

The second marker is at the Payne Chapel Missionary Baptist Church in another tiny Mississippi town. "Queen" Elizabeth Thomas, who claimed to be a former girlfriend of Robert Johnson, told *Living Blues* magazine that Johnson was buried in Quito, south of Greenwood, near an old tree stump. After the interview with Thomas was published in 1990, an Atlanta band called the Tombstones paid to mark the alleged grave. The simple granite rectangle reads:

> Robert Johnson
> May 8, 1911
> August 16, 1938
> Resting in the Blues

The third marker is at Little Zion Missionary Baptist Church in Greenwood, Mississippi. Eighty-five-year-old Rosie Eskridge of Greenwood told Stephen LaVere that her late husband dug Johnson's grave there, though she never saw the body. According to her, Johnson was buried in a shallow grave under a pecan tree with his head facing a path so he could continue traveling. Because it is within a mile of the location of the Three Forks juke joint, where Johnson was poisoned, this gravesite seems the likeliest of the three. In 2002, Sony placed a memorial marker there. The inscription reads in part:

> When I leave this town
> I'm 'on' bid you fare - farewell
> And when I return again
> You'll have a great long story to tell.

Every year, people come from around the world to visit the gravesites. They leave guitar picks, beer bottles, and other small items in tribute, perhaps hoping to connect in some way with Robert Johnson.

Chapter 2

Hello, Satan

As a teenager in the 1970s, I saw Chuck Berry perform at Monticello Raceway, and that show changed my life. It inspired me to pick up my brother Gary's acoustic guitar. I learned the opening riff to "Johnny B. Goode" and I was hooked. My love for the instrument eventually grew into a career and (some might say) an obsession.

I've worked at one of New York's top guitar shops since 1989. In that time, I've sold guitars to professional musicians like Bob Dylan, Patti Smith, Pete Townshend, and Carlos Santana, as well as famous hobbyists such as Johnny Depp and Richard Gere. At the time of that Chuck Berry show, though, I was just an ignorant kid hungry for new music: Led Zeppelin, Derek and the Dominos, and the Who were my early favorites. It took a while before I was able to process the magic of Jimi Hendrix.

Like much of my generation, I got into music backwards from a chronological point of view. The idea of race records was almost incomprehensible by the 1970s. I listened to everything, trying to develop my skills as a guitarist. Every five years or so I would peel back another layer of history, working my way down to the roots.

Years ago, when I studied classical guitar at Brooklyn College, rehearsal rooms were reserved for the orchestral instruments, so I used to practice in the stairwell on the third floor of the music building. No one seemed to mind as long as I stuck to my classical repertoire; all other music was discouraged. I tried to obey the rules, but sometimes when I became frustrated by the difficulty of Spanish composers like Villa-Lobos or Sor, I turned to the blues.

One afternoon I was in the stairwell picking out Cream's version of

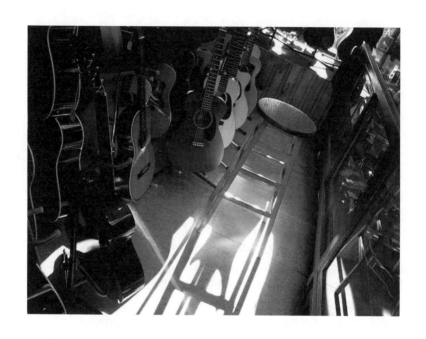

"Crossroads" when I saw someone coming down the hall. I thought I was about to get busted, but I kept playing until I finished the song. When I looked up, I saw a pair of dark blue eyes peering at me from beneath bushy brows: Itzhak Perlman was watching me play. This was like getting busted by Beethoven. I froze, but Perlman smiled at me and said, "Please continue. I love the blues." It turned out he was at the college to teach a master class for violinists and their accompanists. When I asked if I could audit the class, he said it was probably full, but if I walked with him to the classroom, he would ask the professor if it was OK.

The room was packed. Perlman talked to the professor, who took me aside and spoke in severe tones: "Mr. Perlman is going to perform at the beginning of this class. He has requested that you be allowed to watch him play. As you can see, the room is completely full, but we'll find a chair for you and you can watch from the open doorway. This is a master class for violinists and pianists. We are making a special exception for you, but when Mr. Perlman finishes his performance, I ask that you please close the door and leave immediately."

I thanked the professor, and as Perlman entered the classroom, I thanked him too for hooking me up. He shrugged his shoulders and said, "I had to do it, as one bluesman to another. We have to stick together."

He began playing, eyes closed, lost in the music. His violin sounded almost human, first laughing, then slow and mournful. I can't recall exactly what he played; it might have been Tchaikovsky, but as I listened from my seat in the doorway I heard something familiar. I heard the blues.

I left college later that year, having completed my core classes but not a degree, and spent the next few years working at record stores. It was the early eighties and Synthpop bands like the Human League were big sellers. I remember stocking the shelves with debut albums by Stray Cats, Stevie Ray Vaughan, and Madonna. Michael Jackson's *Thriller* and Prince's *Purple Rain* were so popular that we couldn't keep them in stock. After the record stores, I worked at a camera shop and learned about photography.

I also learned that, in the world of sales, knowledge is power. When a customer asked me to explain the difference between a Nikon single-lens reflex camera and a Leica rangefinder, I had to be able to do it, as well as advise them on lenses, accessories, and other gear. A good salesperson knows his stock, and it helps if he likes what he sells. I like vintage gear; it looks and feels cooler than new equipment. There are certain distinct sounds that I associate with vintage gear: the soft hum of vacuum tubes, the solid click of a camera shutter, the subtle hiss at the beginning of a vinyl record, the woody overtones of an old instrument. The mechanical nature of things made long ago appeals to me, as do the rituals that go along with using them. It's satisfying to lift a turntable arm and carefully lower it onto a record, or to open the back of a camera and load a roll of film. There's a sense of accomplishment that comes with watching a photograph appear in a developer tray, or with restringing an old guitar. I like work that lets me hold a piece of history in my hands. It's a way to connect with the past.

In November of 1989, I answered a help wanted ad in the *New York Times* and began working at Matt Umanov Guitars on Bleecker Street in Greenwich Village. Matt was a legend in the world of building, repairing, customizing, and selling guitars. I was excited to work for him, and also to work in the Village. For several decades, this area of New York City had been home base for artists and musicians. The jazz poetry of the beat generation, the protest songs of the folk revival, and the raw sounds of the blank generation all came to fruition here. When I started selling guitars, hair metal was dead, Guns N' Roses was huge, and grunge had yet to lift its unwashed head. Blues wasn't just on the radio; you could go to see it live in the clubs—the Lone Star Roadhouse, Manny's Car Wash, Kenny's Castaways, Dan Lynch, Tramps, and other venues.

I got to know local blues musicians through the store as well as the clubs, and they taught me about their music. John Campbell showed me open G tuning. Chris Whitley gave me a slide that he made from an old bicycle handlebar, and Brian Kramer showed me how to use it. Jon Paris, Big Ed Sullivan, and G. E. Smith taught me Elmore James riffs. Mark Bosch, Arthur Nielsen, and Popa Chubby turned me on to Freddie King and taught me some of his songs. Erik Frandsen explained alternate thumb picking by saying, "Thumb replaces foot." Jimmy

Vivino and Elliot Easton talked to me about Michael Bloomfield, then gave me pointers on his vibrato technique. It was a community of musicians, and I was learning how to speak their language.

I was also learning about guitars, the story behind the sounds. The design, the wood, and the construction of an instrument are integral. It's part of the reason why the classic models of the past, like Fender's Stratocaster, Gibson's Les Paul, Martin's D-28, and Gretch's Chet Atkins 6120 are still being reissued, and why the originals are highly prized by collectors. Also, guitar players worship their idols.

I sold lots of guitars in 1990, but only a few sales stand out. I remember selling Patti Smith and her husband, Fred "Sonic" Smith, a 1976 Martin 000-45 to play at a Radio City AIDS benefit called "That's What Friends Are For." The guitar had a sunburst top with pearl inlays everywhere except the fingerboard. Fred told me it was the most expensive guitar he had ever bought, but it was one of a kind and he sounded great playing it.

I also recall Cait O'Riordan and Elvis Costello buying an instrument. I started to write Cait's name on the receipt, then hesitated and asked her to spell it for me. She said, "C-A-I-T. It's Irish, short for Caitlin." She was sweet, and in late July of that year, when my wife Cathy gave birth to our daughter, we named her Caitlin.

My memory of that summer is hazy because (like most new parents) we weren't getting much sleep, but I remember arriving at work on the morning of August 27 and hearing that Stevie Ray Vaughan had died in a helicopter crash. The blues had lost one of its heroes. The next day, Sony released a box set called *Robert Johnson: The Complete Recordings*. It sold more than a million copies that year and won a Grammy for Best Historical Album. The tale about Robert Johnson selling his soul to the devil at the crossroad made me curious to hear his music, as did high praise from Eric Clapton and Keith Richards.

I bought *Robert Johnson: The Complete Recordings* at Subterranean Records on Cornelia Street. My friend Michael special-ordered it for me on vinyl; the CD version was in stock, but I didn't own a CD player, so I had to wait for the records to arrive. When I first tried listening to Johnson's music, it overwhelmed me. The quality of his guitar playing was undeniable; he sounded like two guitarists playing slightly out of sync with each other. The lyrics were hard to understand, but lines like "Hello Satan, I believe it's time to go" caught my attention. It was creepy listening, but in a good way, like Black Sabbath's first album. The crossroad legend brought me to Robert Johnson and his music kept me there. I kept listening and learned to play some of his songs.

I was working on "Rambling on My Mind" when Jeff Buckley came into the shop. Our mutual friend, Gary Lucas, had introduced us when they were recording songs for Jeff's album *Grace*, and I'd found Jeff soft-spoken and polite. Today he wanted to look at some vintage guitars. I showed him an early 1960s Gibson ES-330 and we talked about music. Jeff told me he had studied jazz and music theory because it helped him to visualize harmony, and that he was into the music of a Pakistani singer named Nusrat Fateh Ali Khan.

"So, Zeke, what have *you* been listening to?"

"Robert Quine gave me some tapes I've been checking out, Blind Willie Johnson and Bukka White. I'm also really into Robert Johnson."

"Feel like playing something?"

I picked up an old National Duolian and played "Aberdeen Mississippi Blues," then passed Jeff the guitar and my slide. He played Bukka White's "Parchman Farm Blues" and Robert Johnson's "Preachin' Blues (Up Jumped the Devil)." Jeff was a very good guitar player with an amazing voice. He had a poetic, trippy style that I liked.

We weren't the only ones trading blues songs across the counter. The success of the Robert Johnson box set motivated record companies to remaster and reissue the music of Charley Patton, Skip James, Blind Willie Johnson, and other early blues artists. Guitarists were discovering their roots.

In 1992, Eric Clapton appeared on *MTV Unplugged*. In the aftermath of his son Connor's death, Clapton's heartfelt performance of "Tears in Heaven" touched everyone who heard it, and his acoustic version of "Layla" became a standard for guitarists. He also played "Walking Blues" and "Malted Milk," both written by Robert Johnson. Eric Clapton's *Unplugged* album sold ten million copies in the US, won six Grammy awards, went to number one on the *Billboard* Top 200, and became a bestseller worldwide. Needless to say, after the show aired, acoustic guitar sales soared.

I started to hang out more at the store's front counter, where we kept the high-end acoustics, and I spent time talking to folk music icons including Richie Havens, Odetta, John Sebastian, Pete Seeger, John Cohen, and Dave Van Ronk. They had personally known Skip James, Son House, Bukka White, and Mississippi John Hurt, and they shared my respect for these men and their music. They agreed that Robert Johnson was a phantom; nobody really knew who he had been or what had happened to him.

It was a time of learning. As I got deeper into early blues, I realized that Robert Johnson and Blind Willie Johnson were bookends at opposite ends of the spectrum, the darkness and the light. Robert sang about temptation and the wages of sin, while Willie preached salvation. In between them was the scale of human experience. I borrowed records from my friends and discovered the music of Blind Willie McTell, Charley Patton, Blind Boy Fuller, and Blind Lemon Jefferson. It was a revelation. I read all that I could about these men, trying to understand their lives. I played their music, but I didn't know the meaning behind their words.

One day, blues would become so important in my life that I would spend over $2,000 on a tattered old photograph I believed to be a lost image of Robert Johnson. But that was still years in the future.

Chapter 3

Return Again

Four months after Johnson's death, the legend returned.

Columbia record producer and talent scout John Hammond envisioned a concert that would trace the history of African American music. Hammond saw the importance of this music and felt that it deserved to be performed on the same stage as a classical recital. On December 23, 1938, "From Spirituals to Swing" opened to a sold-out house at Carnegie Hall in New York.

In a time of segregation, the idea of presenting African American music to an integrated audience was radical. Hammond had trouble finding a sponsor until the American Communist Party journal *The New Masses* agreed to finance the show. Hammond announced that he would present "American Negro Music as it was invented, developed, sung and played by the Negro himself—the true, untainted folk songs, spirituals, work songs, songs of protest, chain gang songs, Holy Roller chants, shouts, blues, minstrel music, honky-tonk piano, early jazz, and finally, the contemporary swing of Count Basie."

He delivered on his promise with an evening featuring performances by Sister Rosetta Tharpe, Big Bill Broonzy, the Benny Goodman Orchestra, the Count Basie Orchestra, and more. The one musician on the program who didn't appear onstage was, of course, Robert Johnson.

Hammond discovered Johnson's music shortly after he began working for Columbia Records. When considering performers for "From Spirituals to Swing," he sent a scout to Mississippi to search out the elusive guitarist and soon received the news that Johnson was dead.

Hammond started the show with two Robert Johnson numbers,

"Preachin' Blues (Up Jumped the Devil)" and "Walking Blues." He recruited guitarist Big Bill Broonzy to stand in for Johnson, representing the raw, primitive sound of down-home blues. Broonzy was a sharp-dressed professional musician from Chicago who had released more than one hundred recordings. But for the concert, Hammond reinvented him as a simple Arkansas farmhand visiting the big city for the first time. This strategic marketing fit Hammond's personal view of blues as a rural form of music. Broonzy agreed to play the part, and he would play it successfully for the rest of his life. One wonders what would have happened if Hammond had asked Robert Johnson to do the same.

Others, too, saw the importance of documenting rural American music. In 1941, folk music researcher Alan Lomax and musicologist John Work traveled through the Mississippi Delta looking for traces of Robert Johnson. At Stovall Plantation they met Muddy Waters, who claimed to have seen Johnson perform: "It was in Friar's Point and this guy had a lot of people standin' around him. He coulda been Robert, they said it was Robert. I stopped and peeked over, and then I left because he was a dangerous man." Lomax recorded Water's performance of "Country Blues," a song based on Robert Johnson's "Walking Blues." It inspired Waters to take his music to Chicago and led to a series of hit records that shaped the sound of modern blues.

While Muddy Waters, Howlin' Wolf, John Lee Hooker, B. B. King, and Little Walter were lighting up stages in Chicago and Detroit, the seeds of the folk blues revival were being planted. In 1952, Harry Smith's *The Anthology of American Music* sparked the beginning of that movement. The three-volume anthology of rare recordings caught the ears of up-and-coming musicians like the New Lost City Ramblers, Bob Dylan, Joan Baez, and Dave Van Ronk.

By the mid-1950s, the color line was beginning to blur in the world of popular music. In July 1954, Sam Phillips recorded Elvis Presley's version of "That's All Right, Mama," a blues song by Arthur "Big Boy" Crudup, at Sun Studios in Memphis. In Presley, Phillips saw an opportunity to present rhythm and blues music to white audiences. He distributed copies of the record to local disc jockeys, and when Dewey Phillips played the song on his radio show "Red, Hot, and Blue," he received over forty telephone calls from listeners asking to hear it again. Dewey played the song fourteen times on the air that night.

"That's All Right, Mama" sold around twenty thousand copies and reached number four on the Memphis charts. It wasn't a hit nationwide, but it signaled the beginning of a new sound, one that would cross cultural and racial barriers to become known as rock and roll. Presley would soon score his first of many number-one hits with "Heartbreak Hotel," another blues-based song. In his memoir *Life*, Rolling Stones guitarist Keith Richards describes hearing "Heartbreak Hotel" on the radio as a youth: "It was a totally different way of delivering a song, a totally different sound, stripped down, burnt, no bullshit, no violins and ladies' choruses and schmaltz, totally different. It was bare, right to the roots that you had a feeling were there but hadn't yet heard." Those roots, of course, were the blues.

At the recommendation of Muddy Waters, Chuck Berry auditioned for Leonard Chess in 1955, hoping to score a record deal. Berry performed a few blues tunes, but Chess heard something special in Berry's unique take on the Bob Wills song "Ida Red." The idea of a black musician performing a country song was so new and different that they decided to retitle the song. According to Johnny Johnson, Berry's longtime keyboard player, Chess spotted a mascara case on the floor of the studio and said, "Well, hell, let's name the damn thing 'Maybellene,'" changing the spelling to avoid a potential lawsuit from the cosmetics company. On its release in July 1955, "Maybellene" went to number one on *Billboard*'s R&B charts and number five on its rock/pop charts, proving that music could successfully cross the traditional barriers.

By 1957, rock and roll was in full swing. Black and white musicians played side by side on the same stages. Little Richard, Jerry Lee Lewis, Buddy Holly, Chuck Berry, and Elvis Presley were blazing a new trail, but it had plenty of speed bumps. Toward the end of the year, Little Richard gave up music for the ministry. In 1958, Elvis Presley was inducted into the US Army, and Jerry Lee Lewis was blacklisted when the news was reported that he had married his thirteen-year-old cousin. Buddy Holly died in a plane crash in 1959, and later the same year Chuck Berry was arrested for transporting a minor over state lines. The first wave of rock and roll was over, and it would take years for the next wave to arrive from across the Atlantic. Meanwhile, a mellower sound was in the air.

In 1959, Sam Charters, a record collector and musician with a degree in economics from Harvard, helped to lay the foundation for folk blues with his book *The Country Blues*. This book, and a companion record issued by Folkways, inspired a new generation of performers and researchers. Among the fourteen songs on the Folkways compilation was "Preachin' Blues (Up Jumped the Devil)" by Robert Johnson, marking the first time in twenty-one years that Johnson's music had appeared on a record.

Also in 1959, Pete Seeger, Odetta, Joan Baez, Sonny Terry and Brownie McGhee, Earl Scruggs, the New Lost City Ramblers, and Leon Bibb were among the featured performers at the first Newport Folk Festival. The festival's signature blend of folk, blues, and country music would soon become the soundtrack of the Greenwich Village music scene.

Bob Dylan arrived in New York City on a cold January day in 1961. He made the rounds, hanging out and performing in places like Café Wha?, Izzy Young's Folklore Center, and Gerde's Folk City. He met and befriended popular folk musicians including Dave Van Ronk, Fred Neil, Odetta, the Clancy Brothers, the New Lost City Ramblers, and Carolyn Hester. While playing harmonica on Hester's third album, he met John Hammond, who promptly signed him to a recording deal. Hammond had recently convinced Columbia to reissue the recordings of Robert Johnson and he gave Dylan an advance copy. The young singer listened to it obsessively, absorbing it into his poet's heart, even writing out the lyrics in hopes of understanding how the words flowed and how the songs were constructed. He would later say, "If I hadn't heard the Robert Johnson record when I did, there probably would have been hundreds of lines of mine that would have been shut down—that I wouldn't have felt free enough or upraised enough to write."

Even in the midst of the folk blues revival, Columbia's *Robert Johnson: King of the Delta Blues Singers* didn't make the charts, but it had inspired Bob Dylan and it would spark the imagination of some young English musicians who were also in the process of creating a new sound. Mick Jagger and Keith Richards were childhood friends who had lost touch. They met again as teenagers in 1960, at Dartford Railway Station, when Richards noticed Jagger carrying two classic Chess albums: Chuck Berry's *Rockin' at the Hops* and *The Best of Muddy Waters*. The old friends began playing music together and in 1962 formed the Rolling Stones with Brian Jones, whose slide guitar style was inspired by Robert Johnson. Richards remembers:

> Brian Jones had [Johnson's] first album, and that's where I first heard it. I'd just met Brian, and I went around to his apartment—crash pad, actually, all he had in it was a chair, a record player, and a few records. One of which was Robert Johnson. He put it on, and it was just—you know—astounding stuff. When I first heard it, I said to Brian, Who's that? Robert Johnson, he said. Yeah, but who's the other guy playing with him? Because I was hearing two guitars, and it took me a long time to realize he was actually doing it all by himself. The guitar playing—it was almost like listening to Bach. You know, you think you're getting a handle on playing the blues, and then you hear Robert Johnson—some of the rhythms he's doing and playing and singing at the same time, you think, this guy must have three brains! You want to know how good the blues can get? Well, this is it.

Named for a Muddy Waters song, the Rolling Stones became an integral part of a new music scene that was taking shape in the places like London's Crawdaddy Club. The sound was rooted in American blues, flavored by the rock rhythms of Bo Diddley and Chuck Berry, and made larger than life by amplified electric guitars cranked to top volume. At the 1962 American Folk Blues Festival's only date in England, Richards, Jagger, and Jimmy Page were in the audience watching Muddy Waters, Howlin' Wolf, and Sonny Boy Williamson II perform.

The British Invasion of 1964 brought rock and roll roaring back to America. The two bands at the forefront, the Beatles and the Rolling Stones, were largely inspired by American music: the Stones by Delta and Chicago blues, the Beatles by country and rockabilly artists like Carl Perkins and Gene Vincent. While the Beatles' US debut album, *Meet the Beatles*, featured mostly songs they had written themselves (including their first number-one single, "I Want to Hold Your Hand"), the Rolling Stones' first American album, *England's Newest Hit Makers*, included covers of songs by Slim Harpo, Willie Dixon, Jimmy Reed, Chuck Berry, and Bo Diddley. The Rolling Stones' success opened the door for other blues-based groups like the Yardbirds, who took over as the Crawdaddy Club's house band when the Stones left. Three of rock's most influential guitarists—Eric Clapton, Jeff Beck, and Jimmy Page—began their careers with the Yardbirds and helped pioneer the blues rock sound.

By the time Jimi Hendrix arrived in Greenwich Village in 1966, he had spent years on the road as a sideman for Curtis Knight and Little Richard. Blues guitarist John P. Hammond, the son of producer John Hammond, remembers meeting Hendrix. "He had gotten fired from a band that he was playing with and he was hanging out in the Village and I was introduced to him and he heard a recording of mine and was, you know, a really nice guy. I worked some gigs where I hired him to play guitar because he was broke, he was stranded in New York, and we got a gig at this club called the Café-Au-Go-Go for a week and it was packed out every night, and we got guys jamming with us every night, and everybody and their mother came to the club. A guy named Chas Chandler who played with the Animals had a recording studio in England and he came backstage on our last night and offered [Hendrix] a plane ticket to England to record and he looked at me and said, What do you think, John? And I said, Man, if it ain't now it's gonna be soon thereafter, just go for it."

Chas Chandler recruited bassist Noel Redding and drummer Mitch Mitchell to play with Hendrix. They formed the Jimi Hendrix Experience, and Chandler became the band's manager. Their first album, *Are You Experienced*, was a huge hit in England—rising to number two on the charts, right behind the Beatles' *Sgt. Pepper's Lonely Hearts Club Band*—but the band was still unknown in America.

A year or so later, Hendrix returned to New York. John Hammond was playing with his trio at the Gaslight Café when Hendrix showed up and sat in with the band. Hammond recalls, "The next day Eric Clapton was in New York to do his tour with Cream. He was off that week, so he came down to check me out. And there was him and Jimi, and they both wanted to sit in. And so for a week, they sat in with my little group at the Gaslight Café." The three guitarists shared a love of early blues, including the music of Robert Johnson. Clapton covered "Ramblin' on My Mind" on John Mayall's *Blues Breakers* album and played "From Four Until Late" on Cream's debut album *Fresh Cream*. His live version of "Crossroads" on Cream's *Wheels of Fire* brought Johnson's music to a generation of young rock fans.

Yardbirds guitarist Jimmy Page was inspired by the psychedelic blues rock sound of the Jimi Hendrix Experience and Cream. When the Yardbirds broke up in 1968, Page formed a band called the New Yardbirds with Robert Plant on vocals, John Bonham on drums, and John Paul Jones on bass. When legal issues arose over the band's name, they changed it to Led Zeppelin. Their eponymous first album included "You Shook Me" and "I Can't Quit You Baby," both written by Willie Dixon, and showcased the band's sculpted, hard-hitting take on the blues. Sales were good, though the critics disapproved.

The band's second album, *Led Zeppelin II*, was a huge success, reaching number one on the charts in the UK and America. In typically sexual terms, Robert Plant described why: "*Led Zep II* was very virile. That was the album that was going to dictate whether or not we had the staying power and the capacity to stimulate. It was still blues-based, but it was a much more carnal approach to the music and quite flamboyant."

From the opening guitar riff on "Whole Lotta Love" to the last note of harmonica on "Bring It on Home," *Led Zeppelin II* is rooted in the blues. In addition to the Willie Dixon tracks, Sonny Boy Williamson II recorded the original version of "Bring It on Home" in 1963; "The Lemon Song" is derived from Howlin' Wolf's "Killing Floor" and features the line "Squeeze my lemon till the juice runs down my leg," borrowed from Robert Johnson's "Traveling Riverside Blues."

The popularity of blues-based rock bands like Led Zeppelin, Cream, the Jimi Hendrix Experience, and the Rolling Stones motivated Columbia to release a second album of Robert Johnson's recordings. Now considered to be one of the great blues albums of all time, *King of the Delta Blues Singers Volume II* didn't sell as well as its predecessor upon release in 1970. It took twenty years for Robert Johnson's music to return again.

Chapter 4

Mojo

I got a black cat bone, I got a Mojo too,
I got a John the Conqueror root, I'm gonna mess with you.
—Willie Dixon, "Hoochie Coochie Man"

When I first heard Muddy Waters' recording of "Hootchie Cootchie Man," I didn't know what he was singing about, but the song had a menacing feel that captivated me. The next time I heard the word "mojo" was in the song "Little Queen of Spades," when Robert Johnson sang, "Everybody says she got a mojo, man she's been using that stuff."

What's a mojo? I wondered.

A little research revealed that Johnson was singing about hoodoo, a form of folk magic whose origins lie in the Yoruba and Fon religions of West Africa. In America, hoodoo dates back to the beginning of the slave trade. It evolved over time to incorporate some tenets of Christianity and was commonly practiced in the Mississippi Delta region during Robert Johnson's lifetime, a more rural, root-based cousin of the voodoo religion practiced in New Orleans and other Caribbean-influenced US cities.

Practitioners of hoodoo see it as a way to petition supernatural forces, enlisting spiritual help in order to improve their lives. They may visit conjurers and root doctors who perform rituals using oils, herbs, powders, minerals, bones, and, of course, roots. The root doctor helps the visitor to attract whatever it is he most desires. Sometimes the conjurer will give the visitor a bit of flannel tied up with a piece of ribbon or string. This is a mojo bag, and the items placed inside it vary

33

according to what one wishes to attract. For example, a gambler's mojo is filled with items thought to bring good luck in games of chance. The bag would likely be green, representing money, and it might contain alfalfa, sassafras, a John the Conqueror root, a lodestone, a buckeye nut, a mercury dime—or any of a hundred other ingredients associated with money, luck, and control over others. The mojo bag is anointed with a small amount of liquid—usually an herbal oil, but occasionally blood, urine, or holy water—to activate its power and bring it to life.

A mojo bag designed to attract love would contain different items than a bag made for gambling, though the "control" ingredients might overlap. (Control over others is a consistent theme in hoodoo spells.) Made of red flannel, it might contain two lodestones covered in magnetic sand, a slip of paper with the putative lovers' names written on it, rose petals, violets, or a "black cat bone" (sometimes the actual bone of an unfortunate feline, but usually a chicken bone painted black or a type of root). Some practitioners advise that the bag must be carried in secret; if anyone but the owner sees it, they say, it will lose its power. Once activated, mojos are considered living things that need to be fed. When Muddy Waters and Robert Johnson sang about mojo, they were referring to these bags as well as the larger power they convey.

Johnson's lyrics are filled with references to hoodoo. In "Come on in My Kitchen," he sings, "Oh well she's gone I know she won't come back, I've taken the last nickel out of her nation sack." A nation sack is a type of mojo worn by a woman to keep a man faithful to her. By removing a nickel from it, Johnson would have disrespected the woman and the mojo. "Hell Hound on My Trail" includes the verse, "You sprinkled Hot Foot Powder all around your Daddy's door, it keep me with a ramblin' mind rider, every old place I go." In hoodoo, Hot Foot Powder is used to rid oneself of unwanted people and keep enemies away.

In "Sweet Home Chicago," the line "You keep on monkeyin' around here friend boy, you're gon' get your business all in a trick" refers to the hoodoo practice of laying down a "trick," or casting a spell to influence someone's behavior. In this case, Johnson is warning his rival that he'll use hoodoo against him. Another allusion to laying down a trick appears in his song "Stones in My Passway": "Now you tryin' to take my life and all my lovin' too, you laid a passway for me, now what are you trying to do?"

The crossroad features prominently as a hoodoo destination. Magical objects may be left or buried there, crossroad dirt may be collected for spellwork, deals may be made, and (according to one legend) a person wishing to practice black magic may pray to the devil there for nine nights. Johnson's song "Crossroad Blues" immediately brings these rituals to mind, but it may also be seen as a social commentary on the realities of everyday life for a black man in 1930s Mississippi. There is an underlying fear in the lyrics, whether it is fear of the supernatural or of being caught alone in an unfriendly area as the sun goes down.

While hoodoo charms are primarily meant to benefit the user rather than harm others, the practice does have a dark side. Many of the charms and spells are symbolic—nailing the intended victim's photograph to a tree, burying a lock of his hair in a miniature coffin— but some involve the introduction of substances into the victim's food or drink:

> Take a scorpion or a poisonous spider. Impale it on a long needle and let it dry. Pound it up into a powder and sprinkle that powder on the intended victim's food. In time live scorpions will grow in the body, and not only will they cause discomfort by their very presence, but also they will secrete their poisonous venom into the veins.

While ingesting venomous creatures may or may not be harmful, such a spell demonstrates the practitioner's willingness to, essentially, poison his victim. Could this have happened to Robert Johnson? It's only conjecture—and it's as easy to spike someone's whiskey with rat poison as with some esoteric powder from a hoodoo doctor—but certainly hoodoo was practiced in rural Mississippi at the time Johnson died, and one of the major motivations for using the darker charms was sexual jealousy, said to be a factor in his death.

As Robert Johnson surely knew, some guitars have mojo. There's an aura about them; they have a vibe, a kind of magic that hits you even before you play a note. They stand out in a room filled with guitars, tempting you, and when you play them you hear something unique. These guitars usually have stories behind them. Some bear the mark of a previous owner, a name painted on them or a number scratched into the wood. When you look inside their cases, you might find old sheet music, a vintage strap, a slide, or a bag of old picks. Guitar dealers call this case candy.

I've seen some strange case candy and found some weird things *inside* acoustic guitars, including a 1960s Epiphone Caballero that contained a rattlesnake rattle. If you find one of these inside a guitar, tradition says you should leave it there; the rattle is believed to protect the guitar and the owner.

The wildest thing I ever found in a guitar had to be the contents of a rust-covered early 1930s National Duolian I sold to playwright and actor Sam Shepard. The guitar looked like it had spent decades forgotten in an old barn. We had a similar one in better condition, but Sam liked the sound of the rusty one and he decided to buy it. I hadn't met Sam before—Patti Smith brought him in—but I'd read some of his work and thought he would appreciate the fact that the Duolian came with a very unusual piece of case candy. When they began working on the guitar, the guys in our repair shop found a mud dauber's nest inside. Matt asked them to put it in a plastic bag and left it in the guitar case.

Sam and Patti cracked up when I showed them the nest. Sam held it up to the light and examined it. I didn't have to tell him that the nest was part of the guitar's story. He knew it was a totem. It was once alive, and it belonged with the guitar. Mud daubers' nests are a powerful ingredient in hoodoo; they may be used for curses or protection, and even today fetch good money in botanicas and magic shops.

Like all forms of folk magic, hoodoo is flexible, and any object that is meaningful or powerful for you may become part of your personal mojo—like Johnny Depp and the penguin.

National guitars usually have bodies made of metal. A spun aluminum resonator cone inside acts as a speaker, making them louder than wooden guitars. Invented by John Dopyera in the late twenties, they remained popular until World War II, when metal became scarce due to the war effort. Nationals went out of style with the invention of the electric guitar, but they began making a comeback during the folk revival of the sixties. By the early 1990s, National guitars were popular again. I got into them after meeting John Campbell and Chris Whitley, both of whom really knew how to play a National.

I was at the shop, playing slide on a 1930s walnut-burst National Triolian with a decal of a penguin in a top hat on the back, when Johnny Depp walked in with one of his friends. It was cold outside and they were both wearing Navy pea coats and sailor hats. Johnny watched me play slide and said, "That sounds amazing." I passed the guitar to him and he played it, then turned to his friend and said, "It's really great—should I be bad?"

"Why not?" said the friend. "You've already spent too much money today."

I looked Johnny in the eye and said, "If you buy it, don't take the penguin off the back. It's mojo."

Johnny looked at the back of the guitar, then smiled and said, "I want it. I love the penguin."

Years later, while watching the movie *Chocolat* with my wife, I noticed that Johnny was playing the same guitar in the scene where he meets Juliet Binoche. I mentioned this to Cathy, and she asked, "How do you know it's the same one?" A few frames later, Johnny turned the guitar around, and you could clearly see the penguin in his top hat.

Mojo.

Chapter 5

The Stuff I Got

"You're the devil," the little guy in the leather jacket told me, fingering the strings of the guitar I'd shown him.

It was an early-fifties Gibson CF-100E, Gibson's first attempt at a cutaway acoustic-electric guitar, and they usually have structural issues, but this one was perfect. The little guy wasn't perfect by any stretch of the imagination, but he *was* a genius: Lou Reed, cofounder of the Velvet Underground, cantankerous New York poet, and guitar legend. Being able to sell instruments to people like him was gratifying not just because I got to meet some of my musical heroes but also because I knew the guitars were going to owners who could appreciate them.

Lou had a soft spot for this Gibson model, and so did Bob Dylan, probably because it embodied a place in time when Elmore James and Dion DiMucci might meet and jam for a while. Lou bought the guitar, as I'd known he would. It was clean and original, and for collectors, the devil is in the details.

Lou also bought an amplifier: a small Trace Elliot Velocette tube amp made in England, covered in racing-green Tolex with a retro-looking circular grill cloth. He asked me to walk it back to his place, a duplex penthouse apartment nearby on Christopher Street, and I jumped at the chance. He'd turned the entire second floor of his apartment into a music room, one of the most beautiful rooms I've ever been in. On one side, a long row of guitars and amps was neatly arranged before a wall of windows with a panoramic view of the city. On the other side, a recording console and comfortable seating spread out beneath colorful art. The guitars were a mix of old and new, acoustics and electrics. I asked Lou why he had so many, and he asked how many guitars I owned.

"Two."

"See, that's the difference between you and me. Guitar players like you spend years developing a sound. Then they look for a guitar that makes that sound, and when they find it, they're done. I use guitars to write with. I might write a song on one guitar that I wouldn't write on a different one."

He explained that because every guitar was unique, he might play a chord on one with a big neck in a different position than on one with a smaller neck, and that chord could be the inspiration for a new song. He also told me that when you're making a record, it's good to have a variety of sounds to layer into the mix.

Lou Reed helped me to understand what a songwriter looks for in a guitar, which came in handy when Bob Dylan walked into the store. He was wearing a black leather jacket and a grey sweatshirt with the hood pulled up over his head. It was nice outside, so I figured the man beneath the hood was either a criminal or a famous rock star. When I looked under the hood and saw the familiar, piercing blue eyes, I was relieved.

He pointed to a 1950 Gibson ES-125 archtop, and I took it down off the wall. We went into the amp room and I plugged the guitar into a 1956 Fender Champ amplifier. I tuned the guitar and passed it to Bob, then sat down and waited to see what he would play. He played "Stop Breaking Down Blues" by Robert Johnson, and he played it well.

When he finished the song, Bob asked, "Is this pickguard original?"

It was a reasonable question, but unexpected because most people wouldn't care. I took back the guitar and looked it over. "Yeah, the pickguard's original. So are the pickup, frets, tuners, nut, bridge, tailpiece, knobs, and the finish. And it comes with the original case."

Bob peered at me intently, then asked, "Is this a good guitar?"

I thought about it for a minute before I spoke. "It's all original and you sound good playing it. If you like it, then it's good, isn't it?"

"Hmmm . . . OK, my people will call you."

He opened the sliding glass door of the amp room and walked out into the light of day. I stood in the middle of the store holding the guitar, watching him leave, passing my friend David, who happened to be wearing a Bob Dylan tour sweatshirt. David never noticed the real Bob, who was still wearing the hood over his head. I guess the disguise worked.

Matt Umanov came over and asked, "Was that Bob?"

I nodded. "Yeah, his people will call you."

Two hours later, they called and bought the guitar.

Around that time, I showed producer/musician Daniel Lanois a 1950s Fender Champ amplifier. It was like the one I'd used to demo the guitar Dylan bought, but the speaker on this one sounded like it was blown. Dan bought it anyway. I had sold Dan guitars before and he had great ears, so I guessed he must have heard something he liked about the amp's sound, something I was missing.

Several months later Dan went into the studio with Bob Dylan and produced a double album called *Time Out of Mind*. In 1998 it won a Grammy award for album of the year. Dylan ended his acceptance speech by saying, "In the words of the immortal Robert Johnson, 'The stuff we got will bust your brains out.'" It was a line from "Stop Breaking Down Blues," the song Dylan had played when I sold him the old Gibson guitar. The next time I saw Dan, he told me Dylan had been listening to a lot of old blues and wanted to make a record that sounded like Slim Harpo. It turned out that the Fender Champ with the blown speaker helped to capture that sound.

The musicians, the collectors, the record producers, the parents buying their kid a guitar, the famous and the soon-to-be: I asked them what they were looking for, what sounds they wanted to make, and when they told me, I helped them find those sounds. It was all about respect. Pretend you're standing on the other side of the counter, that you're about to pay a lot of money for an instrument and you don't want to be intimidated by a snooty salesman. I had to know it all without seeming like a know-it-all. The kid, the businessman, the subway performer, the rock star—all were the same to me. They wanted to find their sounds, and I helped them.

I didn't recognize Mike McCready and Eddie Vedder when they bought a black 1931 Gibson L-00. Just before they walked in, I'd called Lou Reed's assistant, Beth Groubert, because I thought Lou would want the guitar. Beth told me Lou was in Europe but promised to let him know about it. The guitar looked and sounded unusual. It had a white peghead with the name "E. F. Tiffany" engraved on the truss rod cover and custom inlays. It was expensive, and I told Mike and Eddie that I thought Lou Reed or some other well-known musician would probably end up with it. Mike looked at Eddie, and they both smiled.

"We're in a band," Eddie said.

"Oh yeah? Maybe I've heard of you."

"Maybe."

"What's it called?"

I had to laugh when he said "Pearl Jam."

There are all kinds of reasons why people collect guitars. For some it's about nostalgia: guitars denote their youth, good times past, now fondly remembered. It may be about reacquiring guitars they once owned and lost, or ones they dreamed of owning but couldn't afford. For them, collecting is a way to turn back time. For others, guitars are a way to connect with famous musicians. They collect guitarists' signature models or instruments formerly owned by musicians they admire. There are also collectors who commission custom guitars from world-renowned guitar makers, often displaying the instruments like fine art. Which, of course, they are.

Some of my favorite collectors enjoy acquiring instruments that share a basic theme. My friend Robbie spent years putting together a complete collection of every model of guitar the Beatles played. He was on a mission, and he accomplished it. The only thing missing from his display room was a grey pearl Ludwig drum kit like Ringo's. My friend John collects vintage guitar models used by old blues and country musicians. It's not a large collection, but he owns some of the best examples of early blues guitars that I've come across, and it's nice to know they're in good hands.

Richard Gere wasn't like most collectors. There was no rhyme or reason to what he bought, except that the guitars had to play and sound good. They didn't have to be perfect or rare; they just had to speak to him. I sold him some nice vintage guitars, in particular a Gibson L-1 similar to the one Robert Johnson is holding on the cover of *The Complete Recordings*. Richard liked blues music, and we used to sit at the counter and jam. We usually talked about music or movies he was working on, but we also talked about what was happening in Tibet. Richard once showed me a book of photographs he shot while he was there visiting the Dalai Lama. As I looked at the photos, he told me about the difficulties of daily life faced by the Tibetan people. He said he was trying to help them, and he meant it. On October 11, 2011, 106 of Richard's vintage guitars and amplifiers sold for $936,438 at a Christie's auction. He donated the money to charities that support humanitarian causes in Tibet and around the world.

The 1990s were a decade of collectibles. Cars, guitars, comic books, sports memorabilia, Beanie Babies, Pokémon cards—it didn't matter as long as the demand outweighed the supply and there was some investment potential. It was a time of unprecedented economic expansion in the United States. New developments in technology, especially computers, created jobs and changed the way businesses operate. As corporate earnings increased and inflation dropped, the stock market surged. People made money. Some people made tons of it.

Scott Chinery was one of the lucky ones. He made his millions by marketing a safe alternative to steroids called Cybergenics, which he developed after suffering the consequences of steroid abuse during his years as a college football player. Financial success enabled him to collect whatever he liked, and he liked expensive cars, vintage guitars, and pre-Castro Cuban cigars. I met him in the early nineties when he came in looking for guitars to add to his already-extensive collection. He asked me to show him something great, saying that if he didn't already own one of whatever I showed him, he would buy it. It was an interesting challenge and I accepted it.

The first guitar I showed him was a big, beautiful-sounding 1945 Gibson J-45 Banner, a wartime model with no cracks and no issues. Who could resist it? Scott could; he already had one. No problem—time to step up my game. I took down another guitar and laid it on a black velvet pad on the counter. It was a mint-condition 1951 Martin D-28 with deep brown, straight-grained, book-matched Brazilian rosewood, and it sounded like dark chocolate dipped in espresso. Anyone else would have been all over it, but not Scott. He told me he owned a pre-war Martin D-28 that was very similar, and more collectible. Strike two, but that was fine; I was still at bat.

I unlocked the glass case where we keep the most expensive instruments and removed a small guitar. It was a 7/8-size Baby Dreadnaught Martin 7-42 Custom, made in 1984 for Dick Boak, the director of artist relations at C. F. Martin & Co. It had a sunburst finish with abalone trim, a torch inlaid on the headstock, and Dick Boak's name inlaid on the last fret. It was one of a kind, and there was no way that Scott had anything like it.

It was the right call. When I told Scott about the guitar he said, "Nice, I'll take it. I know Dick Boak—he's a friend of mine. What else can you show me?" I showed him a half dozen more of the best guitars in the store, but none was unusual enough for him.

I only met Scott that one time, and I didn't know his history or realize the magnitude of his collection. In 1996, Outline Press published a limited-edition book called *The Chinery Collection*. It featured 250 of Scott's guitars and chronicled the evolution of American guitars from the first Martin parlor instruments up through modern electrics and custom archtops. Scott expanded on this idea by loaning his collection to the Boston Museum of Fine Arts for an exhibition called *Dangerous Curves: Art of the Guitar*, which offered people a chance to see how guitar design had changed and developed over the centuries. Curator Darcy Kuronen described it thus:

> From courtly musicians serenading sixteenth-century royalty to rock bands blasting megawatts in packed stadiums, the guitar has been an enduring musical icon for over four centuries. To a far greater degree than any other instrument, it has been interpreted with extraordinary variety of form and decoration, always reflecting the aesthetics of the time. This is as true for ornate guitars of the Baroque era, inlaid with ivory and pearl, as it is for twentieth-century electric instruments painted in blue metallic flake. "Dangerous Curves: Art of the Guitar" celebrates this diversity, displaying how changes in fashion, technology, and musical taste have influenced the look of the world's most popular instrument.

The exhibit opened on November 5, 2000, and ran for just over a year. It was a way for Scott to share his enthusiasm with others: "My goal always has been to create a museum that will house the collection and that will allow people to come see and even play these masterpieces anytime and free of charge. These treasures do not belong to me, they belong to history, and I consider it an honor to care for and share these wonderful instruments. I hope that I'll be able to do this within the next few years."

Unfortunately, Scott died twelve days before the exhibit opened. He was forty years old. His efforts have influenced others to follow his example; in 2011, New York's Metropolitan Museum presented an exhibition called *Guitar Heroes*, which traced the history of guitar making from Cremona, Italy, to New York. The exhibit focused on three of the most respected archtop guitar makers of all time: John D'Angelico, James D'Aquisto, and John Monteleone.

I've dealt with all types of guitar collectors over the years. Some were millionaires and celebrities; some had saved for years to be able to afford a particular instrument that captivated them. There's a common thread between the big-time collectors and people like you or me who may only own a few guitars: we all want to find our sounds. Guitars help us do that, and that's why we love them.

Chapter 6

Played It on the Sofa

I don't usually give guitar lessons. There are many reasons, but mainly the responsibility of teaching is more than I can deal with. When someone asks for pointers, I'm happy to share, but if they ask me for lessons, I refer them to a guitar teacher—almost always, but there have been a few exceptions.

I had just finished changing strings on a Gibson J-45 reissue, used but in nice condition, when two young women and a man came in. The man was dark-haired with a goatee and intense eyes. He said they needed a guitar for a young girl who was writing and performing music. I showed him the Gibson I'd just restrung, and he handed it to one of the women, whom he introduced as Amelia. She was tall, thin, and pretty, and her hands looked right on the guitar as she strummed it. When I asked her what style of music she listened to, she said, "I like old blues, like Robert Johnson."

"Yeah? Me too."

"Would you play something for me?"

I took back the Gibson and played the first verse of "Terraplane Blues," which made all three of them smile. Then the man asked Amelia if she wanted the guitar. She demurred, saying it was too expensive, but all of us could see she liked it. Her companions told her not to worry about the price, and they bought it.

Afterward, the man asked if me I would give Amelia a lesson at his place. I thanked him and explained that I was a player and a seller, but not a teacher. He said he understood; could I recommend a guitar teacher who played Robert Johnson like I did? I honestly couldn't think of anybody. So he asked me again if I would do it, adding that he'd be glad to pay for my time. He just wanted to hang out and watch the lesson, because he liked the music and wanted to see how it was made.

Because I'd taken a liking to these folks, I agreed to teach a lesson for free, with the caveat that I was not actually responsible for anyone learning anything. I asked them to have two cold beers in the fridge for me in case I needed them. No problem, said the man.

When they left, one of my coworkers asked if I'd recognized the man. I had no idea who he was. It turned out that the dark-haired man with the intense eyes was David Blaine, the magician who had frozen himself in a block of ice for three days in the middle of Times Square.

On Thursday night of that week, after work, I walked to David's apartment carrying my 1928 Stella guitar with me. He lived in a large building near Washington Square Park with a doorman in the lobby. Four of David's friends were hanging out in his living room. Could they watch the lesson? Sure, no problem.

Amelia wanted to learn Robert Johnson's song "Stones in my Passway," which is in open G tuning, but it's capoed at the second fret to open A tuning. The rhythmic pattern of the song is tricky, and singing over it is difficult. I explained this to Amelia while I showed her how to play the song, telling her it takes time and practice to be able to play along with the record. David watched my hands with those intense eyes, and remarked that it was similar to working with cards and coins. Of course he'd spent years perfecting his own finger control and dexterity.

After about an hour, David and the others decided to go out for food. I wasn't hungry, and Amelia wanted to keep working, so we stayed behind. An hour later, they returned with pizza and we concluded the guitar lesson. I drank a beer, and David thanked me for coming over, then took a thin book from a cardboard box full of copies of the same volume. "You should read this, Zeke. This is my Bible."

The book he gave me was *Man's Search for Meaning* by Dr. Viktor Frankl, a psychiatrist who survived a Nazi concentration camp. He said he thought I would understand the book's message. I thanked him and put it in my guitar case.

I was about to leave when David said, "Hey, Zeke, I've been working on something all week. You just went out of your comfort zone, and I want to do this while you're still here."

Everybody gathered around the couch where David was sitting. He removed a long acupuncture needle from its paper sleeve, held it between his right thumb and forefinger, and slowly inserted the needle into the back of his hand between the tendons of his index and middle finger. As he pushed the needle through the meat of his hand, the tough skin of his palm bulged out in a point about an inch long.

Somebody laughed. Somebody else commented that they felt sick. David seemed preoccupied with figuring out how to force the needle all the way through his palm. "See, this is the problem I've been having all week," he said. "It doesn't want to go through." Then he shrugged. "Well, since Zeke's here . . ." He lifted his right hand and slammed it down hard on the needle, which punched all the way through his palm. We could see the long sliver of steel protruding from both sides of his hand, wavering a little, maybe with his heartbeat.

Amelia shrieked, then laughed as David held his hand up in triumph. If he was in pain, it must have been overshadowed by a sense of accomplishment, because he smiled as he examined his hand.

"Does it hurt?" someone asked.

David smiled even more widely. "Yes."

The doorbell rang, and David himself went to answer it. It was his doorman, come to pick up a signed copy of David's autobiography for his nephew.

"Nice to see you," David said. "I'll get the book, but first, let's shake!" He held out his hand, still pierced by the long steel needle.

The doorman's eyes widened. "David, that's crazy! Why did you do that?"

"Because Zeke agreed to give a guitar lesson."

The doorman looked even more confused as David signed the book for the nephew. When David gave him the book, he went to shake David's hand, but decided to pat his arm instead. "Thanks. The nephew will love it." Then he left in a hurry.

David returned to the couch and we talked about Dr. Frankl's book. Putting the needle through his hand was meant to illustrate its meaning: we are all capable of enduring more than we realize. There was no magic or illusion involved in his attempts to test the limits of his own endurance, David explained. The needle was a test for him and an example for the rest of us.

"Does your hand still hurt?" Amelia asked.

David nodded.

"Why don't you pull it out, then?"

A man relaxing in a La-Z-Boy recliner spoke up. "You want to know why he doesn't pull it out? Because it's going to hurt twice as much coming out as it did going in."

The man laughed, and David laughed too. "He's right!"

He tweezed the end of the needle between two fingers. I watched him slowly draw the needle out of his flesh, leaving a small dark puncture mark on either side of his hand. There was very little blood—just a trickle.

Amelia walked with me to the subway. As I was leaving, she hugged me and said, "Thanks for the lesson, Zeke. Read the book—it will change how you view life."

I don't know if it was the book, but something changed after I met David Blaine and his friends. Maybe it was my outlook, because I decided it wouldn't kill me to give someone a guitar lesson every now and then. There was one catch: I wouldn't accept money as payment. Instead, my students had to trade or teach me something. I traded guitar lessons for dinner at a nice restaurant, a memorable bottle of wine, a hand-bound journal, and life lessons with Chuck Barris.

Barris was a former music producer who created the popular 1970s TV shows *The Dating Game*, *The Newlywed Game*, and *The Gong Show* and wrote several books, including the autobiographical *Confessions of a Dangerous Mind*. The most important thing he taught me was to trust my instincts. He also taught me how to do his classic *Gong Show* move: pull my hat down over my eyes, clap my hands, then point and grin like crazy. I did it whenever I felt uncomfortable walking onstage or into a business meeting; it helped put a different spin on things.

I once traded a guitar lesson for a lesson from Dave Van Ronk. Dave lived near the store, and he used to come in for supplies and to hang out. He always had a joke for us, and I loved when he cracked himself up, because Dave's laugh sounded like the roar of a wild bear. It startled customers, it shook the building, and it made everyone else laugh with him. Dave was a fine ragtime guitarist and a good teacher, so I sent people to him for lessons. We used to sell music books at the store, and one morning when things were slow, I looked at Dave's method book and saw that he had his own system of tablature. Later that day I was at the front counter playing "Devil Got My Woman" on an old National Duolian when Dave walked in. He nodded hello and listened to me play. When I finished the song, he asked, "What is that, Skip James?"

I nodded yes.

"'Devil Got My Woman,' right. What tuning are you in?"

"Open D minor. The same one Skip used."

"You know, I hung out with Skip James at the Newport Folk Festival in 1964, and afterwards I tried to play some of his songs, but I couldn't get them to sound right."

I explained the difference in tuning.

"Damn, no wonder I couldn't get it. Oh well, too late now."

"Don't sweat it, man. You're still a better guitarist than me. Hey, I was looking at your book earlier, and I wondered if you'd explain your tablature system."

He obligingly did. It was just like his playing style, unique and well thought out. I thanked him and asked if he'd sign the book for me. He grinned and wrote "STEAL THIS BOOK! —Dave Van Ronk."

"I won't have to steal it. Matt will probably give it to me."

"Steal it anyway, Zeke, it's good for you."

Dave laughed, and the building shook.

Payment in trade for musical aptitude isn't an original idea. According to legend, Robert Johnson sold his soul to the devil at the crossroad in exchange for his remarkable talent. As we have already seen, the crossroad is a traditional spot for magic and ill-doing. Criminals were hanged at crossroads, and suicides buried there. If pallbearers carrying a coffin to a cemetery passed a crossroad, they would set the coffin down and rotate positions at its corners, possibly to confuse the spirits who were said to gather there. Owned by no one, neither one road nor another, the crossroad is the place where spells are cast and deals are made.

The crossroad legend is found in the religious and folklore beliefs of cultures throughout the world, dating back to ancient times. In Greece, the guardian of the crossroad was Hermes; in Rome it was Mercury. In Africa, Legba was one of many names for the spirit who imparts wisdom and protects the crossroad. In European folklore, particularly the pre-Christian Germanic cultures, one encounters tales of musicians and dancers selling their souls to Der Teufel, the old pagan woods-devil.

For hoodoo practitioners, the crossroad is a place to dispose of the remnants of a magic ritual after laying down a trick. The idea is to leave the herbs, powders, roots, or other items where the intended victim will come in contact with them, then walk away without looking back and dispose of the leftovers properly.

Tommy Johnson, the Delta blues guitarist who wrote "Cool Drink of Water" and "Canned Heat Blues," explained how a crossroad deal may be made:

> If you want to learn how to make songs yourself, you take your guitar and you go to where the road crosses that way, where a crossroads is. Get there, be sure to get there just a little 'fore twelve that night so you know you'll be there. You have your guitar and be playing a piece there by yourself . . . A big black man will walk up there and take your guitar and he'll tune it. And then he'll play a piece and hand it back to you. That's the way I learned to play anything I want.

Blues writer David Evans heard this story from Tommy's brother Ledell. It brings to mind the image of Legba, often represented as a large black man, whose domain is the crossroad and who teaches a skill to those who approach with respect. Over the years, this story became associated with Robert Johnson, but with a twist borrowed from Johann Wolfgang von Goethe: Johnson, like the tragic character Faust, made a pact with the devil. Faust traded his soul for unlimited knowledge and worldly pleasure. Johnson traded his for extraordinary musical talent.

Whether or not the legend is rooted in truth, Johnson's lyrics suggest that he was well-versed in hoodoo. He may have practiced it himself, which wouldn't have been uncommon for the time and area; a great many poor black people carried a lucky root or mojo bag, hoping to beat the odds of poverty and illness. Certainly he embraced his association with hoodoo and had no problem with being perceived as someone who had met the devil. These things lent his music a dark mystique.

Johnson adopted the "hoodoo man" persona after his first wife, Virginia, died in childbirth along with their infant in 1930. Virginia's family, like many who lived on Mississippi plantations, were church people. They disdained the juke joint crowd and the blues musicians who played for them. Blues was the devil's music, and the family blamed Robert for Virginia's death. Their accusations hit him hard, and he left the plantation, outcast and broken-hearted, probably half-agreeing with them that his evil ways had killed his wife and child.

It was likely at this time that Johnson began hanging around the juke joint where Son House and Willie Brown performed. According to House, when they took a break between sets, Johnson would grab one of their guitars and play it, which annoyed people:

> So when we'd get to a rest period or something, we'd set the guitars up and go out—it would be hot in the summertime, so we'd go out and get in the cool, cool off some. While we're out, Robert, he'd get the guitar and go bamming with it, you know? Just keeping noise, and the people didn't like that. They'd come out and they'd tell us, "Why don't you or Willie or one go in there and stop that boy? He's driving everybody nuts." . . . I'd say, "Just leave the guitars alone" . . . [but] we couldn't break him from it, and his father would get at him, dogged him so much that he run away.

In 1931, Johnson married a woman from Martinsville named Caletta Craft. She was ten years older than her new husband, with two children from previous relationships. Caletta was an attentive wife, but she suffered from mental and emotional instability, and Johnson abandoned her in short order. He then went to Hazlehurst, Mississippi, where he met Ike Zimmerman, a highway worker and part-time musician. Zimmerman, a family man with a wife and children, befriended Robert and invited him home. One of Zimmerman's daughters described what happened next: "He came there and lived in our house . . . Robert

Johnson asked my daddy to teach him how to play guitar . . . Okay, well, he came for my daddy to teach, and my daddy taught him. He lived there with my daddy . . . He stayed a long time [because] he was staying to learn how to play the guitar . . . for a long time I thought he was related [to us]. I really did! . . . he just fitted in. I was used to him."

Zimmerman was four years older than Johnson. He took the younger man under his wing and taught him how to play. According to Zimmerman's daughter, he chose an unusual place to practice:

> They would leave and go to that cemetery. He'd sit back there with him. He wasn't at no crossroads. There wasn't no crossroads. [It] was just a path. They went 'cross the road. "Cause you gotta go across [the] road and go to that cemetery . . . [Daddy liked to practice there] 'cause it was still . . . real quiet. Real quiet. But he'd come back and tell them he played for the, he said haints. He said I been up there playing for the haints. They'd make a big laugh out of it. They sure would . . . And I think when he was carryin' Robert up there, it was so Robert could really concentrate on his guitar . . . He wasn't never scared, but he wasn't meeting the devil neither.

As Johnson's musicianship progressed, he began accompanying Zimmerman on his playing route at nearby lumber camps, fish fries, and juke joints. Sometimes Johnson would go out alone to try his hand at playing solo, then return a few days later. When Zimmerman felt he had taught Johnson the skills he needed, the two of them left the Hazlehurst area and set out for the Delta.

Zimmerman stayed for a short while and then returned home. Johnson went to the juke joint where Son House and Willie Brown played to show them what he had learned. House described what happened:

> Me and Willie, we was playing out at a little place called Banks, Mississippi. I looked and I saw somebody squeezing in the front door, and I seed it was Robert. I said "Bill, Bill." He said, "Huh." I said, "Look who's coming in the door, got a guitar on his back." . . . He said, "Oh, that's little Robert." I said, "Yeah, that's him." I said, "Don't say nothing." And he wiggled his way through the crowd, until he got over to where we was. I said, "Boy, now where you going with that thing?

T'annoy somebody else to death again?" . . . He say, "This your rest time?" I say, "Well, we can make it our rest time. What you want to do, annoy the folks?" He say, "No, just let me—give me a try." So I said, "All right, and you better do something with it, too," and I winked my eye at Willie. So he sat down there and finally got started. And man! He was so good! When he finished all our mouths were standing open. I said, "Well, ain't that fast! He's gone now!"

Son House could scarcely believe that Johnson had transformed himself from a terrible musician into a virtuoso in such a short amount of time. Whether one believes his talent came from the devil or Ike Zimmerman, it's still difficult to comprehend how he got so good so fast. Some of the best guitarists in the world have tried to replicate Johnson's style, but nobody can, because his timing and phrasing are so perfectly out of sync. His sound is unique and belongs only to him. Its origins remain a mystery.

Chapter 7

Some Joker Got Lucky

I threw a guitar pick straight up into the air and it stuck in the ceiling. It was a Fender Heavy Triangle pick, the kind no one used except for Richie Havens and a friend of mine named Dudeman.

My nasty pick-throwing habit began when I started working at the store. My coworker Carlo Tonalezzi and I would throw picks across the counter at each other, usually hitting other people in the crossfire. One day, Carlo threw a pick at the ceiling, trying to make it stick. It seemed impossible; the pick kept bouncing off and dropping to the floor. Over the years, I saw many people try to do it without success. But on Thursday, June 2, 2005, I threw a pick straight up into the air and it stuck in the ceiling. Maybe it was a sign.

After work, I rode the train home and then ate dinner with my wife and daughter. Later, while Cathy helped Caitlin study for a test, I checked my e-mail. Nothing. I was bored and killing time, so I logged on to eBay, thinking I might find a guitar for Tom.

Tom Crandall worked in the repair shop above the store, and he was a friend. I sometimes found unusual old guitars on eBay for him to buy. He would repair and sell some, while others ended up in guitar purgatory: a large stack of instruments waiting eternally to be fixed and played again.

I typed "old guitar" into the eBay search box. There were no interesting guitars on the first page, or the second. On the bottom of the third page I noticed an odd listing: "Old Snapshot Blues Guitar B. B. King??? AAMUS." Not a guitar, and probably not a photo of B. B., but still worth a look.

I clicked on it and the page appeared with a photograph and description:

Old Snapshot Blues Guitar B. B. King??? AAMUS

Looks like a very young B. B. King to me . . . but a very rare circa 1930 photo of a blues musician nonetheless! In poor condition, as you can see . . . but of historical interest and a wonderful early image. The Blues Image auction on eBay consists of a large collection of African-American performers in antique photographs. SEARCH "AAMUS" to see all 22 images listed in the auction, all will end June 8. All original, never reproduced and all unique, the images range from early CDV and tintype images to real photos, snapshots and publicity photos. For the most part, the photos are anonymous and depict the entire African-American musical experience in the United States during the late 19th and early 20th Century, A once in a lifetime opportunity to purchase historical original RARE vintage and period images of Blues Musicians, Early Rock and Roll performers, Minstrel and carnival performers, wandering "songsters" banjo and guitar players, street performers . . . as well as early Black string bands, jazz performers gospel and MORE. An extraordinary collection of 22 images, each selected for their authenticity and historical interest, all being listed on eBay starting June first and running 7 days, ending June 8. Of interest to African-American collectors, institutions, museums, and anyone who enjoys historical images depicting vernacular and roots music in natural settings, the auction and collection illustrates the variety of African-American musical experience throughout American History and dispels many myths. All images offered with little or no reserves, but competition is expected so place your bids accordingly, add enough to cover last minute bidders and ENJOY. All images are as shown from a scanner, no "sharpened" images. Detail photos are shown for most photos. Payment by winning bidder by check or money order, no Paypal. All sales are final. Enlarge pics and ask questions if you like. Little or no reserves, but make sure to bid enough to cover any last minute bidders, a collection like this will not come along again in a long time. Thanks!

I didn't read the entire description at first. Instead I clicked on the photo to get a better view. The emulsion was damaged in the center of the guitarist's head. The left corner was torn and jagged, and the surface was covered with specks of dirt and discoloration. The photo looked haunted, like it had been to hell and back.

I used the enlargement function to look carefully at the guitarist's hands, then at his face. His hands were huge, with long, spidery fingers. You never see anyone with hands like that. When I looked at his face, I knew who he was, because I had spent the past fifteen years studying the only other two known images of the man who was holding the guitar in the photo.

"That's not B. B. King," I said to myself, "because it's Robert Johnson."

Impossible.

It sure looked like him, though.

I stared at the image on my computer screen for a long time, then went to the bookcase where I keep signed books. In 1998, Dave Rubin had given me a copy of a book he edited, *Robert Johnson: The New Transcriptions*. On the first page, he wrote: "To Zeke—Who better to have a copy? Like the song says, when you've got a good friend." The cover of the book features a blowup of the Robert Johnson "cigarette photo," minus the cigarette, which was Photoshopped out by Hal Leonard for some reason.

I compared the face of the man on the screen with the face of the man on the book cover. They looked identical. I thought about the pick stuck in the ceiling and its possible connection to the appearance of a third photo of Robert Johnson. Maybe this is dumb, but it reminded me of an episode of *The Twilight Zone* called "A Penny for Your Thoughts." A man tosses a coin onto a table to buy his morning newspaper. The coin lands on its edge, perfectly balanced, and the man is suddenly able to hear other people's thoughts. This felt almost as weird.

I pictured Rod Serling smiling as I read the description of the photo. The phrases "rare," "large collection," "22 images," "African-American musicians," "real photos," "dispels many myths," and "once in a lifetime opportunity" were intriguing. I would take a look at the other photos in the auction tomorrow, but right now I needed another opinion on this one.

"Hey, Cat, can you look at this?"

My wife compared the two images, then said, "It's the same face."

Caitlin came over to look. "It is. You should buy it, Dad. How much is it?"

"I don't know."

I scrolled to the top of the page. The starting price, or minimum opening bid, was $25. There were no bids and seven days to go until the end of the auction. Anything could happen.

The next morning, after two cups of black coffee, I went on eBay and looked at the photo again. It was Friday, my day off, so I took my time and tried to think it through. The man holding the guitar still looked like Robert Johnson in the famous cigarette photo, but there was another photo to consider.

I dug out my copy of *Robert Johnson: The Complete Recordings*. The cover features the "suit" photo of Robert Johnson taken in Memphis at the Hooks Brothers photography studio in 1935. The lighting is severe, creating high contrast that makes Johnson's complexion appear lighter than in the cigarette photo. It also makes the sunburst 1929 Gibson L-1 guitar that he's holding look washed out. The harsh lighting exaggerates Johnson's lazy eye, which looks unnaturally out of sync with his other eye. Some writers have described him as looking like a deer caught in the headlights in this picture.

When I compared the suit photo with the image on eBay, it still appeared to be the same man. The lighting and angle of the face were different, but the features were the same. The stylish suits, huge spidery hands, and body language matched too.

The next question was, who is the other man in the photo, the one in the white suit? My first thought was that it could be David "Honeyboy" Edwards, the old friend who was there when Johnson died. Another possibility was Johnson's student, Robert Lockwood Jr. The man in the white suit was very young, and all the photos I'd seen of Edwards and Lockwood were taken when they were much older. Maybe there was a clue in the booklet that came with the box set.

On page eight, I found a reproduction of Johnny Shines' *Standin' at the Crossroads* album cover. Smiling confidently, Shines looks poised and professional in a white jacket and matching fedora. I noticed that the guitar slung across his shoulders was a mid-1960s Gibson B-25, a good choice for playing the blues. The dramatic lighting in this cover photograph creates a spotlight effect similar to that in the eBay photo.

The body language, white clothing, and similar lighting convinced me to take a closer look. With a magnifying glass, I could see that the shape of Shines' eyes, nose, cheekbones, and chin seemed to match those of the second man in the photo. Of course, my task was made more difficult by the thirty years or so between the two images. Also, although I had heard of Johnny Shines, I knew almost nothing about his life or his music. With six days until the end of the auction, I had some homework to do.

I went to work on Saturday and didn't tell anyone about the photo. When I got home, I logged onto eBay and studied the photo again, combing it for evidence to either prove or disprove that the two men were Robert Johnson and Johnny Shines.

The listing described the photo as three by four inches, a common size for the mid-thirties. I knew this because I used to sell vintage cameras. I wasn't as sure about the clothing. The suits in the photo looked like zoot suits, and the hats had wide brims, which I thought was a later style. I Googled zoot suits and learned that they were popular in black communities years before white people caught on to the style. So the mid-thirties was a likely time period for the clothing, too. I didn't have to research the guitar in the photo, because I had seen so many similar ones over the years. There was no name on the headstock, but I was sure the guitar was made by Harmony in the mid-thirties.

I Googled Johnny Shines and found out he had been born in Arkansas in 1915. One article said he met Robert Johnson in 1933, while another said they met in 1935. Both articles agreed that Shines claimed to have traveled with Johnson and described Shines as an excellent singer and guitarist. Johnny Shines died in 1992 at age seventy-two. An online discography listed several albums. I couldn't understand why no one had ever told me about Johnny Shines, and I decided to hunt down some of his CDs.

Based on the time period and the facial features, I felt there was a strong possibility that the man in the photo standing next to Robert Johnson was Johnny Shines. If the photo was taken in 1935, Shines would have been twenty years old, and Johnson would have been twenty-four. It all worked.

It was after midnight, and I needed some rest. I looked at the photo one more time. The starting price was still $25. No one had bid on it in the past two days. I decided to do something that I wouldn't normally have done because it seemed sketchy. I e-mailed the seller an offer and asked if he would consider ending the auction early.

I got a return message the next night. The seller thanked me for my offer but said he couldn't accept it. He explained that ending an auction early was in violation of eBay's rules and reminded me that he had twenty-one other photos currently up for sale, which he had collected in hopes of eventually using them for a book about pre-war African-American musicians. He had abandoned this idea because he didn't think he would ever find enough photos to fill a book. He told me the photo I wanted probably wouldn't sell for much because it was in poor condition and suggested that if I bid on it, I might get a bargain. He also wished me good luck.

The message was polite, but it wasn't what I wanted to hear. I'd figured ending an auction early might be against the rules, but I hadn't been sure. At least the seller seemed honest, and I was glad he mentioned the other photos that he was selling, because I had been so focused on my detective work that I'd forgotten about them.

I spent the next two hours looking at the seller's other photos, and they transported me back to an earlier time. There was one of a guitar player in front of an old railroad station, standing next to a horse-drawn peddler's carriage, that was especially compelling. I noticed that the current high bid on it was over $100, and that the starting prices on most of the other photos were higher than that of the one I wanted. Several had been bid up into the hundreds.

It was after 1:00 a.m. now and I was tired, but I clicked once more on the photo that had initially caught my interest. It was the best of the lot, and still at only $25. I could hardly believe nobody had bid on it yet.

I listened to Robert Johnson's music on my train ride to work the next morning. As I listened, I thought about the various accounts I had read of his strange, short life and tried to imagine where the eBay photo had come from. Perhaps it was taken when Johnson and Shines traveled together, but where had they been, and who was the photographer? This was Monday morning, and the auction was ending on Wednesday night. There wasn't enough time for me to find answers to these questions. I wondered if there ever would be.

I got off the train at West 4th Street and walked along Bleecker. I probably bought a cup of black coffee at Rocco's on my way to work, and I probably sold a guitar or two that day. I don't remember; my mind was elsewhere. When I got home, after dinner, I checked the auction. The price was still $25. There were no bids. I turned off the computer and watched TV with Cathy and Caitlin.

The next morning, on my way to work, I thought about how much I was willing to pay for the photo. What was it worth? If it was an original, unpublished photo of Robert Johnson, then it was priceless. I had recently sold my early-1920s Stella guitar to my friend Greg for $2,000, and I'd saved another $1,100 from working extra days. The total came to $3,100. I wondered if I should spend that much on an old photo.

I decided to sleep on it, but I didn't sleep very well. My mind wouldn't shut down. I kept thinking about why I really wanted the photo. It wasn't about reselling it for money. Anyone who knows me would tell you I'm not someone who chases dollars. It also wasn't about personal recognition. I like being part of a scene, but I don't like being the center of attention. So why did I want it? Two reasons: I wanted to hold the photo—a piece of history—in my hands. And I wanted to protect it.

Robert Johnson was a walking bluesman. He traveled from town to town, from the arms of one woman to another. He played music for money. His stage was a street corner or a juke joint; it didn't matter as long as there was a crowd. He traveled light, always moving, in search of something, lost or running from demons.

I knew his story and I loved his music. I thought if I could hold his photo—his actual image, made in some backstreet photography studio—then I might feel a connection, some kind of spiritual thing. If I could hold it, I would know if it was real, and I could protect it. This almost felt like a responsibility. It was a fragile antique in rough condition, and if someone mishandled it, it could be lost forever.

When I got out of bed that morning, I drank some coffee with Cathy and confessed that I was thinking of bidding $3,100 on the photo. The auction was going to end at 9:00 that night, and I had to decide what to do. Cathy said I should buy it and even offered to take money from our savings if I needed to bid a little higher. It was sweet of her, but I didn't want to use the rent money or Caitlin's college fund. I told Cathy that $3,100 was enough; if someone bid more than that, they surely knew it was a photo of Robert Johnson, and it would be in good hands. Someone else could curate this piece of blues history.

What I didn't say was that some part of me didn't want the job. The blues world is filled with people who like to argue about the music and lives of their heroes. There's an abundance of self-proclaimed scholars who believe their opinions overshadow those of everyone they encounter. I had seen this over and over again. Claiming to own a third photo of Robert Johnson was like painting a bull's-eye on your forehead. It was not a job for the faint-hearted. I also didn't mention to Cathy that in these days of Photoshop, it was possible that the photo was a fake.

On the train ride to work, I kept debating with myself whether to tell Tom, my repair shop friend, about the photo. I'd wanted to say something all week, but I hadn't. It wasn't a matter of trust. It was a less-rational thing: What if the photo carried some kind of bad mojo? What if it got disproved and people started saying bad things about everyone connected with it? I didn't use eBay much. Tom usually did most of the bidding for me, and he had a near-perfect record of winning auctions. He also knew Delta blues history. It would be interesting to get his take on the photo, but even if he disagreed with me, I was still going to bid on it.

I got off the train, went upstairs, and bought a cup of coffee at Rocco's. I probably unpacked some guitars that UPS or FedEx delivered. I might have sold something, and I'm sure I went to lunch. But again, I don't remember. Around 3:00, with a few minutes left on my break, I asked Tom if he would place an eBay bid for me. He asked what I wanted to buy, but I wouldn't tell him. All I said was that I wanted to bid $3,100 and that I had the money to cover it.

We went to the computer in the back of the store. Tom logged on to eBay and I gave him the item number.

"What kind of guitar is it?"

"It's not a guitar."

The photo appeared onscreen, and Tom asked me who it was. I

told him to take a closer look. Tom examined the photo, and his eyes widened. "Robert Johnson!" He stared at the screen for a moment, then asked, "Who's that standing next to him, do you know?"

"I think it's Johnny Shines."

"You know, I once saw him play live. I think you're right, it's Johnny Shines."

Tom agreed to bid on the photo for me and I asked him not to tell anyone about the photo until the auction ended.

As soon as I got home that night, I checked the auction. Two people had bid on it, and the price was now $88, with twenty minutes to go. Cathy brought me something to eat, and I went into the other room and picked at it. The auction was about to end, I told her. The price was still under $100 and I didn't want to watch.

Two minutes before the auction's end, I went back to the computer and clicked refresh. The top bid was still $88. With less than a minute to go, I refreshed the screen again. Now there were two more bids and the price had gone up to $355. I knew that Tom was going to place my bid in the last few seconds, but it was still nerve-wracking. With ten seconds until the end, I clicked refresh again, but before the screen could reload, the auction ended. I signed in and checked my completed auctions to see how it had played out.

Six bids had been placed on the photo, and Tom was the high bidder at $2,176.56. It was a lot of money, but I owned the photo.

PATTI SMITH
GONE AGAIN

AFTER SHOW

Chapter 8

Kind-Hearted Woman

The first person I ran into after I bought the photo was Patti Smith. I was on my way to work, walking up the stairs of the West 4th Street subway station, and there she was, directly in my path, heading downstairs. When I hailed her, she smiled and said, "Funny, I was thinking of you yesterday. I found some photos you might want."

Photos again! These were pictures that Oliver Ray had shot of me holding his 1929 Gibson L-1. This guitar was similar to one of Robert Johnson's. I explained this to Patti, then said, "This is really weird, because last night I bought an original photograph of Robert Johnson."

"What? Where?"

I told her the whole story. Patti knew that $2,200 was a large amount for me to spend, and she offered to cover me if I needed money to get by. I said thanks, but I had enough because I'd sold my acoustic guitar.

The train platform was unusually empty, and we talked for a few more minutes. Patti advised me to talk to a lawyer after I received the photo. She told me to call her and said she'd help me.

The last question Patti asked me that morning was, "Zeke, are you sure it's Robert?"

I looked at her sideways and grinned. She laughed, then smiled at me and said, "Sometimes life is just perfect. Of course it's real, and it went to the right person. You should have it."

As the uptown train pulled into the station, Patti said, "Remember this, Zeke: the guardians of history will be rewarded, becoming history themselves."

The doors opened and she got on. I watched the train pull away, then went upstairs and bought a cup of coffee. When I got to the store, no one was there yet. I let myself in and sat quietly at the front counter, thinking about the second time I'd met Patti.

It was on New Year's Eve of 1994, half an hour before closing. Patti came in and told me she was looking for a small guitar to write with. I noticed that she looked tired and very sad. I asked where Fred was, and her expression told me all I needed to know.

"I guess you didn't hear. Fred died in November."

I hadn't heard. "I'm so sorry. Are you OK?"

"No, I'm not."

She told me she was staying nearby with friends, and that she just wanted a simple guitar to help her get through the holidays. She had started to cry and I didn't know how to help, so I looked at the guitars we had behind the counter, trying to find the right one. Finally I handed her a small brown 1950s Martin 0-15. She played a few chords, smiled a little, and said she liked it.

It was near closing time and everyone was getting ready to go. Patti decided to buy the guitar. She looked through her pockets and realized she had left her credit card and checkbook at her friend's house. I explained the situation to Matt and asked if I could walk Patti home and take her check for the guitar. It was an unusual request, but he agreed to let me do it.

I went upstairs and found a copy of Patti's book *Seventh Heaven* I'd stashed away. I slipped it into my coat pocket and returned to tell Patti we were good to go. When I got back to the front counter, she was strumming the guitar and singing quietly, "The silence of a falling star lights up a purple sky . . . and as I wonder where you are . . . I'm so lonesome I could cry."

The only ones who heard this lovely impromptu performance were me and an intoxicated man who had just wandered in. He must have heard the whole song, because he said, "Thank you, that's beautiful, sweetheart," and gave her a dollar. I couldn't help laughing when he left. Patti shrugged and said, "Hey, a gig's a gig."

I put the guitar in its case, put on my coat and hat, and walked Patti to her friend's house. She was staying with entertainment lawyer Rosemary Carroll. Patti gave me a check for the guitar, and when I asked if she could sign my copy of *Seventh Heaven*, she wrote a nice note inside.

"You going to be all right for New Year's Eve, Zeke?"

"I'm spending it at home with my family," I admitted, feeling a little guilty because she couldn't do the same. I felt sad on the subway ride home, and grateful to see my wife and daughter.

I saw Patti again a few months later. She stopped by the store to tell me she was staying at the Chelsea Hotel and working on her guitar playing. I handed her a guitar and asked her to show me. When she strummed a few chords in waltz time, it was clear that she had been practicing.

"Pretty good!"

She smiled. "I'm writing, too."

I was happy to hear it, because it was a sign that she was finding her way. When a creative person starts working again after a loss or tragedy, they are resuming life.

One of Patti's favorite hangouts was a coffee shop nearby, so she often stopped by the store. She had good and bad days, but I was always glad to see her. Later that year she introduced me to Oliver Ray, who looked as if he had just stepped from the pages of Charles Dickens. He was young, pale, thin, and ragged, a Victorian waif you could easily picture asking for another bowl of gruel. During our first conversation, I realized he was also smart, and we soon became friends.

We hung out, played guitar, listened to old records, and drank coffee. Oliver was a natural poet with a good eye for photography. His guitar skills were basic, but I enjoyed playing music with him because he had an odd sense of timing and he liked using unusual chord shapes. Oliver was sincere in his desire to create art and to develop as a musician. Some people found him difficult to deal with, but we got along fine, maybe because some people find me difficult to deal with too.

At the end of August 1996, Oliver came to the store to tell me that Patti was going to play a benefit show as part of the Central Park SummerStage series. Tom Verlaine was in Paris, and Patti thought I should play his slide guitar part on one of her songs. It was an honor to be invited to perform with Patti, and I decided to give it a try.

On September 5, the night of the show, Cathy, Caitlin, and Patti's son Jackson met me at the store. I left work ten minutes early and we took a taxi to Central Park. When we got there, crowds of people were headed toward the stage. Caitlin was hungry, so I bought her a hot dog, but she didn't like it. There were no garbage cans in sight and it was a long walk to the show, so I threw the hotdog down a sewer grate.

"Zeke, that's so disgusting!" Jackson yelled.

I laughed. "Not as disgusting as that hot dog. At least it won't go to waste—the rats will eat it."

We got to the stage area, but none of us had ID. Jackson asked the security guard to find his mom, and Patti's assistant, Andi Ostrowe, came to let us in. There were two trailers with food and drinks in a fenced-off area near the stage. I took a bottle of water and washed down a Benadryl because I had a cold. Yik, the band's guitar tech, tuned my guitar and we did a quick sound check. People were beginning to come in. I hung out with Cathy, Oliver, and Jackson, watching Caitlin and Patti's daughter Jesse as they ran around the trailers. The show was going to start late because we were waiting for Patti's mother, Beverly, to arrive, but Patti, ever thoughtful, said I could play early in the set so I could take Caitlin home if she got tired.

Oliver introduced me to a tall, long-haired, bearded man, a biker type in a big straw hat and a black leather vest with matching pants. His name was Steven Sebring and he was filming the show with a vintage 16mm camera. Patti's mother finally made her entrance, and as the show began, Oliver took me upstairs to watch from the side of the stage.

"Mother has arrived," Patti said, and read her poem "Piss Factory." The band played "Radio Ethiopia," followed by Patti's spoken-word version of "People Have the Power." They launched into a loud and powerful rendition of "Gone Again," and then it was my turn. I stood there wondering how I would play a ballad after such intense music.

Patti introduced me as her friend Zeke from Matt Umanov Guitars. She said I had sold her a beloved guitar and that she couldn't remember my last name. I walked over and whispered it to her. She said, "No wonder I couldn't remember, it's too beautiful. Shine, Zeke Schein."

I looked down at the crowd below and saw my friend Lisa. She waved hello, and suddenly it felt good to be onstage. Patti sang her song "Wing," and I played the most beautiful slide guitar part I could manage. I was trying to invoke the spirit of Robert Johnson for a crowd of nine thousand people. *Can't you hear the wind howl . . .*

When the song was over, I hugged Patti and walked down the stairs to where Cathy was standing. "OK, I'm impressed," she said, and hugged me. She said she'd had a hard time seeing the show because a woman standing at the top of the stairs had blocked her view. She pointed out the woman. It was Courtney Love.

We stayed for the whole show. Two highlights for me were when Jackson joined the band to play "Smoke on the Water" and when Thurston Moore came out for the encore and played guitar on "Rock and Roll Nigger." After the last song, Jackson and Oliver came offstage and hugged me. I thanked Patti for the opportunity to play with her and the band. As Cathy, Caitlin, and I left Central Park, several people came up to say they had enjoyed the show. We took a taxi to Bleecker Street and had coffee and pastries at Rocco's before heading home.

The show left no doubt that, after eighteen years, Patti Smith was back. She would spend most of the next several years touring and recording. I kept in touch with Patti, and from time to time she would stop by the store or we would run into each other in the neighborhood, as we had in the subway this morning. I really appreciated her offer to help me with the photo. I'd call her when it arrived, but right now I had to open the store.

I went upstairs to get a bottle of water from the fridge. Tom grinned at me from his workbench, and we talked about how the auction had played out. There were five other bids, and two of them were pretty heavy, so someone else may have known what they were bidding on. Tom gave me a slip of paper with the seller's contact information. His name was Jim Linderman, and he lived about a mile away from the store. Tom also showed me a message Jim Linderman had forwarded to him from the second highest bidder: if I didn't want the photo for any reason, he would match my bid.

I told Tom I would e-mail the seller to let him know I definitely wanted the photo. Before heading downstairs, I said, "Thanks for helping me. I might not have gotten it without you. Let's hope it's not cursed."

Tom laughed, but I wasn't joking. Later that night I e-mailed Jim Linderman offering to buy him lunch and pay him in cash if he would bring the photo to the store instead of mailing it. He didn't get back to me, so I sent him a cashier's check via registered mail and waited. Three weeks passed and the photo still hadn't arrived. I was concerned that the photo might have gotten lost, so I e-mailed Jim, but he didn't reply. At this point, I didn't even want to consider the possibility that I might have gotten ripped off.

On a hot July afternoon almost a month later, our postman handed me a large stack of mail held together with two rubber bands. On the bottom was a slightly bent Priority Mail envelope addressed to me, return addressee Jim Linderman. I was relieved that the photo had arrived, but I couldn't believe he had sent it uninsured in the US mail.

I finished helping a customer, then took my lunch break. I brought the mail upstairs, but no one was there. Tom wasn't at his bench because it was his day off. Matt was out running errands, and Jean, our bookkeeper, was also off, so I sat at her desk and opened the envelope. Inside were four pieces of white cardboard encasing a large plastic sleeve, which contained five old black-and-white photos. The photo of Robert Johnson and Johnny Shines was the smallest, and it was on top of the others, pressed up against the plastic sleeve. It was hot outside and the plastic was warm. I was concerned that the photo might be stuck to the sleeve, so I waited a few minutes before removing it. Luckily, it was fine. The photo was in rough shape, though—torn, cracked, spotted, and dirty. I didn't know where it had been, but one thing was certain: it was a survivor.

There are moments when time slows down, when your heart beats an unfamiliar rhythm, a strange pulse. It's a shaky feeling, but it's good because you know something surreal is happening, like when you dream you're falling, but instead of hitting the ground you start to fly. I stared at the photo for as long as it took me to level out, then carefully lifted it by its edges and held it in my hand.

I felt an immediate connection, an energy, as if I were there in the room watching the photograph being shot. When I put it down, things were normal again.

I turned the photo over to look at the back, hoping to find a photographer's stamp or an inscription. There were two pieces of cellophane tape on the back. A single strand of short, curly black hair was stuck to one of them. There was also a piece of faded red paper stuck to one side, as if the photo had been pasted in an album or a frame. The back was as rough-looking as the front.

My lunch break was almost over and I still had to get a coffee, so I set the photo aside and looked at the other four. They were interesting, but nothing special. I noticed that one of the pieces of white cardboard had a note written on it: "THANKS ZEKE. AS I RECALL, I BOUGHT THE PHOTO IN ATLANTA, GA. A FEW YEARS AGO. I TOSSED IN A COUPLE LEFTOVERS FOR YA. Thanks, Jim."

That explained the other photos. It was also a possible lead for future research. I placed everything back inside of the envelope except for the photo of Robert and Johnny, which I put in an archival-quality acid-free sleeve. Then I went across the street for a black iced coffee. It totally hit the spot.

Chapter 9

Wind That Thing

I was on the twenty-second floor of the Woolworth building in the offices of Pelosi, Wolf, Effron, & Spates, LLP. Several months earlier, Patti Smith had referred me to Rosemary Carroll for legal advice about the photo. Rosemary was sweet and provided some guidance, but I soon realized that I needed more help. Wendy Wills steered me to John Pelosi.

John was taller, darker, and handsomer than me. He was also smarter than me and made more money than I do. But I didn't feel too bad despite all that, because I had the pale, skinny, guitar-player-wearing-a-fedora thing going on. Oh yeah . . . I had plenty of that.

"So, how do you know Wendy?" John asked.

"We used to play together. The first time I saw her, she was playing in a Starbucks on West 30th Street. A few days later she came to the store to get her guitar fixed. It was pretty messed up, but it meant a lot to her because it used to belong to her brother, you know?"

"He passed away, right?"

"Right, and I felt bad telling her the guitar was toast, so I mentioned that I'd caught her show and thought she sounded good but needed a better guitar. I showed her a few, and then we talked for a while and decided to try playing together. We became friends, and you know how she is, sort of spacey, but in the best possible way. Did she tell you why I came here?"

"She said something about a photo of a musician—Robert Johnson. Aren't there only one or two photos of him?"

"Two, and that's why I'm here. I think I've found a third."

I removed a copy of the photo from a manila envelope and handed it to John. He glanced at it and asked, "Who's standing next to him?"

"I'm pretty sure that's Johnny Shines. He traveled with Johnson in the mid-thirties. He was also a great blues player."

John asked me about the provenance of the photo. Did I know the photographer's identity? Where it was shot? Was everything about it period-correct? Where did the original owner say he got it?

As I answered John's questions, he continued to study the photo, comparing it to copies I'd brought of the two other Johnson photos. When he finished, he looked up at me and said, "Zeke, I'm sure you know more about this than I do, but frankly . . . I don't see it."

I was disappointed, but tried not to show it. "That's OK. I understand, but I bet if you live with it for a few days, you'll see it's the same man in all three photos. The camera angle and lighting are different, that's all."

John stood up and came around his desk to walk me out. "It would help if you had some proof."

"I know. I'll leave a copy of the photo with you. Live with it for a few days and call me if you if you see the shot. Thanks again for everything."

I left John's office and walked down Broadway into the chill of a wintery New York morning. I bought a black coffee to warm up, then caught the uptown train to West 4th Street, arriving at the store ten minutes early. You never know how the day will go. It might be busy, or it might drag on. You also never know who might walk in. It could be a return customer stopping by to say hello, or a family of European tourists, or someone really famous. It doesn't really matter; my goal is to have every customer walk out happier than when he or she first came in.

It was a slow morning, and by mid-afternoon I was feeling down. I don't know what I'd expected John to say, but I had hoped he would want to get involved. Now that seemed like a long shot. He was right; it would help if I had more proof. I was thinking about that when my friend Kevin Delaney walked in. We began chatting as he fingered a Gibson Banner J-45. When I told him about the photo, Kevin suggested that I contact the History Detectives. At first I thought that he was joking, but he explained that there was a PBS television show called *History Detectives*. In each episode, the Detectives research an artifact to determine whether it's authentic. Surely they would want to do a show about a mysterious lost photo of Robert Johnson.

Watching a few episodes convinced me that the History Detectives knew their stuff. Their aid and expertise might uncover a clue that would prove the photo's authenticity, but it might also be proven a fake. I was willing to roll the dice, so I e-mailed them.

A week later, John Pelosi called to tell me that after studying the photo and comparing it to the others, he believed it to be the real thing. I was glad to hear it. John represents some heavyweight photographers and musicians, and also plays guitar. He was my kind of lawyer.

In June of 2006, a TV producer named Dave Jacobs contacted me to say the History Detectives might be interested in doing a show about the photo. I mentioned that I had stumbled upon a promising new clue. On the website for *Can't You Hear the Wind Howl*, a documentary film about Johnson, I found a quote from director Peter Meyer: "Robert Johnson's traveling companion, blues legend Johnny Shines, claimed that there was a photo taken of himself and Johnson by a woman named Johnnie Mae Crowder in Hughes, Arkansas, in 1937 and later published in a local newspaper. However, this photo has never surfaced."

"Whoa, Zeke."

"That's right, Dave. That's what it said."

"Did you follow up on it?"

"Yeah, I e-mailed Pete Meyer, and he said his source was Johnny Shines himself."

"You should ask if he knows anything about the photographer. Is she still alive? Where does she live? It could help."

I e-mailed Pete again to let him know I'd recently bought what might be the very photo Shines had mentioned, and asked if he had any knowledge of Johnnie Mae Crowder's whereabouts. Pete got back to me two weeks later.

Hey Zeke—Sorry I haven't responded sooner to your e-mail—we've been on a much needed holiday. This is fabulous news about the photo—unfortunately I don't have any current information on Johnnie Mae Crowder. I seem to recall it being mentioned to me that she lived in or around St. Louis with her family. Naturally, I would be very interested in seeing this photo—I would love to use it in a re-edit of my film—but you need to get it copyrighted.

I called Dave Jacobs and relayed the information about Johnnie Mae

Crowder. Dave agreed to pitch the story to the show if I agreed to let them debut the photo.

About a week later, John Tefteller, a record collector from Oregon, stopped by the store. John buys and sells some of the world's rarest records, specializing in prewar blues 78s and early rock and roll discs. His collection is impressive and vast. I first met him when we began selling his Blues Images calendar at the store. The 2004 cover featured a long-lost full-body photo of legendary delta bluesman Charley Patton, which John had unexpectedly found among piles of Paramount Record Company promotional art he had purchased. The Patton photo blew me away. His oversized suit and snappy two-tone shoes perfectly matched his raucous sound, while the unusual overhanded way he held his cheap Stromberg-Voisinet guitar reinforced all the stories painting him as a wild, crazy performer. John was interested in my own photo discovery. He said he was only in town on a short business trip but would contact me when got back home.

Talking with Dave Jacobs and John Tefteller inspired me. Being around guys with drive and ambition always makes me feel like the slacker that I am, and usually I'm fine with it, but not this time. Owning the photo of Johnson and Shines came with certain responsibilities. I had to learn more about it and share it with others, just as John had done with the Patton photo.

I fell asleep with that idea on my mind. When I woke up, the idea had blossomed into an obsession, as if watered by a platoon of beer-helmeted dream fairies. I awoke wondering how I might go about doing some history detective work, but who was I kidding? I was never going to do it by myself. I hate to work alone, so I called my old friend Lonnie Jackson, hoping to convince him to go with me to the New-York Historical Society. It didn't take much convincing, as Lonnie loves this kind of stuff.

Lonnie lives in Park Slope, Brooklyn, a few miles closer to Manhattan than my neighborhood. We met in our usual place, the last subway car of the uptown Q train. It was Friday and I had the day off, so of course it was raining. Lonnie had the good sense to carry an umbrella. I never carry an umbrella, which meant I was wet and cranky on the train ride in while Lonnie was cheerfully dry.

When we got off the train at 81st Street, it was still raining. I tucked my notebook under my jacket as we began walking along the western perimeter of Central Park. We had walked less than two blocks when a loud thunderclap exploded and rain started pouring down. We ducked beneath an underpass in the park. I was cursing and Lonnie was laughing at how ridiculous our situation was. We waited half an hour for the rain to subside before finally arriving at our destination.

Aside from the life-size bronze figures of Abraham Lincoln and Frederick Douglass near the entranceways, from the outside, the New-York Historical Society doesn't look like much. But inside it's impressive: time—neatly displayed behind glass showcases in the museum—and history that you can reach out and touch in the library. It seemed like a place where even two wet, scruffy, neophytes like Lonnie and me might find a clue.

I told the librarian that we were researching an old photograph and asked her to bring us an assortment of Sears Roebuck catalogs from the 1930s. They were soon wheeled out on a wooden cart and the librarian showed us how to use a table stand to support their heavy weight.

We thanked her and opened the first volume, a 1936-1937 fall/winter catalog from Chicago. Of course, I went right to the pages of guitars first and saw that the headstocks, bridges, and tailpieces on some low-end models were a match. We turned to the pages that featured men's suits ranging in price from $9.00 to $16.95. The pants were high waisted with two-button closures; most had pleats and cuffs. The jacket lapels were wide and some of the ties had bold striped patterns. Square (tank) watches were priced from $3.98 up to $45.00. I looked at the photo of Johnson and Shines for comparison. Their outfits were similar, but somehow slicker. I opened the next volume.

This was a 1937-1938 fall/winter catalog from Boston. The guitars were mostly fourteen-fret archtop models. A few inexpensive twelve-fret flat tops like the guitar in the photo were priced at $3.65. The suits were different, more conservative than those in the Chicago catalog. The style didn't match—the shoulders were padded and the lapels were wider.

When I reached for the 1936 spring/summer catalog from Chicago, I noticed that Lonnie was already immersed in the amazing Technicolor world of the 1937 spring/summer Chicago catalog. We were both in the same room of the library and in the same city in the catalogs, but Lonnie had traveled back in time exactly one year ahead of me. He seemed to be enjoying himself there, so I left him and dove headfirst into 1936.

In his song "Sweet Home Chicago," recorded in 1936, Robert Johnson referred to Chicago as "the land of California." I hadn't thought about that when I looked at the first catalog, but now that I had, I decided to take my time leafing through this one. The catalog featured thousands of products. It was a mind-blowing, endless array of supplies for everyday life in the big city. For Robert Johnson, Chicago must have been sweet indeed—geographically close to Mississippi, but worlds away from the plantation life that he had left behind.

The wide-brim hats, the wide-lapel suits, the crisp high-collared shirts, the classy ties, the two-tone wingtip shoes, the tank watches with steel-link bands—all were represented in this catalog. In Chicago, in the spring of 1936, Sears was one-stop shopping for the man about town. The guitars were identical to those in the winter catalog, and some were similar to the one Johnson holds in the photo.

Lonnie and I switched catalogs, then looked through the remaining three the librarian had brought us. An hour later we were sitting in a cafe near Central Park, drinking coffee and comparing notes. We agreed that everything in the photo matched the time period of the catalogs, but Johnny Shines was wearing a suit that looked way cooler. Who knows where he got it, but surely it wasn't Sears.

Chapter 10

Ramblin'

The problem with research is that it usually ends up leading to more research. I found myself waist deep in a pile of exasperating questions. What was Johnny Shines' story? Where did he and Johnson first meet?

I dug deeper into the past and found a few more pieces of the puzzle.

Johnny Shines was born in Memphis in 1915. He began playing guitar as a teenager, performing at juke joints and on street corners. In 1932, at age seventeen, Shines moved to Hughes, Arkansas, where he supported himself working on farms and soon met Robert Johnson.

As Shines tells it:

> The first time I came to Helena [a town two counties over from Hughes] was 1932, I think it was. That's the time I met Robert, the first time. Well, I was playing with a boy M&O and for some reason or another he was looking for somebody to cut Robert's head . . . I think he was thinking that Robert was a little too high for himself, you know, and he kept begging me to 'Come down here and meet Rob, come down here and meet Rob. He think he's the best in the world.' You know and all that kind of stuff. But that was my game then, cuttin' heads, you know, so finally one day we hopped a train and come on down here. What I was aiming to do, well that's what happened to me. He stole my crowd. In other words, he cut my head.

Most accounts agree that Shines began traveling with Johnson in 1935. In interviews, Shines described Johnson as a loner who preferred to perform solo. "I tagged along with him cause I knew he was heavy and I wanted to learn . . . He'd go one way, and I'd go the other. We'd work in the streets. I'd go over here and start playing, and he'd go over there and start playing. He'd draw his gang; I'd draw mine."

When asked what style of music he and Johnson played, Shines recalled that they played all types of music, everything from polkas to pop tunes, juggling their repertoire based on where they were and what the crowd wanted to hear. They took their music where the money was. "It was pretty rough at times; we didn't know where the next food was coming from or where we'd stay that night," Shines recalled. "Robert and I would travel anywhere to play and make some money. We'd hear about a sawmill going to pay off at a certain time, and we'd be there; we'd pick up maybe seven dollars just playing where the payday was. And then some guy might hire us to play somewhere for four dollars a night and all we could drink. Different guys'd give us a quarter to play this piece or that piece, so we'd end up with twenty-five or thirty dollars."

In terms of musical ability, Shines described Johnson as a natural genius. "He'd hear something on the radio that he liked, sometime that night later on he'd play it chord for chord, note for note, lick for lick, word for word, just like you'd hear it on the radio. I never saw him practice."

As a person, Shines described Johnson as "a very nice guy when he wasn't drinking too heavy, which was very seldom." In contrast to that, he said that when Johnson would "get a lot of whiskey in him, then he'd start messing with folks. It's a wonder my head isn't as big as a garbage can, the way he used to get my head knocked in. 'Cause he'd mess with people, mess with people's wives, and things like that—women. He didn't have no respect for nobody when he got to drinking."

My research convinced me that Shines knew Johnson about as well as anyone could have. I was impressed with his candor about "tagging along" with Johnson and playing separately on opposite street corners. His humility was endearing, and his stories rang true.

Shines had mentioned that they occasionally hit a good payday, so at times they could afford an extravagant purchase, but where did Shines buy his custom-made suit? He and Johnson had traveled together, but where to? According to Shines, they had been to Chicago, Texas, New York, Canada, Kentucky, and Indiana.

While in New York, Shines might have visited Harlem. He could have won the suit playing poker with one of Cab Calloway's horn players. Calloway's band wore similar suits in the 1933 film *International House*. Shines might have gotten a good deal on it from a pawnbroker, perhaps trading his own suit and three dollars for it. We can make up all kinds of stories, but in reality we can only venture a guess where Shines got his sharp suit.

In 1938, Robert Johnson, Johnny Shines, and Shines' cousin Calvin Frazier left Mississippi and went to Chicago, then Detroit. In the latter city they met up with blues pianist Big Maceo Merriweather and Elder Clarence Leslie Morton Sr., a minister with his own radio show. *Elder Morton and His Radio Chorus* aired twice weekly on CKLW, a radio station in Windsor, Canada.

Shines said that he, Frasier, and Johnson played on the radio and performed at personal appearances with Elder Morton. When asked if he played blues with Elder Morton, Shines laughed and said, "No, no, no, I was playing gospel music . . . regular old gospel songs like 'Ship of Zion,' 'Stand by Me,' 'When the Saints Go Marchin' In,' and 'Just Over in Glory Land.'"

Shines' account of three bluesmen traveling and performing with a singing preacher reminded me of the scene in the movie *O Brother, Where Art Thou?* where the Soggy Bottom Boys (George Clooney, John Turturro, Tim Blake Nelson, and Chris Thomas King) sing the song "Man of Constant Sorrow." The film is set in rural Mississippi in 1937, and Chris Thomas King's character, Tommy Johnson, first meets the others when they stop their car to give him a ride. When asked what he's doing in the middle of nowhere, he explains, "I had to be at that there crossroads last midnight to sell my soul to the devil."

The scene as written by Joel and Ethan Coen is affecting, but what truly makes the film brilliant is T Bone Burnett's Grammy-winning soundtrack. It sold several million copies and helped to popularize traditional bluegrass and country blues music. Needless to say, I liked the soundtrack. Apparently I wasn't alone, because two years after the film's debut, my customers were still talking about *O Brother, Where Art Thou?* and buying banjos, mandolins, and steel guitars to play Ralph Stanley and Skip James songs.

I was sitting at the front counter playing Skip James' "Hard Time Killing Floor Blues" when a sleek black limo pulled up to the curb outside the shop. The driver got out and opened the rear door. I immediately recognized the tall, elegantly dressed man who emerged from within. T Bone Burnett walked in like Rhett Butler, perfectly groomed, in a tailored black waistcoat and a high-collared white shirt. He stopped to listen as I finished playing the song.

"Skip James, what is that, 'Hard Time Killing Floor'?"

"Yeah, wow, nice to see you."

"You too. What tuning are you in, open minor?"

"Open D minor. Skip also used it for 'Devil Got My Woman.' He used it most of the time."

I asked T Bone what he was in town for. He was on his way to do an interview with the Coen Brothers to promote *O Brother, Where Art Thou?*, and he wanted to buy a guitar to use for the interview.

He asked to see two black 1960s Silvertone guitars, both model 1420s. One had two pickups, the other a single. We went into the amp room and I plugged the guitar with two pickups into a 1959 Gibson Skylark amp.

T Bone tuned the guitar to open D minor and asked, "Is that the tuning Skip used?"

"Yeah, D-A-D-F-A-D, from low to high."

"Would you mind showing me how you play 'Devil Got My Woman'?"

Would I mind? I plugged the other guitar in and tuned it. We sat across from each other and I taught him the song. When he was satisfied that he could play it, T-Bone smiled and said, "Did you ever wonder where Skip got that tuning?"

"I did. Where do you think he got it?"

I was hoping that T Bone wasn't going to say "From Satan," because that would have freaked me out. Instead he said, "From the gypsies."

"What gypsies?"

Instead of giving me a direct answer, T Bone began to talk about Mississippi—a Mississippi of the past, shrouded in folk magic and lore. He talked about root doctors and mojo bags, about altars and spells, about hoodoo and the place where music and magic meet.

And then T Bone played a song for me. It was his own song, but it was timeless. It was hauntingly beautiful, and it was terrifying. If I had any doubt about bluesmen and gypsies playing together after deals were done, it was gone now. T Bone's song had convinced me. I asked him to teach it to me and he did. After that, T Bone bought both of the Silvertone guitars. I carried them out to the limo and we thanked each other.

Yeah, some days I like my job.

Chapter 11

Stones in My Passway

"So, what do you think?"

It was a question I would find myself asking time and time again. Owning the photo was frustrating. I wanted to show it to others to get their input, but I had to be careful because I still hadn't copyrighted it.

On the morning after the photo arrived, I went upstairs to the repair shop and showed it to Tom, Matt, and Darrell Gilbert, an old friend who worked at the shop. They all agreed that it looked like Johnson; the lazy eye and the huge hands were especially convincing. Matt said we might be able to prove or disprove it by examining the ears. He pointed out that ear shapes, like fingerprints, are unique to an individual and that no two people have identical ears. Matt took the photo into his office and studied it with a high-quality jeweler's loupe. Ten minutes later, he handed the photo back to me and said, "I don't know what to tell you, Zeke."

I passed the photo to Tom, who inspected it under a bright light with an old-school Sherlock Holmes magnifying glass. "It looks right to me. What do you think, Darrell?"

Darrell looked at the photo for less than a minute before asking, "Did any of you geniuses notice that there are no strings on the guitar?"

"What?—No!—Let me see."

My heart skipped a couple of beats as I looked.

"Wow, no strings, no nut, no tuners on one side, busted tuners on the other."

Tom looked at it again, "Amazing. Maybe it was broken in a juke joint fight."

"Or it's a prop." Darrell surmised.

"It could be either one," I said. "In interviews, Johnny Shines mentioned that he broke up more than a few barroom brawls that Robert Johnson got himself into."

I spent my lunch break showing the photo to Dave Rubin, who believed it was the real deal. I'm not big on eating lunch. Usually I just get coffee and a scone, so it wasn't a problem for me to show the photo on my break. After Dave Rubin, my next meeting was with Frank DiGiacomo, a writer for *Vanity Fair*. Frank was an old friend of John Pelosi's, and John thought Frank might want to pitch the story to his editor. When John told me that he thought *Vanity Fair* was the right place to debut the photo, I didn't understand why. I knew it was a quality magazine, but in my mind, *Rolling Stone* was a better choice. Besides, I had already told Dave Jacobs that *History Detectives* could have first shot. I agreed to meet Frank anyway, because John wanted me to.

We met at the store and walked over to Rocco's. I liked Frank right away. I don't know if it was his John Lennon glasses, his cynicism, or maybe because he ordered a double espresso and a plate of pignoli cookies. He said he wanted to pitch the story to his editor and that he would be in touch.

My next lunch meeting was a month later. John Tefteller e-mailed me wanting to see the photo. In town on business, he asked if I could meet with him and his friend Ralph DeLuca, a major player in the world of rare movie memorabilia. I was fine with that.

Once again, I chose Rocco's as the meeting place. Their barista, Joe, slung mean caffeine, and who doesn't like bingeing on cookies and cannoli? John showed up with Ralph and I brought along Tom and Dave, so there were five sturdy guys in black jackets sitting at the table. To anyone watching, it must have looked like a sit-down, especially when I pulled out a copy of the photo, because we all lowered our voices and looked over our shoulders as we passed it around.

By the end of the meeting, both John and Ralph agreed that the photo appeared to be authentic. John is a heavy hitter when it comes to collecting early blues music, so I wasn't surprised when he mentioned that he had been one of the six lower bidders in the original eBay auction. He had placed a low bid on the photo because he thought it was interesting, but it hadn't occurred to him that the young men in the photo might be two bona fide blues legends. John was interested in debuting the photo on the cover of his Blues Images calendar, and I was glad to hear it, but I let him know that I had prior commitments. John said that he was going to do more research on Johnnie Mae Crowder, the woman who may have shot the photo. He also advised me to keep the photo under wraps—which is exactly what I did until the night of May 7, 2006.

Two weeks earlier, Dave Rubin had called to let me know that David "Honeyboy" Edwards and Robert Lockwood Jr. were scheduled to play a show at B. B. King's club on West 42nd Street. Dave, who had done an instructional video with Honeyboy Edwards, asked if I would like to go with him.

"Yeah, of course I want to go," I said. "Hey, let me know if this sounds crazy, but do you think we could get Honeyboy and Lockwood to look at the photo?"

I could hear the wheels in Dave's head turning.

"It's not crazy, Zeke. I think it's a good idea. Who knows, they might remember where it was shot."

"Do you think you could make it happen?"

"I'll find out. I know Honeyboy's manager, Michael. I'll give him a call and get back to you. Are you sure you want to do this?"

It was a serious question, and although he didn't say it, I understood exactly what Dave was implying. Edwards and Lockwood had known Johnson and Shines personally. What if I showed them the photo and they told me that it wasn't the real deal?

"Yeah, Dave, I'm sure. It's probably the only chance I'll get. They're like, what, ninety years old?"

"That's right, and it's worth going to see them play. They still sound great and it will be interesting to get their take on the photo."

Dave called later in the week to let me know that we were both on the guest list and that Michael had agreed to let me show the photo to Honeyboy Edwards.

On the afternoon of the show, my friend Eli Smith showed up at the store with his roommate Steve Strohmeier. I had known Eli since his early teens. Even as a kid, he knew more about music history than anyone four times his age. On top of that, he could also play guitar. Usually Eli came by to buy strings or just hang out, but this time he came by to let me know that he and Steve had picked up Honeyboy Edwards and Michael Frank from the airport and had just dropped them off at the club. Michael had told them that I was going to show the photo to Edwards and Lockwood. Steve showed me a video camera and asked me if I wanted him to document what happened. Sure, why not?

After work, Eli, Steve, Tom, and I caught the uptown A train to 42nd Street and walked over to B. B. King's. We met Dave there and he introduced me to Michael. After we found our seats, Michael asked to see the photo. I showed it to him and he said, "I don't know, it doesn't look like him to me, but I don't have an eye for these things. We'll show it to Honey and see what he has to say—he'll know."

I had hoped to meet Edwards and Lockwood before the show began. They were both ninety years old, and I figured I should show them the photo early in the night, when they would be more focused and alert. Of course, it didn't work out that way. Michael said I would have to wait until after the show. When I asked if Steve could film their response, Michael said no. He also insisted that I wasn't allowed to ask Edwards or Lockwood if the men in the photo were Johnson and Shines, because that would be "leading them." Michael was running the show and I was his guest, but I was annoyed.

"So I can't ask them a direct question?"

"No. You can't mention their names."

"If I can't ask whether this is a photo of Robert Johnson and Johnny Shines, then what do you want me to say when I show it to them?"

"Just ask them if they knew the men in the photo. Otherwise I won't let you show it to them."

There were too many jokers in the deck, but these guys weren't getting any younger and I only had one shot at this. I couldn't dismiss the possibility that Edwards or Lockwood might actually have been in the room when the photo was shot. They might know the story behind it. I considered that and then said, "OK, Michael."

I enjoyed the show. Honeyboy Edwards came out playing an aluminum-topped, cutaway electric Martin Alternative X guitar. Eli, who had seen Edwards perform twice before, said that this was by far the best show. There was a heartwarming instant, after Edwards played "Sweet Home Chicago" and then began to play it again, when the crowd cheered him on. Edwards was great and Michael's harmonica playing was spot-on.

The second half of the show featured Robert Lockwood Jr. accompanied by a bass player. Lockwood played his blue semi-hollowbodied twelve-string guitar with the dexterity of a man half his age. It was inspiring to watch him weave blues and jazz together to create his own distinct versions of Johnson's repertoire. By the end of the set, I wanted to meet him just to say thanks.

Half the audience probably felt the same way, because after the show almost a hundred people lined up to meet the two bluesmen. They were waiting for autographs; I was there to show the photo. I was still keeping it under wraps, so I went to the back of the line.

It was close to midnight by the time I got to meet Honeyboy Edwards. He was seated at a folding table in front of the stage, looking tired but in good spirits. I thanked him for the show and asked if he would mind looking at an old photo I'd found. I handed him an enlarged scan of the photo, and he studied it briefly before saying, "It's cool, where did you get it?"

"From a collector. Can I ask you a question about it?"

"Sure, you can ask me."

I paused and bit my tongue out of frustration, because the question that I wanted to ask was "Is this a photo of Robert Johnson and Johnny Shines?" But I had agreed to play by Michael's rules, so instead I asked, "Did you know the men in this photo?"

Edwards looked at it again. He pointed to Johnny Shines and said, "Yeah, I knew him. He was from the Hill Country."

His answer surprised Michael, who quickly came over and asked, "Honey, do you remember his name?"

Edwards shook his head from side to side. "No, I can't recall, but I seen him around. Yeah, I knew him."

I was optimistic and uneasy as I asked Edwards whether he knew the man holding the guitar. But my heart sank when he said, "No, I couldn't say who the guitar player is." I thanked him and asked for an autograph, which he gladly signed.

Robert Lockwood Jr. was at another table with his family, getting ready to leave, when I approached him. "Excuse me, I know you're headed out, but would you mind looking at a photo I just showed to Honeyboy? It will only take a minute."

Lockwood looked me up and down, then sighed wearily and said, "OK, let's see it." He looked at the photo for less than ten seconds, then placed it on the table. "What do you want to know?"

"I apologize for the way that I'm being allowed to ask this, but did you know the men in this photo?"

Lockwood looked me in the eye and held my gaze as he answered. "You know, two years ago a guy showed me a photo that was supposed to be Robert Johnson. It wasn't him, and I told that guy, right there on the spot, that isn't Robert Johnson. You remember that, Honey?"

Edwards answered, "Yeah, I remember that."

Lockwood continued to look me in the eye, and I didn't look away as I asked, "What about my photo?"

He glanced at it one more time before saying, "I don't know."

"That's it? You don't know?"

"No. I don't know who's in your photo."

Michael's brother smiled and said, "Well, I guess that settles that." I didn't understand why he and Michael seemed so pleased, unless it was because they wanted to see me and the photo get shot down. Eli, Steve, and Tom, by contrast, seemed disheartened by the way things had turned out. As we left the club, I looked at them and said, "Too bad they couldn't confirm it, but neither one said, 'That isn't Robert Johnson in your photo.'"

On the train ride home, I stared at the photo wondering what my next move would be. My grandmother used to say, "Men make plans and God laughs." It was an old expression and it was right on. In the weeks and months that followed, all my plans imploded. *History Detectives* bailed on the story, citing "time and budgetary constraints" as the reason. Shaky legal footing, lack of copyright, and inconclusive evidence were more likely the cause.

Dave Jacobs was thoughtful enough to call and let me know that his research had turned up information on Johnnie May Crowder (it turned out May was spelled with a y, not an e). She married a man named

James Brown on November 9, 1935, in Little Rock, Arkansas. Crowder and Brown were both twenty-one years old at the time. In 1935, Johnny Shines would have been twenty and Robert Johnson twenty-four. Dave pointed out that the time frame and location supported the possibility that Crowder might have been the photographer.

Unfortunately, he also told me that—like Johnson—Crowder had died young, in April 1940. Dave found her death notice in the *Arkansas Gazette*. A few days later, John Tefteller called to let me know he had traveled south in search of information on Crowder, and he corroborated what Dave had already told me.

Meanwhile, in spite of Frank DiGiacomo's best efforts to get some traction for the story at *Vanity Fair*, that project had stalled too. The clock was ticking and I was trying with all my heart, but there were stones in my passway.

Chapter 12

I May Be Right or Wrong

Almost two years had passed since I bought the photo. I felt like I was spinning my wheels, going nowhere. I was tempted to post the photo online and watch from the sidelines as everyone battled it out, but I respected Robert Johnson too much to do that. *Vanity Fair* wasn't off the table, but it seemed unlikely to happen. In May of 2007, Frank DiGiacomo told me he would understand if I decided to pursue other options.

It was time for another meeting at Rocco's. As usual, Joe was brewing the good stuff to wash down the pignoli cookies, but this time I was the only one eating them. Four of us were seated at the table. Dave Rubin was digging into a slice of decadent-looking chocolate cake. Sean McDevitt, a writer at CNN, was munching on a mix of mouth-watering pastries, while across the table from us, Tom Crandall was appeasing his sweet tooth with chocolate chip cookies and two creamy cannoli. When the sugar and caffeine kicked in, we talked about the photo. Dave and Sean said that if *Vanity Fair* fell through, they would pitch the story to *Rolling Stone.*

Another possibility for the photo's debut was on the cover of John Tefteller's Blues Images calendar. John told me that he wanted it, but only if I let him have first use. When I mentioned it to John Pelosi, he advised me to go with *Vanity Fair.* I deferred to John's wishes because he wouldn't let me pay him for his work. When I brought it up, he said, "If this all works out, you can buy me a guitar." John told me that in college he had owned a Fender Telecaster, but he had to sell it. If all went well, Robert Johnson and I would buy John the guitar of his choice.

But if all didn't go well, then what? I couldn't waste time thinking about that. I had better things to do. Like what? Well, I could watch

TV with the sound turned down and mess around on guitar, or I could do what I should be doing: more research.

Every time I looked at the photo, I thought I must be missing something, a clue hiding in plain sight, something obvious. The guitar in the photo made no sense. It had no strings; one strip of tuning pegs was broken, the other gone. There wasn't even a logo on the headstock. Still, it looked like an early- to mid-thirties Harmony twelve-fret. What about Johnson's other guitars? What were they?

In the famous cigarette photo, he's holding a Kalamazoo KG-14 made by Gibson. According to the liner notes in the box set, the cigarette photo dates from the early 1930s, which would mean that Johnson was younger in that photo than in the one on the box set cover where he's holding a 1929 Gibson L-1. I looked at both photos as I had done many times before, but this time it occurred to me that the Kalamazoo KG-14 is a fourteen-fret guitar, a later style than the twelve-fret Gibson L-1 in the other photo.

So when did Gibson start making the KG-14? According to *Gruhn's Guide to Vintage Guitars*, production began in the fall of 1936—which meant that the cigarette photo wasn't from the early thirties; it was from 1936 or later. OK, then what year was the photo on the cover of the box set taken? It was shot at the Hooks Brothers Studio in Memphis, circa 1935. That seemed crazy, because Johnson looks older in the Hooks Brothers portrait than in the cigarette photo. It was also food for thought, because it supported my theory that the photo that I owned was from 1935 or a bit later, based on similarities to Johnson's appearance in the cigarette photo.

Some might find these details uninteresting, but blues historians live for such minutiae. When I saw George Barkin a few days later, I shared my theory about the order of the photos. I also told him that Johnson had probably played the Kalamazoo KG-14 in the cigarette photo, taken at his first recording session in San Antonio, Texas, on November 23, 1936. George would have bought a 1936 Kalamazoo KG-14 on the spot if we'd had one for sale.

When George asked me how things were going with *Vanity Fair*, I told him the project had stalled.

"Is that a fact? You know, I had lunch with Graydon this week."

He was talking about Graydon Carter, the editor of *Vanity Fair*.

"Really? How was lunch?"

"It was good. I told Graydon about your photo, but I guess I should have emphasized its significance. I'll give him a call."

I had no idea that George knew Graydon Carter, but it didn't surprise me. George knows lots of people. Soon afterward, he called to let me know that he'd spoken with Graydon. George had compared the photo to "a lost quarto" and said that Keith Richards and Eric Clapton would certainly be very interested in seeing it. After that, Graydon told George that *Vanity Fair* was probably doing the story. A week later, John Pelosi sent me an email saying, "V.F. is on for the story."

Soon afterward, Frank DiGiacomo e-mailed me, "Excited to do the piece." He wanted to discuss it over dinner. We met at Maremma, a restaurant on West 10th Street named after a cowboy region of Italy located on the Tuscan coast. I brought Tom along, and Frank introduced us to chef Cesare Cassella, who told us that most of the ingredients on the menu came from his farm upstate. Frank ordered a bottle of wine while I looked around at the pictures of Tuscan cowboys and longhorn cattle decorating the walls. Cesare brought some ciabatta bread and olive oil for us to snack on while he explained the menu. It all sounded rich and heavy, but when the food arrived, I was surprised at how easily it went down. We had fresh heirloom beans, followed by Tuscan chili with chicken-fried pork, spaghetti and lamb meatballs, and pappardelle with wild boar ragu. Cesare's food paired well with Johnny Cash's music playing softly in the background.

Frank had asked me to bring a hard copy of the photo and a digital file. At Frank's request, my friend Jimmy, a computer whiz, had placed banners across it stating, "This Image Is Copyrighted" and "Unauthorized Use Prohibited By Law." It was a bluff because the photo wasn't copyrighted yet, but it looked intimidating enough to work. Frank had also asked for a list of people he could contact for comments. I handed him an envelope containing everything as we finished off our espressos.

The story was scheduled to be 2,500 words long, and Frank had one month to complete it if it was going to be included in the November 2007 music issue of the magazine. It didn't seem like enough time, but at least things were in motion.

A few days later, Frank e-mailed to let me know he was heading to Mississippi. He planned to show the photo to the Johnson family and Steve LaVere, which was potentially dangerous. Claud Johnson, Annie

Anderson (the niece of Carrie Thompson, who was Robert Johnson's half-sister), Annie's nephew Robert Harris, and Steve LaVere were involved in a legal tug-of-war. It was a complicated mess that had been going on for years. The winner would own the name, likeness, and image of Robert Johnson, meaning not only that they would own the two other known images of Johnson, but that they could possibly lay claim to mine. As unbelievable as that sounds, it was a fact. If I allowed Frank to show the photo, I risked losing it, but I was willing to take the chance.

Almost overnight, things went from motionless to hyperdrive. Frank had a deadline to meet, and he was on a tear. He e-mailed me with questions. "Do you have a contact for Honeyboy?" "Do you remember the name of the eBay seller who sold you the photo?" "How can I get in touch with John Tefteller?" and lots more.

Frank's calling John must have touched a nerve, because John contacted me afterward to warn me that it was dangerous allowing Frank to show the photo without having the copyright in place. He was trying to protect me, and he was also trying to protect the photo so he could use it for his calendar. I thanked John for his advice, and he asked me to have my lawyer contact him.

I don't know the exactly what they talked about, but it must have been heavy, because the next day John Pelosi sent me an e-mail: "Can I get a copy of the photo—watermarked in an attachment. I am going to get a copy to Robert Johnson's estate and work out a deal."

Later that afternoon, Frank called to let me know he was back from Mississippi. "Zeke, I showed the photo to Steve LaVere."

"Yeah, how'd that go?"

"He picked it up, looked at it, and put it down several times before telling me that he doesn't think it's Robert Johnson, but he asked me to keep him updated."

"That figures. Who else did you show it to?"

"Dick Waterman. He was skeptical but thinks that it might be Johnson and Shines."

"Cool, you know he was Johnny Shines' manager."

Frank had also contacted Michael Frank, who "talked about Johnson and turnarounds, but wouldn't allow Honeyboy to view or comment about the photo." At the end of the call, Frank asked me for John

Hammond's telephone number, which I gave to him. When I showed Hammond the photo months earlier, he'd said, "It's the most beautiful photo that I've ever seen of two young musicians."

August was off to a good start. The store was slightly busier than usual, and Steve Earle was back in town. Steve lived around the block on Jones Street. When he wasn't on tour, he liked to hang out at the store with us. Steve's stories are great because he knows everyone and he's been everywhere. He's way into early blues, yet somehow I hadn't shown him the photo. Frank thought it would be good to get Steve's take, so when he came by that afternoon, I pulled it out.

"It's definitely him," Steve said. "You can tell by the eyes."

I e-mailed Frank that night and he got back to me almost immediately. He had talked to several of the contacts I'd given him, and they had spoken well of me and the photo. The first draft of the story was due in a week.

Two good things happened later that week. The first was that Chuck Barris and his lovely wife, Mary, came in for a hug. Chuck's taste in music leans toward classic pop, rock, and soul. He's not big on Delta blues, but Chuck's a hero of mine and has been ever since I first saw him on *The Gong Show*. I wanted Chuck to be a part the story, so when he asked me how things were going, I told him about *Vanity Fair* and asked him to send a comment to Frank. Here's what he sent:

> Frank:
> Just a few words about my good friend Zeke Schein and his remarkable photo, although what I have to say has nothing to do with his remarkable photo. I just want to tell you that Zeke taught me how to play the guitar. Zeke was about twelve and I was thirty-eight. Zeke's lessons are the reason why I never mastered the instrument. After Zeke, I still played badly but with a certain flair. Between you and me Frank, I blame the Gong Show's cancellation on my guitar playing.
> Thank you for your understanding.
> Chuck Barris
> P.S.: Zeke sold me a Les Paul guitar. Do you know how heavy they are?

That was hard to top, but the second good thing that happened was equally cool. John Pelosi called to let me know that the Johnson estate had contacted a forensic artist named Lois Gibson. She had identified Robert Johnson in the photo!

Chapter 13

What Evil Has the Poor Girl Heard?

The internet is a mixed blessing. It's great for research, but it's also full of distractions. After about an hour of goofing off watching music clips on YouTube, I remembered why I had originally logged on. I wanted to learn about Lois Gibson.

According to her website bio, Lois holds the Guinness Book of World Records title as the world's most successful forensic artist. She graduated from the University of Texas at Austin with a BFA, then completed the FBI Academy forensic artists' course. Lois has won numerous awards for her work and has been profiled on *Dateline NBC* and in *O, The Oprah Magazine*. She had street cred, but the thing that really hit me was this line: "Her near-death experience as a victim of a serial rapist/killer fuels her passion for catching criminals."

I wanted to know more, so I bought *Faces of Evil*, a book Lois had coauthored with Deanie Francis Mills. After reading it, I was able to fully appreciate what Lois Gibson does for a living: she catches monsters. She listens to horror stories and absorbs nightmarish crime scene images, translating darkness, interpreting evil. Lois helps victims of violent crime remember the faces of their attackers. Her sketches put murderers, rapists, and child molesters in jail.

In her book, Lois describes her early family environment as similar to that of the old TV series *The Waltons*. She grew up in Kansas City, the second eldest of five children, in a loving, low-income household. When it came time for Lois to attend college, her family was unable to afford tuition. Struggling to balance work and school, Lois moved to Los Angeles, hoping to find a job that would enable her to save enough money to attend college full-time. Soon after her arrival, she found work as a model. The modeling led to a job as a go-go dancer on a local TV show. Life was going well, but everything changed when a man pretending to be her neighbor knocked on Lois's door. When she opened it, the man attacked her. He strangled Lois several times to the point of blackout, then raped her.

The attack traumatized Lois, but she didn't report it to the police, fearing that they would say that she brought it on herself by working as a dancer. Instead she spent weeks isolated in her apartment, afraid to go outside. Eventually, she returned to work. In a strange twist of fate, while driving through an unfamiliar part of town, Lois saw the police handcuff and arrest her attacker. "He was fighting and struggling against the cops the same way I had fought with him." An officer at the scene told Lois that the man was being arrested for possession of six kilos of cocaine and that he would serve serious jail time.

Witnessing her attacker's arrest set Lois on her life's path. "That feeling, that amazing, jubilant, triumphant feeling I had at that moment— the relief and joy, that at long last justice had indeed been found . . . is a feeling that I want to give to every victim of violent crime."

Lois has been successful in this goal. Her sketches have helped law enforcement to solve more than 1,300 criminal cases. Amazing, but I still wondered why John Kitchens had approached Lois to identify Robert Johnson in the photo. Why use a police sketch artist?

It turned out that Lois had been involved in projects other than police work. John contacted her after reading an article about how she identified the sailor kissing the nurse in Alfred Eisenstaedt's iconic V-J Day photo. I remembered reading the same article. Over the years, several men and women had claimed to be the kissing couple, but Lois' detailed forensic analysis determined that the kissing sailor was Glenn McDuffie. McDuffie was able to identify fellow shipmates in the photo and pass a series of polygraph tests. I understood why John Kitchens had chosen Lois to weigh in on the Johnson photo. She thinks outside the box and, unlike others in her field, she isn't afraid to be definitive. She trusts her instincts and her eye.

Shortly after e-mailing to let me know that Lois had identified Johnson in the photo, John Pelosi called to tell me that the Johnson estate believed in the authenticity of the photo. They were prepared to stand behind it and were interested in negotiating a deal. John talked about probable terms and conditions, but I told him I needed to sleep on it—which I did, and had a most unusual dream.

My dream was in color and it unfolded in real time. I was in a juke joint in the Mississippi Delta. The place was dark and small. It looked and smelled like an East Side dive bar, but not quite the same. There was a different alcohol smell, somewhat harder, mixed with tobacco, perfume, and sweat. There was sawdust on the floor. I was sitting at a small table wearing my usual outfit: a black T-shirt, jeans, Chuck Taylors, and a stingy-brim fedora. My clothes seemed too modern for the setting, but I didn't care.

The place was empty except for a man who was sitting in a corner, holding a guitar. He got up, and as he approached, I saw that he was well-dressed, wearing a dark suit and a nicer hat than mine. He was slim and lanky. His movements were fluid and smooth. When he got closer, I realized that I was looking at Robert Johnson. He grinned at me and laughed. His laugh echoed—"Ha-ha-ha-ha"—then began to continuously loop, changing speed and tonality, faster and lower-pitched until it sounded like a dog barking. And then Robert sang over it, "I got to keep moving-moving-moving, blues-blues, falling down, like hail-hail-hail . . ." It was eerie, music from a dead man's mouth. I've never heard anything like it. Unfortunately, I woke up in the middle of the song.

Later that morning, after two cups of black coffee, I called John. "Hey, I think we should assign the copyright to the estate."

"OK, Zeke, if you're sure that's what you want, I'll set it up."

"I'm sure. It's a photo of Claud Johnson's father. He should decide where it goes, not me. But I want to keep the original."

"Of course. It's valuable and you found it. It's yours."

"Yeah, owning it is as close as I'll ever get to meeting Robert Johnson," I said, still thinking about the otherworldly dream.

Chapter 14

Can't You Hear That Wind Howl?

Frank and I were at the Cornelia Street Café. *Vanity Fair* was picking up the tab because Frank was interviewing me for the story. I was trying to relax, but the tape recorder on the table wasn't helping. I noticed the waitress eyeing it and felt a bit self-conscious, wondering why anyone would care what I had to say. For me, it was all about the photo. I was prepared to do whatever it took to get it out there.

Frank sipped his espresso and waited for me to take a few bites of my eggs florentine before asking his first question. "So, Zeke, can you tell me why you decided to buy the photo? Was there a specific reason why you wanted to own it?"

"Yeah, there were two reasons. The first was that I wanted to protect it."

"Interesting. What was the other reason?"

"I wanted to hold it in my hands."

I asked the waitress to refill my coffee, then explained to Frank about the responsibility I felt toward the photo and the legacy of the men pictured in it. The photo had to be handled delicately, both physically and intellectually. Owning it involved more work than one might imagine. Holding it was like holding an antique lace doily, small and fragile. I realized that scanning it was a good idea, but that had to be handled by a professional. I'd mentioned it to Patti Smith, who hooked me up with Steven Sebring.

As I continued eating, I told Frank about the day I'd gone to Steven's studio on Little West 12th Street to have the photo scanned. Although I'd been there before, I had trouble finding the place. It's confusing when you go that far west. The cobblestone streets all look similar and they're haphazardly arranged.

I finally found his studio and went upstairs. Steven's assistants, Bijou and Yargan, let me in and told me that Steven was away working on a photo shoot for Coach. I'd been hoping to see him, but I didn't have to explain why I had come. Patti had called ahead and arranged everything. When I showed the photo to Yargan, he smiled. "That's a million-dollar photo." Then he looked at me seriously and said, "I'm going to scan it slowly. I hope we don't fry it."

I placed the photo gently facedown on the glass of the scanner and I held my breath. Fortunately, the scan turned out fine. I left Steven's studio with an 8 x 12 work print and DVD containing two high-resolution scans.

Frank seemed amused by the story. "So what happened after you got it scanned?" he asked.

"Nothing, until John decided that we should have it digitally retouched."

"Who did the retouch?"

"John had me bring it to Robert Polidori's studio."

"Really? I know Robert. Amazing. Did you meet him?"

"Yeah, he's great. He gave me a book that hit me hard."

"I have to hear about it. Tell me what happened."

I explained that John Pelosi had arranged for me to go to Robert Polidori's studio in Chelsea. It was a spacious loft with hardwood floors, clean and dimly lit. Robert's assistant, a cute brunette named Jennie Ross, invited me in and told me that Robert was traveling in Europe. Jennie showed me a mural-sized photo Robert had shot. Despite its huge size, it was flawless. Jennie's job was to make sure of that.

I handed her the DVD from Steven's studio, which she loaded into an expensive-looking computer. When the image of Johnson and Shines appeared on the screen, I saw Jennie's jaw drop. She studied it, assessing the amount of time and effort it would take to retouch something so damaged. I knew she was up for the challenge when she turned to me and said, "Wow, he's really handsome," referring to Robert Johnson. Yeah, I thought to myself, the ladies still loved him.

Jennie and I spent all day retouching the photo, discussing small details, figuring out what to touch up and what to leave alone. It was painstaking work, but after eight hours, most of the photo was restored.

The next day, late in the afternoon, Jennie called to let me know she was close to completing the job. Johnny Shine's hand was hard to do, and the sleeve of his jacket was also a problem. She said that she could do it, but it would take another day. I didn't want to abuse Robert Polidori's generosity, and I had already taken up too much of Jennie's time. I told her I was nearby with my wife and daughter and we would come by to get everything.

When we arrived at the studio, Jennie showed us how far she had gotten with the retouch. We were gazing at it when we heard a loud "hello" from the doorway. Robert walked in, looking as dapper and disheveled as any globetrotting photographer worth his salt should.

After the introductions, Robert looked at the photo. As a blues fan himself, he was excited to see a new photo of Robert Johnson. He was also curious to see what his assistant had done to it. Jennie showed Robert the before and after images. He studied them clinically, then suggested some small changes to improve it. Jennie was happy to let him have a go, and Robert spent ten minutes working his magic. When he was satisfied, he called us over to see what he had done. It looked great and I told him that I appreciated his help. As a gesture of thanks to Jennie, I discreetly slipped her some cash to use for a night out with her friends.

"Nice, but what about the book that Robert gave you?" Frank asked as the waitress refilled my coffee for the second time and cleared away the plates.

"Oh yeah—on my way out I told Robert I liked his cityscapes and he gave me a huge book in a white cardboard box. I opened the box so that he could sign it and I saw that the cover was a picture of a dirty old car in front of a cheap wooden house with pigeons on the roof. The image had nothing in common with the glamorous cityscape on the wall of Robert's studio. It was dull and ordinary, except for the clouds behind the house. They looked ominous."

The title of the book was *After the Flood*. When I got home and looked inside, my heart sank. The book was filled with images of devastation in New Orleans: houses blown apart as if bombs had imploded them, upended cars buried beneath fallen trees, flooded streets, shattered windows, splintered furniture, deadly-looking mold covering the walls of uninhabited Victorian shotgun houses. Page after page chronicling the destruction Hurricane Katrina and the failure of the federal levee system had wrought. Halfway through, I was moved to tears and had to put the book down. I realized that there were no people in Robert's book, maybe because no photograph could capture what the people of New Orleans went through during and after the flood.

Frank paid the check, and as we got ready to go I said, "You know, it's like what happened when David Blaine gave me that book *Man's Search for Meaning*."

"How so?"

"Well, after reading it I saw things differently. The same thing happened with Robert's book. It made me realize I had spent too much time struggling to restore a photograph when I should have been paying attention to a city struggling to restore itself."

Chapter 15

Last Fair Deal Gone Down

On September 14, 2007, Cathy woke me with a "Happy birthday!" and a cup of coffee in bed. I thanked her and sipped the ebony brew, trying to clear the cobwebs from my mind. I'd been out late the night before.

When I finished my coffee, I grabbed a small stack of papers off the end table. I didn't bother reading them; I'd already spent several days looking them over. I turned to the last page and signed my name next to Claud Johnson's signature. Then I shook my head in disbelief and smiled. It was my forty-seventh birthday and I had just signed a contract with Robert Johnson's son.

I had agreed to assign the copyright of the photo to the Johnson estate; it was the right thing to do. The estate believed it to be an authentic photo of Robert Johnson and would represent it as such, but when it came to splitting the profits, they wanted the lion's share. When John Pelosi explained why it was a fair deal, I thought of a line from Robert Johnson's song "Last Fair Deal Gone Down": "If you cry about a nickel, you'll die 'bout a dime." So true, but for me it wasn't about the money. It was about the mission: chasing a phantom.

It was also about respect. I was concerned that the contract didn't include Johnny Shines' family. Legally it didn't have to, but out of respect it should have. Robert Johnson's heirs owned the rights to his name, likeness, and image, but Johnny Shines' heirs didn't own similar rights. When I suggested that we include the Shines family, no one wanted to hear it. I didn't argue when they pointed out that while Shines was a talented musician, Johnson was a legend.

I went to the kitchen and poured myself a second cup of coffee. It any previo...

...l or oral understand...

...executed the Agreement as of the date first

CLAUD L. JOHNSON as Heir at law:

Claud L Johnson

was Ethiopian Yirgacheffe and it was good. Caitlin was making her morning tea. She hugged me and said "Happy birthday, Dad."

"Thanks, kid."

My day was off to a good start.

I settled back onto the couch and called John Pelosi. "Hey, I just signed the contract. Do you want me to drop it off?"

"Hey, good. Aren't you playing the Beacon tonight with Patti Smith?"

"Yeah, she's doing a birthday tribute show for Fred. It's my birthday too, so she invited me to play, but I can stop by your office on my way."

"No, enjoy your birthday. You can bring the contract on Monday. Have fun tonight."

Good, I could hang out and take my time getting to the Beacon. I was tired from working at the store yesterday and rehearsing for the show afterward, but it had gone well. I had fun playing slide on Patti's cover of "Gimme Shelter," especially when she told me to turn my guitar up louder. After the rehearsal, I walked south toward Bleecker Street with Lenny Kaye. We talked about early jazz and blues musicians, and Lenny schooled me on a New Orleans trumpet player named Buddy Bolden.

Bolden suffered a nervous breakdown during a performance and was taken to a mental hospital, where he spent the rest of his life. His flamboyant style influenced Louis Armstrong and changed the shape of jazz, yet there are no known recordings of him. There's only one known photo of Buddy Bolden. Like Robert Johnson, he remains somewhat of an enigma, and fictional versions of him crop up from time to time. In Louis Maistros' novel *The Sound of Building Coffins*, Bolden is imagined as a sort of conduit or vessel through which music mystically flowed: "Listen, this jass [jazz] thing—it mighta passed through me its first time round, but that don't make it mine. Or nobody else's neither." The same might be said of Robert Johnson.

It was unusually warm that night, so I decided to wear an old button-down shirt with a torn "Free Tibet" T-shirt underneath and a pair of faded Levis, Kurt Cobain style. This wardrobe decision proved prophetic, because at the show I ended up playing on "Smells Like Teen Spirit" instead of "Gimme Shelter." Rich Robinson was scheduled to play, but his child was sick and he didn't think he would be able to make it. When he showed up at the last minute, Patti asked me to switch songs. "You love Kurt," she rationalized, "and Rich wants to play on the Stones song."

"And I want to hear him," I said.

Patti seemed relieved that I wasn't bothered by the change. "Thanks, Zeke. You can also play on 'People Have the Power.'"

She was busy preparing for the show, so I didn't tell her that I had never tried to play "Smells Like Teen Spirit" or "People Have the Power." Instead, I quickly sat down and taught myself both songs. I was about to play them live in front of three thousand people.

At the sound check, Patti introduced me to Flea. He was playing bass and trumpet that night. No kidding; he played trumpet on "Smells Like Teen Spirit." Flea told me he was a Robert Johnson fan and that his band, the Red Hot Chili Peppers, had recorded a cover of Johnson's song "They're Red Hot." I'd brought a copy of the photo because Patti told me Flea wanted to see it. When I showed it to him, he saw the resemblance right away and thanked me for finding it.

The show went well. It was a poignant tribute to Fred on his birthday, especially the last performance of the night, when Patti sang "The Jackson Song" accompanied by her daughter Jesse on ukulele. After the show, I had birthday cake with my family and friends. I never told them about the napkin I had surreptitiously placed on the music stand beside me. Before the show, I'd written charts for both songs on it. When you're onstage at the Beacon, it's better to be safe than sorry.

Frank DiGiacomo called me at work the next day to say he'd been in the audience and enjoyed seeing me play. He was still compiling comments for the story and said his talks with Billy Gibbons and Steve Earle had gone well. The story was shaping up.

On Monday morning before work, I stopped by John Pelosi's office with the contract and two prints, one original and one retouched, to submit to the copyright office. John was out, so I left everything with his assistant, Danny. The next day, John Tefteller e-mailed to ask again about using the photo for his blues calendar. I told him I had assigned the copyright to the Johnson estate and he could contact them. I'd put in a good word, but it was out of my hands.

I still owned the original photo, but I no longer controlled who got to use it; that decision was now up to the Johnson family. That was our deal. It made me wonder about the deal Robert Johnson had made—not the one with the devil, but the other one, the deal with his record company. How much of Johnson's soul did they get?

Johnson got his record deal through H. C. Speir, a music-store owner in Jackson, Mississippi. In addition to running the store, Speir was a talent scout who had arranged recording deals for many of the musicians who had influenced Robert Johnson, including Charley Patton, Son House, Skip James, the Mississippi Sheiks, and Tommy Johnson. By 1936, when Robert Johnson auditioned for him, Speir had grown disillusioned with the business. He referred Johnson to Ernie Oertle, a young talent scout and salesman for ARC Records, who took him to Texas to record in November of 1936.

At San Antonio's Gunter Hotel, Oertle introduced Johnson to recording engineer Art Satherley and producer Don Law. Law, who was in charge of the session, would later describe Johnson as a shy kid of seventeen or eighteen. (Johnson was twenty-five when they met.)

Besides Robert Johnson, Satherley and Law recorded several other artists. The sessions yielded smooth western tunes from Zeke Williams & His Rambling Cowboys, the Crystal Springs Ramblers, the Chuck Wagon Gang, and the Light Crust Doughboys, as well as lilting Mexican melodies from duos Andres Berlanga y Francisco Montalvo and Hermanas Barraza y Daniel Palomo.

Johnson recorded sixteen songs in a three-day session that started on Monday, November 23, and ended on Friday, November 27. He didn't record on Tuesday or Wednesday because the local police had arrested him for vagrancy. Sprung from jail by Law and lodged in a local boarding house, he completed the sessions that gave birth to some iconic blues recordings, among them "Sweet Home Chicago," "Crossroad Blues," "I Believe I'll Dust My Broom," "Come on in My Kitchen," and "Terraplane Blues."

Johnson recorded again in June of 1937, this time in the sweltering heat of downtown Dallas. At a two-day session on the third floor of the Brunswick Records Building at 508 Park Avenue, Johnson recorded thirteen songs, including "Me and the Devil Blues," "Hellhound on my Trail," and "Love in Vain Blues."

Johnson's known recorded output consists of twenty-nine songs and thirteen alternate takes. With the exception of "Terraplane Blues," these songs weren't commercially successful during his lifetime, but they had massive impact on future generations. So what kind of deal did Johnson make with the record company?

According to Pete Meyer's website for his Johnson biopic *Can't You Hear the Wind Howl*, the American Record Company probably paid Robert Johnson $10 to $15 each for the songs. Altogether, he probably made about $300 from the San Antonio and Dallas sessions, with no royalties forthcoming.

Was it a fair deal? Johnson may have thought so. In post-depression America, $300 went a long way. A loaf of bread cost nine cents. You could rent a house for $26 a month, or buy a new car for about $750. In 1937, the average annual wage was $1,780.

Looking at these figures made me wonder about my deal with Johnson's family. Was it fair? I hoped so, but only time would tell.

Chapter 16

Come on in My Kitchen

Seventy years earlier, Robert Johnson had visited Dallas for his second recording session. I was going there to buy guitars. I've been to lots of guitar shows, but the Dallas International Guitar Festival proves the old saying that everything is bigger in Texas. Twenty thousand people were expected to attend the April 2008 show at the Dallas Market Center.

In celebration of the show's thirtieth anniversary the previous year, Paul Reed Smith had sponsored the "Holy Grail" exhibit, a display of ultra-rare guitars including two iconic Fender Stratocasters, Stevie Ray Vaughan's "Lenny," and Eric Clapton's "Blackie." Clapton's Gibson ES-335 from his Cream years was also on display, along with four 1950s Gibson Les Paul gold tops, a 1954 Fender Strat, and a 1958 Gibson split-headstock Explorer. The exhibit helped bring in the crowds, and over $3 million traded hands at the show. Matt and I had bought about two dozen guitars at that show, and we hoped to do it again this year.

Every show has its own flavor, and they're all wacky, especially Dallas. Maybe it just feels that way because I'm from New York, but then again, maybe not. As Matt and I walked out of our hotel into the bright sunny Dallas morning, everything seemed normal, but when we walked through the entrance to the show, a sign over a small booth caught Matt's eye: Touch a Thug, Change His Life. We had to ask the guy under the sign what he was selling. His reply, "Stun guns," caught our full attention. "And knives." Even better. And they were cheap, so who could resist?

The booth next to Mr. Touch-a-Thug was a large, fully stocked bar serving beer, wine, and mixed drinks. It was way too early, and we were on the clock, so we took a pass on that. At the third booth, we found homemade

beef, buffalo, and turkey jerky and bought two packs of each.

The guys at the next booth were still setting up, but I could tell that the unopened cases on their table contained high-end, collectible guitars. In my line of work, you need to know what's inside a case before you open it. The early bird gets the "rare bird" at guitar shows. Judging by their cases, the birds at this booth were too rare for our taste, so we moved on.

Although theft is almost unheard of at guitar shows, it occurred to me that this show was perfectly laid out for a would-be robber. Weapons at the first booth, liquid courage at the second, beef jerky at the third to snack on in the getaway car after stealing pricey guitars from the fourth booth. There was even a restroom conveniently located by a nearby exit in case the thief needed to make a pit stop.

The first day of the show is Dealer Day. It's for loading in and setting up. On the second day, the show opens to the public. The first day is less noisy and crowded, but there's a frenetic energy as dealers wheel in carts stacked high with guitars and amps. Everyone wants first shot at the new arrivals. The competition on Dealer Day is well-mannered but intense; you have to be accurate and decisive. I've bought lots of cool guitars quickly and discreetly because I recognized their cases before others did. Unfortunately, that doesn't always work. Sometimes the guitar and its case are mismatched, or even worse, the case is empty. Certain guitars are so iconic that a knowledgeable collector can easily identify them by their cases alone. The brown Gibson case with pink lining for a 1959 Les Paul is valuable because the guitar can sell for over $200,000. Other examples are silver Rickenbacker cases and the tweed cases that 1950s Fender guitars came with. At a crowded show, a rare case ideally contains a rare guitar, but sometimes dealers sell the empty cases because they still have some collector value.

Dealer day played out well. We came, we bought, we schmoozed. Never underestimate the power of the schmooze. One of the dozen instruments we bought involved an unusual trade. After five minutes of talking about food while bartering over the price of a vintage Gibson, Matt realized that the guy was hungry, so he threw in a pack of turkey jerky to close the deal.

That night we had Tex-Mex for dinner and washed it down with Shiner beer at the hotel bar. An hour later, I walked into a different bar five miles away with my friends Corey and Tony. Upon seeing us, a vivacious woman in a tight white tank top clapped her hands and shouted joyfully,

"Yay, Tony's band is here!" Nice, except that we weren't a band and we'd never played together. Of course that never stops me. Tony was into it too, but Corey decided to play it safe and sit this one out. Safe is smart, but gonzo is way more fun, as long as you don't crash and burn.

Tony and I joined the band onstage, and one of the guitar players handed me his Telecaster. We looked completely out of place, but Tony's longhaired Jersey-metal style and my Delta-grunge look were so weird that everyone wanted to hear us play. Tony did his Robert Plant thing while the band and I did our best to channel the spirit of Robert Johnson. Maybe we did, because we sounded better than we had any right to.

The next morning, after four cups of coffee and breakfast with Matt, we hit the show floor for day two. By the end of the day, we had bought four more guitars, two basses, two ukuleles, a mandolin, a lap steel, and two amps. It was a good haul, and despite the occasional jerky break, we had worked up an appetite.

I had been looking forward to tonight's dinner for months. Chef Dean Fearing had recently opened his own restaurant, Fearing's, in the Ritz Carlton after twenty years of helming the kitchen at the Mansion at Turtle Creek. Dean is a friend and a guitar aficionado. I had sold him a few instruments, and if his food was as good as his taste in guitars, we were in for a treat.

Matt and I met up with six other dealers and crammed into the smallest car in Texas. None of us had thought ahead to call for a second car, and we didn't want to wait for one. I spent the next half hour bouncing around like the family dog in the car's hatchback.

At the Ritz Carlton, eight punchy, hungry, half-hysterical guitar dealers piled out of the tiny clown car. Our laughter died down as we handed the keys to the valet and looked around at the young, elegantly dressed patrons waiting for their tables. We gave our name to the maître d' and were instantly seated at a prime outdoor table with a great view. Dean appeared within minutes, wearing his chef whites and a broad smile. I could tell he was genuinely glad we were here. Matt and I had shown Dean the best we had to offer, and he was about to do the same for us.

The tasting menu Dean designed for us that night was beyond anything I could have imagined. In a perfectly choreographed presentation, eight servers simultaneously poured broth over the components of Dean's signature tortilla soup: crisp cabbage and radish rounds, creamy avocado slices, and crunchy deep-fried tortilla strips.

I can't remember everything that we ate, because we also drank several bottles of wine, but some of the highlights were seared scallops with leeks, bacon, peas, and kumquat marmalade; maple buffalo tenderloin on jalapeno grits; and Wagyu beef with chicken-fried lobster. I passed on the desserts—banana pudding with homemade vanilla wafers, passionfruit cupcake with strawberry parfait—but I couldn't resist downing an espresso as I watched everyone else indulge.

On the ride back, I wondered how far we were from 508 Park Avenue, where Robert Johnson had done his second recording session. For that matter, how far away was San Antonio and the Gunter Hotel? I thought about the fine food we had just enjoyed, and it brought to mind a story Don Law told about how Robert Johnson had interrupted his dinner at the Gunter.

In 1961, while writing the liner notes to the album *Robert Johnson: King of the Delta Blues*, Frank Driggs contacted Don Law looking for information about Johnson. Law described Johnson as a "medium height, wiry, slender, nice-looking boy, [with] beautiful hands." He believed Johnson was shy and self-conscious because, while recording, Johnson sat in a far corner of the room facing the wall.

On his first night in Dallas, after an all-day recording session, Johnson was arrested, beaten, and thrown in jail for vagrancy. The Bexar County police telephoned Don Law, who retrieved Johnson, found him a room at a boarding house, and told him to get some rest. He gave Johnson forty-five cents, enough for a hearty breakfast.

A bit later, while enjoying a meal in the Gunter Hotel's dining room, Law received another telephone call. He was probably relieved to hear that it wasn't the police again. This time the caller was Robert Johnson.

"Mr. Law, I'm lonesome."

"You're lonesome. What do you mean, Bob?"

"There's a lady here. She wants fifty cents and I lacks a nickel."

So on his first full day in San Antonio, Robert Johnson recorded eight songs, including the classic "Sweet Home Chicago" and his biggest seller, "Terraplane Blues." After that, he was beaten and thrown in jail. Yet he still had enough left in him to pick up a prostitute.

And some people wonder why he's my hero.

Chapter 17

They're Red Hot

Some people smile a lot. I don't know why; maybe they're happy, or maybe just stupid. Growing up in Brooklyn taught me that if you went around smiling for no visible reason, someone would smack the smile off your face. Then they would smile, and so would the five other goons standing behind them. So I have an aversion to smiling, and because of that, I always feel awkward having my photo taken.

Three days after my return from Dallas, Gasper Tringale shot two hundred photos of me for *Vanity Fair*. I never smiled once. When Gasper paused to reload, I tried not to squirm as his assistant applied makeup to my face. I wondered if Robert Johnson had felt equally uncomfortable during his photo session at the Hooks Brothers studio, because he looks stiff in that picture, seeming to force a smile for the camera. In the photo booth shot, maybe he wanted to look tougher, so he stuck a cigarette in his mouth instead of smiling. I like how edgy he looks in that photo, but his warm, open smile in the photo I found is even better.

In the months leading up to the photo's *Vanity Fair* debut, rumors began appearing in online forums like International Guitar Seminars, Blindman's Blues Forum, WeenieCampbell, and the Unofficial Martin Guitar Forum. Dozens of posts shared all sorts of misinformation about who was writing the story, its supposed editorial slant, and where and when it was scheduled to appear. Though I didn't take any of this material too seriously, I was a little disturbed by the posts of an IGS forum member named "bluesprof" who opined that "after seeing the photo" he thought its subject "looked too young" and that his clothing was "from the wrong time period." In addition, bluesprof claimed to have done "digital comparisons that didn't match the other photos." In his opinion, the forensic evidence pertaining to the photo was "specious," and he didn't believe it to be authentic.

The problem with online forums is that anyone can post almost anything while hiding anonymously behind a made-up screen name. I didn't know who bluesprof was, but I soon found out. Dave Rubin called to let me know that *Living Blues* had published an article about Robert Johnson's guitar teacher, Ike Zimmerman. After reading it, I called Dave to thank him for the heads-up. We agreed that it was a well-written, informative piece. Soon after that, Dave sent me an e-mail. He had spoken to Bruce Conforth, the author of the article, who was interested in trading information about Zimmerman for a scan of the photo. I declined because I didn't want to risk the photo showing up online prematurely.

Bruce's proposition struck me as odd, so I Googled him to see what his deal was. According to his bio, he was the first curator of the Rock and Roll Hall of Fame and a professor at the University of Michigan. It took me three more minutes to find out that Bruce Conforth had posted several times in online forums under the screen name bluesprof. So there was no way bluesprof could have done "digital comparisons," because Bruce obviously didn't have a scan of the photo, and I had dodged a bullet by declining to supply him one.

Dave sent Bruce an e-mail calling him out for his lack of discretion and his claim that he had done digital comparisons. A responsible scholar, Dave pointed out, would have waited to read the *Vanity Fair* story before going on the attack. Dave is a gentleman, so he ended his e-mail by letting Bruce know that we had both enjoyed his Ike Zimmerman piece. Dave's words must have touched Bruce's conscience. Soon afterward, bluesprof commented on the IGS forum: "[B]ased on new information, I now believe in the authenticity of the photo. It is a major find."

Another blues writer who couldn't wait for the story to come out before debunking it was Elijah Wald. Eli Smith had called to ask if I would show the photo to Elijah. Upon seeing it, Elijah said almost exactly what Michael Frank had said months earlier: "I don't see the resemblance, but then again I have no eye for these things." He also pointed out that the odds of me finding a third photo of Johnson were astronomical, so therefore it probably wasn't authentic. If the Johnson estate had really wanted to put forensic artist Lois Gibson to the test, he said, they should have shown her six random photos of African American men, including mine, and then had her compare them to the two known photos of Robert Johnson.

Out of respect, I held my tongue and didn't tell Elijah how ridiculous I thought his suggestion was. It was like putting six random Gibson Les Pauls in front of me and asking me to pick out the 1959 "Brock-burst" on the cover of Tom Wheeler's *American Guitars*. I could do it easily and I would find it insulting if someone questioned my ability to do so.

My interactions with Elijah Wald, Bruce Conforth, and Michael Frank left no doubt in my mind that I had upset three tribal chiefs in the inner sanctum of the blues world: they who had "no eye for these things," the elder statesmen of the forums, the blues police poised and eager to debunk a new photo of Robert Johnson. It had to be a fake, because if it were real, then *they* would have found it.

Meanwhile, the *Vanity Fair* story kept growing. It went from 2,500 words to 6,000, and Frank was still writing. As the deadline kept getting pushed back, I finally had to let John Tefteller know he wouldn't be able to use the photo for his 2009 calendar. Needless to say, he was very upset.

At the store, it was business as usual. Vintage small-bodied Gibson acoustics were the flavor of the month. I sold Sean Lennon a 1940s LG-2, then sold similar ones to Ryan Adams and Citizen Cope, then a 1950s LG-1 to Chris Robinson. I also got to meet and jam with one of my all-time musical heroes, Dion DiMucci. The first single I ever bought was by Dion, on a trip with my brother to a record store in the Times Square subway station that specialized in selling golden oldies. I wanted Dion's "The Wanderer," but the store was sold out of it, so I bought his single "I Wonder Why" backed with "Teen Angel" and played it until the grooves wore out.

I wasn't surprised when Dion told me he was a big Robert Johnson fan. His early records, he explained, were a form of blues that teenagers could relate to. My mind was blown that day when Dion invited me to jam along with him as he played "Dust My Broom." He was still great, and we sounded like we had been playing together for years.

It's interesting how you connect with certain people. Something resonates; there's an empathetic vibe. That's how I felt meeting Dion. It reminded me of when I first met Chuck Barris. I knew that we would become friends. Over the years, Chuck would stop by and we'd talk, usually about nothing too serious, and then I'd show him guitars. Sometimes he'd buy one; sometimes he'd buy an ice cream cone across the street and offer me a lick. Yeah, I just said that, and it's true.

After the photo shoot, and after I met Dion, Chuck brought his Gibson ES-330 to have it set up (sort of like a tune-up for guitars). While I wrote the repair tag, Chuck entertained himself by looking at a Kamaka Pineapple ukulele, which he decided to purchase. As I was writing the receipt, Chuck turned serious. "Hey, Zeeker, I need you to do a favor for me."

"Sure, Chuck, what is it?"

I looked up, and Chuck locked eyes with me. "I just finished writing a manuscript and I want you to read it. I can drop it off next week when I pick up the Gibson. After you read it, let me know what you think. I trust your opinion."

A week later, Chuck came by with the manuscript. It was titled *Wasted—The Death of a Daughter*, and it was about his daughter Della, a precocious girl who had moved out on her own at sixteen and died from an overdose of alcohol and cocaine at thirty-six. After reading it, I e-mailed Chuck to say I thought the book was deep and sad, and very good. It read as if written in Chuck's own blood and tears. I told him I'd had a hard time getting through it, but that I wouldn't change a word.

Chuck e-mailed me back,

Zeeker,

My favorite reader, guitar player, hat wearer, etc. etc. etc., I can't sell it the way it's written. I'm very glad that you read the "original sin" version of my book. Now you can read the revised version and tell me what you think. I'm out of the house for the next month or so working on the revised version of Della. You will be the first to read it. Take care of your bones.

Your buddy,
Chuck

By the end of May, after dozens of e-mails back and forth, Frank told me the *Vanity Fair* piece was finally happening. He was done writing it, and now we would wait to see when it hit the newsstands. Meanwhile, I needed to find a guitar for John Pelosi. Two lightweight butterscotch Fender Custom Shop '51 Nocaster Relics had just arrived at the store. John picked the one he liked, and I bought it for him as my way of saying thanks.

Spring turned to summer, the story got pushed back again, and life went on. Cathy and I celebrated our twenty-first wedding anniversary. Caitlin graduated high school. The weather was nice and we went to see a few shows. Sam Shepard invited us to see him play at Joe's Pub, a blissful cacophony of Sam and Peter Stampfel singing wildly over a nine-piece jug band. It was a good time, and I've learned to cherish those, because too often they are followed by sad news. Shortly after Sam's show, a close family friend passed away. Two weeks later I saw *Dream of Life*, Steven Sebring's film about Patti Smith, and remembered why I hate looking backwards. It affirms how quickly the hands of time move.

At the Philadelphia guitar show in July, several people asked me when the story was coming out. I had to tell them I didn't know, but I came home to an e-mail from John: the piece was scheduled to appear in the November 2008 music issue of *Vanity Fair*, and they would be sending someone to the store with a print for me to approve.

I spent my birthday walking around the West Village with Cathy and Caitlin. It was a hot, humid day, and we took it slow and easy. The girls bought me a vintage jacket and a western shirt at Rags-A-Gogo. Afterwards we went for iced coffee and dinner. When I got home, I saw that Frank had e-mailed me some fact-checking questions. When I called him the next day to see if the story was still scheduled to run in November, Frank laughed and said, "I don't want to jinx it. I'll call you when it closes."

Nine days later, Frank called to let me know the story had closed. It would definitely appear in the November issue of *Vanity Fair*. The piece was 10,000 words long and featured a full-page reproduction of the photo. The magazine would be available in New York and Los Angeles the following week, in the rest of the US in two weeks. Later that afternoon, Steve Earle invited me to his show at the Judson Memorial Church. Steve's show was the cherry on top of a good week.

I believe worrying is pointless. The way I see it, when you set something in motion, it takes on a life of its own. Whatever happens after that is out of your control. Of course I could be totally wrong about that, but the idea helps keep me calm.

On the evening of Tuesday, September 30, *Vanity Fair* posted the story online. I read it, then showed it to Cathy and Caitlin. They were happy that it was finally out, but I guess I didn't look so happy, because Cathy asked me, "What's wrong?"

"They didn't mention you or Caitlin in the story."

"That's OK."

"No, it's really not. And they also didn't mention Tom."

"Why do you think they did that?" Cathy asked.

"Probably because the editor wanted to portray me as a misanthropic oddball who spends his lonely nights searching the internet for buried treasure."

Cathy laughed, and I was glad she thought it was funny. I just hoped Tom wouldn't be too upset.

The next morning when I arrived at work, Tom grinned at me and handed me a freshly printed copy of *Vanity Fair*. He said that he wasn't upset that his name wasn't included in the story, but in truth we were both annoyed and there was nothing we could do about it. Well, that wasn't exactly true. We could do what guys do in these situations: we could go out after work for beers. And so we did.

First we hit the Spotted Pig, and I gave a copy of *Vanity Fair* to my friend Dan, who bought us a round of their malty, smooth cask beer. Next we went to Vol de Nuit, a Belgian bar owned by our friend Sham. I gave him a copy of the magazine and he treated us to a round of sweet-tasting Leffe Brown. We closed out the night at the Blind Tiger with my friend Sara. When I gave her the magazine, she hugged me, and soon two delicious Imperial IPAs magically appeared.

I got home late and slept like a dead man. Surprisingly, I didn't wake up with too much of a hangover, and after two black coffees I felt well enough to turn on my computer and read the story again. It had taken me three years to get the photo out. I'd done the best I could to research, authenticate, and respectfully share it. Frank had written a great, long story. It was solid, and the reproduction of the photo was beautiful. I thought *Vanity Fair* had done it right, and many others agreed. But of course some didn't.

Later that afternoon, I checked online to see if anyone had commented on the story. The blues forums were overflowing with negativity. I'm not sure what motivates people to join internet forums. Maybe they're bored and lonely. I'm sure some of them are nice enough, but way too many are full of pent-up anger. Maybe they've exhausted the patience of their former friends and spouses, so the forums are their last chance at human contact. I picture them alone, late at night, sitting in their underwear crouched in front of their computers, spewing expertise, waiting salaciously for some poor, lonely soul to voice an opinion. If he's foolish enough to join the conversation, the experts will invariably gang up and trounce him.

Bloggers are a different breed, often exhibiting more advanced social skills than the forum dwellers—not least because they usually attach a real name to their work. While the photo and I were getting thrashed in the forums, I noticed that several blogs with links to the *Vanity Fair* article were more receptive. Some part of me knew that I shouldn't take any of it personally, but it was hard not to.

The next morning, my friend Michael Wincott came by the store. I've known Michael since long before he was cast as the villainous street boss who battles Brandon Lee in the movie *The Crow*. Michael high-fived me when I told him the story was finally out, then called Keith Richards to let him know about it. After Michael left, Steve Earle and Allison Moorer stopped by to offer their congratulations, as did Dion and his wife, Susan, and John Leventhal and Rosanne Cash. Late in the day, Chrissie Hynde came in and we talked for a while. I gave her guitar advice and she gave me some insight on how to deal with being in the public eye.

I spent that weekend at the Four Amigos Guitar Show in Arlington, Texas, where Matt and I bought some unusual guitars. My favorite was an early-sixties Carvin electric with the name Clay in gold foil letters on its pick guard. It resembled one of Paul Bigsby's early models, and it just oozed rockabilly. As I walked around, lots of people congratulated me on the story, even those who had their doubts about the photo's authenticity. At least we all agreed that it was great to see blues featured in a mainstream magazine.

That's really what mattered most to me: representing a legend. Sure, the personal accolades were sweet, but I preferred to have the focus centered on the photo rather than me. Some days it felt as if the photo were afloat in a stream, and I was just there to move small branches and other obstacles out of the way in order to keep it moving. Meanwhile, I kept believing the photo would find its rightful destination. It was like a dandelion wish: take a deep breath, blow, and watch the seeds fly away. They land where they will.

Two days later, Eli Smith and I met at Cocoa Bar on Seventh Avenue in Park Slope. It's quiet and they know how to make a proper Americano, so it was the right place for what we had planned. As we drank our coffees, Eli interviewed me for his *Down Home Radio* show. Our conversation centered on the photo and the musical community surrounding Matt Umanov Guitars. I told Eli that if John Campbell, Chris Whitley, and Brian Kramer hadn't introduced me to slide guitar, then I probably wouldn't have studied Robert Johnson's music, and I would never have bought the photo. John and Chris died way too young, and Brian had relocated to Sweden. Maybe the photo found its way to Bleecker Street because their spirits were still here. That resonated with me somehow, but it didn't explain why I was the one who ended up with it.

The following morning at work, I got a telephone call from someone I'd never met. He introduced himself as Davey Williams and told me that Johnny Shines had taught him how to play guitar. He made me laugh when he said, "Zeke, I knew Johnny Shines really well, I spent a lot of time with him, I can tell you how he liked to eat his spaghetti." Davey believed I had found an early photo of his teacher. At the end of our conversation, he said, "Thank you for doing what you did. I never thought I would see a photo of Johnny Shines in *Vanity Fair*. You know, I think he would have liked it too."

On my lunch break, I got a coffee and headed over to Raffetto's on West Houston to buy some fresh linguini and pesto for dinner. I stopped to watch a group of kids playing roller hockey in the schoolyard nearby and noticed that one of them was way taller than the others. In rollerblades, Tim Robbins looked almost seven feet tall. When he noticed me, he skated over to say hello. "You sell any good guitars lately?"

"Yeah, I just sold a '65 Candy Apple Red Jazzmaster. You playing music?"

"Yes, we're in Electric Lady this week, recording."

Though best known for his film work, Tim also records and plays live with his band, the Rogues Gallery. I told him about the *Vanity Fair* story and how unprepared I felt to deal with the all the attention. He understood, and he offered me some advice: "Whether it's good or bad, don't read your own press."

Tim was right. I needed to disengage my ego and listen to what was in my heart instead of what others were saying. In theory, it should have been easy to do; but in reality, it was hard. Given the daily chaos each of us deals with, it's amazing that we're able to function at all. Combine that with a teaspoon full of ego, add a dash of controversy and a pinch of media coverage, then shake well and take a big gulp. Swallow it and tell me if you like the taste. I didn't, so I tried to follow Tim's advice, but my respite from the online chatter was short-lived.

It ended with an e-mail from Frank, who had written a follow-up piece for *Vanity Fair* called "A Disputed Robert Johnson Photo Gets the *C.S.I.* Treatment." Early on, I had told Frank that no matter how convincing a case we could make for the photo's authenticity, there would always be doubters and haters. I warned Frank that some people in the small but contentious blues world would see his story as a target on my forehead, and if he decided to stand beside me, he might want to Kevlar up too. Frank probably thought I was being overly dramatic, but I wasn't. I guess I was trying to tell him that if you open the lid of Pandora's Box, you shouldn't be surprised when monsters show up at your door.

Frank and I were like the two guys who worked in the medical supply warehouse in the movie *Return of the Living Dead*. When they accidentally released a poison gas into the air, they had no way of knowing that the vapors would reanimate the dead. Frank and I had a similar situation on our hands. We had released a portrait of a phantom, and the image had awakened the zombies.

Frank's follow-up article was concise and on point. In an attempt to disperse the naysayers, Frank had persuaded *Vanity Fair* to publish key portions of Lois Gibson's forensic analysis. In four different examples, Gibson illustrated how my photo compared with the two other known photos of Robert Johnson. She said the photos "show almost identical feature placement." When comparing the foreheads, she cited a "square bony eminence" that was "extraordinary" and visible in all three photos. After superimposing the right side of Johnson's face in my photo over the photo booth shot, Gibson concluded that comparison "shows almost a perfect fit." Superimposing it over the Hooks Brothers photo, she stated, "The features on the vertical plane line up exactly as possible." As Frank had reported in the original story, Lois Gibson believed that if my photo was taken about the same time as or a little earlier than the photo booth shot, "it appears that the individual is Robert Johnson. All of the features are consistent if not identical. The only differences are due to the different angle of the camera on the face and/or the lighting." She left herself a bit of wiggle room by saying, "My only problem with this determination is the lack of certainty about the date of the questioned photo." I was fine with this equivocation, because my research showed that the time period was correct.

When I called Frank the next day to compliment him on a second compelling piece, he apologized for not taking my warnings seriously. In all his years as a journalist, he said, he had never experienced negativity of the kind that the photo had generated. I was prepared for it. Frank wasn't. He didn't understand what we had unleashed, and while I appreciated his effort to contain it, I knew that as far as the blues world was concerned, his follow-up article was too little, too late. It was a kerosene torch, and we were dealing with Frankenstein's monster.

Chapter 18

Goin' to the 'Stil'ry

A few days later, Frank and I met up at Caffe Reggio on MacDougal Street. Reggio opened in 1927, the first cafe in America to serve cappuccino. They still do it perfectly, but I prefer my coffee straight-up, no milk, no sugar. Frank does too.

After we ordered, Frank handed me an envelope with multicolored French postage stamps on it. "Here, read this and let me know what you think."

The letter was two pages long. Its author said he had enjoyed reading the story and seeing the photo. He had some theories about what brand the guitar in the photo might be, but his guess was off base. He also suggested that we show the photo to B. B. King, just to make sure that it wasn't a photo of him. I looked at Frank and said, "You know what they say about a little knowledge? Well, this guy knows a little about guitars, but not enough. The guitar in the photo was made by Harmony, not Regal or Orpheum. I can tell by the shape of the headstock and the style of the tailpiece. I wish there was a logo, but there isn't."

"I know, it's driving you crazy, right?" Frank cracked a smile. "It's funny that he suggested showing the photo to B. B. King. It doesn't look like him to me."

"Me neither."

"Just so you know, I showed it to King's manager and her opinion was that it doesn't look like him."

"She would know. Hey, was this the only letter that you got?"

"No, there were more. I didn't want to mention this, but since you

asked, maybe I should. There was a letter from a guy in Montreal who believes that the photo was printed in reverse."

"Why?"

"Because Johnny Shines is wearing his watch is on his right hand instead of on his left. The guy also noticed that the buttons on Shines' pants and jacket were on his right side, like they would be on women's clothing, and that the ticket pocket on Robert Johnson's jacket was also on his right side instead of the left where it would normally be. What do you think?"

Our waitress brought our espressos. I sniffed at my cup and took a sip, then looked at Frank and half-smiled. "Well, he has a point."

"So if it's reversed, wouldn't that mean the guitarist is left-handed?"

"No, he might just be holding it backwards for the photo. It's broken and there are no strings on it. I don't know. There were no left-handed guitars back then."

"What about the eyes?"

"Even reversed, they'd still look mismatched. Listen, if the guy holding the guitar in the photo was standing on his head, then it would look like a photo of Robert Johnson doing a headstand. You know what I'm saying?"

Frank chuckled at the thought. "Yes, I see your point."

When I got back to the store, Steve Earle was at the front counter drinking a Diet Dr Pepper. I asked whether he thought the photo might have been printed in reverse and was surprised to hear him say that he believed it was. He told me that the photo of Bob Dylan on the cover of his first album was printed in reverse because it looked better that way. That didn't mean that Dylan was left-handed, and the fact that he's not fingering a chord didn't mean he wasn't a guitar player or wasn't the real Bob Dylan. Steve said that, even reversed, he believed that the man holding the guitar in my photo was Robert Johnson.

Later that night, I found myself staring at a high-resolution image of Robert Johnson's face on my computer screen. I zoomed in on his eyes, not sure what I was looking for—perhaps a small cataract he was said to have had. Or maybe I was hoping to find a piece of his soul. I scrolled down to Johnson's hands, once again marveling at their size and the remarkable length of his fingers. Johnson's hands are as distinctly recognizable as his eyes. When I first saw the photo, I noticed that Johnson was wearing what appeared to be a pinky ring. I was always curious about it. Viewed now at slightly larger than life-size, it was oddly shaped and worn just below the middle joint of the finger. I've never seen another like it, yet somehow it reminded me of Chris Whitley's ring slide.

As I continued my examination, I was struck once again by the overall damage and wear the photo had sustained over the years. When magnified, the overall effect was creepy. For some reason the scan had a redder hue than the original print. The dirt and discoloration looked like spattered blood, and the rips and creases in the emulsion added to the effect.

I thought about my conversations with Frank and Steve as I looked at Johnny Shines' watch and the buttons on his clothing. They appeared to be backwards, so I reversed the photo. When I did, Shines' clothing and watch looked correct, but the stripes on Johnson's tie were now backwards. His ticket pocket and handkerchief were where they should be, but now he was holding the guitar backwards, as a left-handed guitar player would. I didn't know what to make of it. I felt like I was looking into an antique funhouse mirror while someone somewhere was laughing.

The thought made me smile. My situation was ridiculous. I realized I was chasing smoke. I could grab all I wanted, but I would never be able to get hold of it.

My epiphany was interrupted by the phone ringing. It was my brother Gary calling from Las Vegas to congratulate me on the *Vanity Fair* story. "Hey, I just read it and it's great, but you know what the best part is?"

"No, tell me."

"At the bottom of the photo, in tiny white letters, it says 'Portrait of a Phantom.' Now that's cool!"

Gary asked if I had any plans for where to display the original photo. When I told him I was still thinking about it, he said, "If I was you, I'd put it in the Rock and Roll Hall of Fame, right next to Alan Freed's ashes."

"OK," I said. "I'll do that."

Chapter 19

Like Consumption

I envisioned it in the center of a wall, surrounded by a hundred handwritten pages. A tiny picture framed with a thousand words by musicians, artists, writers, filmmakers, and historians, all inspired by the legacy of Robert Johnson. The wall would be a tribute to Johnson on the centennial of his birth. It would take time to create, but two years seemed sufficient. On May 8, 2009—Johnson's ninety-eighth birthday—I e-mailed James Henke, the curator of the Rock and Roll Hall of Fame, to see if he might be interested. To improve my chances, I attached a link to the *Vanity Fair* story.

A week later, I received an e-mail from Meredith Rutledge, an assistant curator at the Rock and Roll Hall of Fame. "Thanks so much for reaching out. What an amazing story—the enigma of Robert Johnson is fascinating and it's great to have more to add to the story. I'd love to discuss some ideas for what we could do around Mr. Johnson's 100th birthday."

She asked if there had been any progress in authenticating the photo. I sent her links to Frank's follow-up story and the Robert Johnson Blues Foundation home page, which featured a photo of Claud Johnson sporting a T-shirt printed with the photo and the caption *Robert Johnson, King of the Delta Blues*. Claud clearly believed I had found a photo of his father.

In early June, Meredith e-mailed to let me know she had spoken to Lauren Onkey, the vice president of education at the Hall, who was "excited about the prospect of putting something together around the photo . . . she would like to talk to you about this so I passed your info on to her and she will be giving you a call."

On June 22, I stumbled across an entertaining online interview called

135

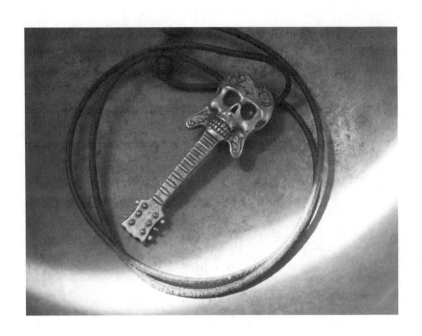

"An Hour with Jack White/Pamela Des Barres." I especially enjoyed how their conversation unfolded after Jack explained that there is only one known photo of the great delta blues man Charley Patton:

> Pamela: How about Robert Johnson, isn't there only one photo of him too?
> Jack: There were two, and they just found a third one. It was in *Vanity Fair* a couple of months ago, it was crazy. It was on the kitchen table and I'm flipping through *Vanity Fair* and I'm like, "Is that a new picture of Robert Johnson?" Some guy found it on eBay.
> Pamela: Wow!
> Jack: "Unknown blues singer. B. B. King maybe??" on eBay and some guy bought it and it was Robert Johnson. And he looks so good. Just a good-lookin' guy.
> Pamela: Yeah, he got in trouble for that, I guess.

I got a kick out of this. It made me laugh and inspired me to keep working.

In mid-August, Lauren Onkey called. We spoke briefly, and she promised to talk to her associates and get back to me soon. Two weeks later she sent me this e-mail: "I've been talking to our folks here about some events that we might put together around your photo of Robert Johnson, and everyone is very excited—and we're especially glad that there's time enough to put something interesting together. The director of our Library and Archives is especially excited. We're thinking about some kind of one-day symposium either on blues research or on photographic resources and rock/blues research, and we love the idea of a web site idea. So let's think about next steps. Should you or I contact the estate about their cooperation?"

I told her I'd do it, then called Robert Johnson's grandson Steven, who said he would talk to the rest of the family and get back to me. A week later, Cathy Gurley, who handled licensing for the Johnson estate, called to say that I had their support.

Cathy Gurley and I were also working with a visual artist named Tom Zotos, who had worked with Warner Brothers and Disney to produce the "Art of Walt Disney" collection and the "Speechless" tribute to Mel Blanc. Zotos contacted me after reading the story in *Vanity Fair* to say he loved the blues and his son Zack was a guitarist. He wanted to create and sell art based on the photo. I liked his artwork, so I put him in touch with Cathy and they worked out a deal. After that, I didn't hear from Zotos for several months, and I didn't think about it again until Dave Rubin forwarded me an e-mail from our friend Doug Redler.

Attending a show at the House of Blues, Doug had noticed that the club was selling T-shirts featuring the third photo of Robert Johnson for $22. I called them and bought two shirts, one for Tom Crandall and one for myself.

Ten days later, Cathy Gurley sent me this press release:

THE REEL BLUES FEST
HONORS JAMES COTTON AT THE BOSTON HOUSE OF BLUES
ROBERT JOHNSON FOUNDATION
PARTICIPATES IN COMMEMORATION

BOSTON- The House of Blues will present a special evening of music and art to honor the lifetime achievements of Grammy winner James Cotton. Cotton and his music will take center stage on the evening of October 29, with tributes by Huey Lewis, James Montgomery, J. Geils, and a plethora of Blues greats. The event will benefit the Reel Blues Fest, a non-profit 501 (C3) organization which raises money for musicians in need of health care but without the resources and educational film related projects.

Prior to Showtime there will be a VIP reception with a "meet and greet" in the foundation room where attendees will experience *"The Birth of the Blues"* art show by pop artist Tom Zotos. Zotos has worked on 150 movies with an expertise in licensing. He also was instrumental in the merchandising of the House of Blues brand in the early years of the franchise. The Art Show will also run on Friday, October 30th.

Zotos recently entered into an agreement with the Robert Johnson Foundation to develop unique usages of the newly discovered photograph of the famed Mississippi Bluesman, Robert Johnson (1911-1938). The photograph of Johnson is one of only three known images of him.

A highlight of the October 29th event will be a special presentation of the photograph to Cotton by Steven Johnson, grandson of Robert and Vice President of the Robert Johnson Foundation in Crystal Springs MS.

Zotos called to invite me, but it was short notice and I wasn't able to go. After the show, he sent me a group photo of Kim Wilson, Huey Lewis, James Montgomery, J. Geils, and Steven Johnson holding a poster-sized blowup of my photo. They had signed it and presented it as a gift to James Cotton. The group photo was cool, so I sent it to Lauren Onkey. Two months had gone by since we last spoke. It was almost

Thanksgiving now, and I was curious to see if there was any progress on her end.

It turned out that there wasn't. Lauren e-mailed to let me know everyone at the Hall of Fame had just finished working on their biggest event of the year, American Music Masters. This year's honoree was Janis Joplin. "I wasn't planning to do anything with the Johnson photo until we were done," Lauren wrote. "I will reach out to them soon; we haven't planned anything yet, however."

It was a bit of a red flag, but I wasn't going to sweat it yet. There was still plenty of time to put something together. Thanksgiving rolled around and we celebrated it with friends. My sister Cindy called from Vegas to wish us well and remind me to call my brother and parents. My mom had undergone cancer surgery earlier in the year, and Gary was also having health problems. I called my folks, listened to my dad tell an old joke, and spoke to my mom, who told me she was worried about my brother. When I talked to Gary, he sounded terrible. I told him to see a doctor, but he didn't want to. I knew it was useless to argue, so instead I wished him a happy Thanksgiving and told him to call me if he needed anything.

Everyone knows that the weeks between Thanksgiving and Christmas are the busiest time of the retail year. Tons of people visit New York for the holidays, and dealing with the crowds is exhausting. It always goes by in a blur, and by Christmas Eve, I'm usually wiped out. I didn't have the time or energy to think about the photo, but I kept thinking about my brother. I called him on New Year's Eve and he sounded really sick. I urged him to go to the hospital, but he refused. He was convinced that if he checked himself in, he would never leave.

Gary told me that he didn't want to die, but that if he did, he wanted to be cremated and have me bring his ashes back to New York. He wanted them scattered in the ocean. It was the last thing he ever said to me. On January 15, 2010, Gary died. I flew to Vegas and brought his ashes back home. On a cold, windy afternoon, I honored his final wish. Gary's ashes took off like a paper kite, like smoke dissipating, and then he was gone.

I had lost my brother, my oldest friend. Gary was crazier than me, yet I had followed his lead for most of my life, until he walked down a path so dark I couldn't allow myself to explore it. I had my own demons, but my way of dealing with them was less toxic in the short run. My drinking was becoming a problem because it wasn't fun anymore. I was hurt and trying to go numb, and some days I succeeded. I woke up and went to work, but my heart wasn't in it. I felt time slipping through my fingers like sand, like ashes.

By the end of March, I began to regain my footing. Picking up where I'd left off with the photo, I reached out to Cathy Gurley to see where we stood, but she told me Lauren Onkey hadn't contacted her. When I asked what was happening with Tom Zotos, she said the Johnson estate was exploring other options for licensing the photo. I e-mailed Lauren to check in, but she didn't reply, so I waited until May 8 (Robert Johnson's ninety-ninth birthday) before trying again. She got back to me two days later, saying she'd kept it on the back burner because the museum would be in the midst of a redesign in 2011 and she wasn't sure how that would affect programming. She would talk to Curatorial, she assured me, and make a plan. I was caught off guard. A year had gone by, and I was back at square one.

In a follow-up e-mail to Lauren, I described the tribute wall I had envisioned. She replied that the museum redesign would preclude the possibility of an exhibit. As an alternative, she suggested programming. "What we could do is to bring in a couple of speakers to talk about Johnson—a symposium kind of format—and we could show the photo in our theater during the panel and display it outside the theater for the day or something like that. Give that some thought and we can talk next week."

I did what she said. I thought about my job, and about others who had told me they were influenced by Robert Johnson. I thought about the past and the future connecting. I thought about time and ashes. "If I was you, I'd put it in the Rock and Roll Hall of Fame, right next to Alan Freed's ashes," my brother had said. I sent Lauren another e-mail explaining why Robert Johnson deserved an exhibit on his centennial. If it wasn't possible to do it at the Rock and Roll Hall of Fame, then I would take it elsewhere.

Lauren got back to me quickly. "We had another RJ meeting today. We still want to do a symposium here sometime in May of 2011, and we would like to feature the photograph in our sessions, especially by focusing on photography and blues/early roots music research, which will connect well to Library and Archives. While we can't do the kind of exhibit that you're proposing, our curators did come up with a couple of interesting ideas to exhibit the photo."

It was worth talking about, so I agreed to take a conference call with Lauren and two of the curators, James Henke and Howard Kramer. I didn't have an office, so I called from the phone in the basement of the store. They wanted to use the photo to promote the opening of their new Library and Archives. It would be featured on their website and would be the centerpiece of a symposium about photography and early blues and roots music. It wasn't exactly what I had wanted, but it sounded worthwhile, so I agreed. When I sent Lauren contact information for the Johnson estate, she replied, "I passed it on to our curators James and Howard, as they have to handle everything re: exhibiting the photo."

Five weeks later, in mid-July, I hadn't heard from anyone. I checked in with Cathy Gurley, who hadn't either. I found it strange that no one had contacted her, so I suggested she reach out to James Henke. We also discussed a few ideas for licensing the photo. Cathy was working on something with Getty Images, and I told her I would ask a friend of mine for merchandising advice.

Looking back at that summer, I realize that I took my eye off the ball. I had a life outside of the photo and I believed that Cathy and James, two professionals, were capable of planning things without me. I guess I assumed they would let me know if they needed my help.

In September, on my fiftieth birthday, my wife and daughter and a dozen of my friends surprised me with a little celebration at Vol de Nuit. Everyone knew I had been through a rough year, and I appreciated their sharing a toast with me on my birthday. As I said before, you have to enjoy the good times because sad news often follows.

On October 24, my sister called to tell me that our mother had died. I flew to Vegas for her funeral, and later that night at my sister's house, my father collapsed. I stayed in Vegas for a few days until he stabilized and then returned home. I felt beaten. It was like after a fight, when you're lying on the ground, still conscious but badly hurt.

I returned to work, not knowing what else to do. While I was in

Vegas, Cathy Gurley had e-mailed me regarding a licensing deal I had set in motion. She mentioned that James Henke had never gotten back to her after she contacted him months earlier. I told her that I would reach out to him, and I did.

Here's how he responded:

Hi Zeke,

Thanks for the e-mail. I think we are going to pass on the Robert Johnson photo. We have two other images of him here at the Museum, and one is going to be blown up quite large. So I think we will pass on the other one.

Thanks again for the offer.
Happy holidays,
Jim Henke

My reply to him was, "Unbelievable ... but not unexpected." I also sent Lauren an e-mail that said, "Two years later . . . not cool."

Lauren got back to me with an apology. She blamed the museum redesign and explained that the curators decide what will be exhibited, not her. As a gesture of consolation, she offered to display the photo onstage at a one-day event. She had already reached out to some speakers, but she could put the brakes on that if I didn't want to do it.

I thought about it and realized I was too messed up to make other arrangements. I e-mailed Lauren and let her know what I had just been through. I told her I accepted James's decision, but I didn't understand it.

There had to be another reason why James decided to pass on the photo. Maybe someone had talked him out of it. I said I understood Lauren's position and agreed to let her put together an educational event around the photo. She replied, "Thanks. I'll look at our calendar and get back to you on Monday."

She never got back to me, and I didn't really care. I had more important things to deal with. My father was dying. It seemed as if he was unable to recover from the shock of losing my mom. In the weeks that followed, my sister called me every day, crying because my father's body was shutting down and there was nothing we could do about it. At his doctor's recommendation, I consented to have my father's feeding tube removed, and two days before the change of the year, he died. I have no words to describe how I felt.

Chapter 20

Business All in a Trick

"Mr. Johnson, Mr. Johnson!"

I was on the West 4th Street subway platform heading to work. I turned to see a goth kid in a motorcycle jacket trying to flag me down. He looked like Marilyn Manson, but prettier and more petite.

"Mr. Johnson, I just wanted to say hello. I'm a fan of your music."

OK, I thought, *I have no idea what's happening here.* I considered the possibilities. Either the kid was crazy, or on my subway ride in I had mysteriously transformed into Robert Johnson.

"Who do you think I am?" I asked. I was almost afraid to hear his answer.

"You're Matt Johnson of The The," the kid said.

I was tempted to tell him he was right, and I might have done so if I could fake an English accent. After all, who would it hurt? Once at JFK airport, some stoner kids mistook me for Tom Waits and I played along. I bet it made their night, too. While I could almost pull off Tom's raspy, poetic drawl, an English accent was out of my league, so I decided to come clean with this kid. I tried to let him down easy, saying, "Hey, yeah, you know, I like that band too. But I'm not Matt Johnson. Sorry."

I could see the kid's disappointment, and it was one of the few times I ever wished I was a rock star.

"But you're a musician, right?"

"Yeah, I play guitar. I'm not famous, but I sell guitars to famous people."

Upon hearing that, the kid perked up. He asked me where I worked, and when I told him, he said, "Oh, you must know my Uncle Carl."

"Wow, Carl Luckert's your uncle? Yeah, I work with him. We're friends."

I didn't see a family resemblance. Carl looks like he should be hanging out in a speakeasy with Bix Beiderbecke, whereas this kid was a modern vampire. It turned out the kid's name was Nick Kushner, and he was an artist. Nick's choice of medium wasn't acrylic or oils. He painted in his own blood.

After that, I occasionally ran into Nick on our morning commute and we'd talk on the train. Nick's day job was web design. He was a friend of Marilyn Manson's and he had designed Nachtkabarett, a website dedicated to uncovering the occult imagery and symbolism in Manson's work. Nick had also designed a website for his friend Rudy Coby, a comedic magician who, like Manson, played by his own rules. In his own way, Nick was following their lead, and I respected that.

I was working with Cathy Gurley on a licensing deal with a company out of Nashville called Dreamer Media. My friend Barry Perlman, one of the founders of Lucky Brand, referred me to Dreamer's CEO Dean Gelfand. Dean had put together a successful run of Bob Dylan T-shirts for Lucky Brand, and his list of clients included Billy Joel, Aerosmith, Paul Simon, and Kiss. Dean understood marketing and he was a nice guy. Cathy and Dean were close to signing a deal, and it occurred to me that Nick was the right person to design a T-shirt for Robert Johnson's centennial. When I told Nick about the third photo of Johnson, I noticed a gleam in his eye.

"Isn't he the guy who sold his soul to the devil?" he asked.

"Yeah, that's what they say."

"Do you believe it?'

"I believe he had his demons."

I told Nick about the pending deal with Dreamer and asked if he was interested in helping me design a shirt.

"Of course. What did you have in mind?"

I described my idea. I imagined the photo in an antique ebony picture frame carved with images depicting the struggle between good and evil. Underneath, in small letters, would be Johnson's and Shines' signatures.

Nick tried, but despite his best efforts, the picture frame's carvings looked wrong. Instead of a carved frame, we decided to go with one made of wood that looked like it had been salvaged from the Bates Motel. Nick used more than one hundred layers of Photoshop to create an eerie, incredibly realistic image. It was finely detailed and I didn't know if it was right for a shirt, but it looked cool, so I sent it to Dean and he liked it.

In mid-January I took a conference call with Dean, his assistant Mary Jo English, and Cathy Gurley while sitting at the shipping bench in the basement of the store. I was still grieving over the loss of my father. Johnson's one hundredth birthday was four months away and I needed to pull myself together and focus. As foolish as it might sound, I didn't really care about the terms of the deal. I just wanted a cool shirt to wear on Johnson's birthday. I spaced out during the call, so I don't know what was discussed, but it must have ended well because everyone seemed pleased. All we needed to complete the deal was for the Johnson estate to sign off.

It never happened. A month later, we were blindsided by the news that the Johnson estate had signed an exclusive licensing agreement with Sony. The deal with Dreamer was over before it had begun. Dean was a good sport about it, assuring me that he knew the merchandising executive at Sony and that I would be in good hands. I had my doubts about the estate's decision, but there was nothing I could do about it. I knew the deal wasn't going to work out well for me, because Steve LaVere, who owned the other two photos of Johnson, had long-standing ties with Sony and it wasn't in his best interests for Sony to promote a third photo.

Shortly after inking the deal, Sony announced plans to release *Robert Johnson: The Complete Original Masters: Centennial Edition*. This was a $400 limited edition vinyl box set that came with two bonus CDs, a DVD, and a twenty-four page booklet. When I asked John Kitchens, the Johnson estate's lawyer, if Sony planned to use the third photo for the box set, he replied, "Sony does not intend to use the photo for the new release. Everything for the release is set in stone and Sony isn't entertaining any more images." I wasn't surprised to hear that, but it still stung, because I expected at least a bit of loyalty from the estate. Oh well; I didn't have a law degree, but street smarts had gotten me through some dirty fights in the past, so I used them. Sure enough, when the box set came out, the photo was included.

Apparently I had ruffled some feathers, because Sony featured the photo on a page in the booklet surrounded by discredited photos of men who vaguely resembled Robert Johnson. The accompanying text read, "Over the years a number of photographs of Robert Johnson have been 'discovered.' Though only two have ever been verified and universally accepted, a third seen here (center photo) was recently acknowledged by a forensic expert hired by the Robert Johnson estate as being Robert Johnson. Still the mystique and debate continues."

It was a cheap shot, and although I had won the first round, I had a black eye to show for it. Sony won round two by excluding the photo from the double-CD, mass-marketed release of the centennial collection. I'd like to believe round three was a draw, but in truth, I got hit hard.

In February, Sony's vice president of merchandising, Mat Vlasic, asked me to send him a scan of the photo suitable for making T-shirts. When I sent the scan, I included Nick's design, hoping Sony would use it. I didn't hear back from Mat and I didn't sweat it. I had other things on my mind, like where I might wear my Robert Johnson T-shirt on Johnson's hundredth birthday. B. B. King's would be nice, not too big or noisy, and my friend Karl Schwarz worked there. I contacted Karl, who pitched the idea to the club's talent buyer. Before too long, tickets for the show were for sale on B. B. King's website.

I was also thinking about a hosting a smaller show at Caffe Vivaldi. It would be fun to get the neighborhood out for a night of blues. I imagined it as a moment out of the 1960s Greenwich Village music scene: an event where anyone could perform, a free show where everyone was welcome. I talked to my friend Ishrat, who owns Caffe Vivaldi, and we set a date for the show.

By the end of March, my T-shirt and two events to wear it at were in the works. While leafing through music magazines in the Union Square Barnes & Noble, I was surprised to see the photo prominently featured in the April issue of *Guitar World*. The article, "Devil in the Details," was written by Alan Di Perna. In a six-page tribute to Johnson that included quotes from Keith Richards, Eric Clapton, Robert Plant, and Billy Gibbons, the magazine captured the essence of my vision for the ill-fated wall at the Rock and Roll Hall of Fame.

Seeing the photo in that context gave me some hope. It was a glimmer of light in a dark time. The shock of losing my brother and my parents had at first left me numb, but as time passed, numbness turned to pain. I dealt with it by going out drinking on Thursday nights, so most Fridays I was hung over. It was a bad way to spend my day off.

By mid-April, I still hadn't heard from Sony about the T-shirts. They were, however, collaborating with Dogfish Head on a beer to commemorate Robert Johnson's centennial. "Hellhound on My Ale" was an IPA made with centennial hops and lemon. At 10 percent alcohol by volume, it was strong, and it probably tasted good too. Despite its goofy name, I wanted to try "Hellhound," and the perfect opportunity soon presented itself.

I noticed an announcement for an exhibit of photographs by Dick Waterman at the Chelsea Market. I was a fan of Waterman's work and he was scheduled to make an appearance, so maybe I'd get to meet him. As if that wasn't reason enough to go, Sony was sponsoring the event, providing free Hellhound on My Ale for the occasion. The show's opening night was April 21, a Thursday. Perfect.

After work that night, Tom and I headed over to the Chelsea Market at West 19th Street and 9th Avenue. It's not far from the store, and I figured we'd get there early to look at Waterman's photos before the crowd arrived. The place was almost empty except for a few late shoppers. I began to wonder if I had gotten the date wrong. We walked around until we spotted one of Waterman's photos, and then they seemed to be everywhere.

In 1964, Dick Waterman, along with Phil Spiro and Nick Perls, rediscovered the legendary Delta blues musician Son House. Waterman later formed Avalon Productions, the first agency to manage and promote exclusively blues musicians. After forming Avalon, Waterman went on to manage Son House, Skip James, Booker White, Mississippi John Hurt, and a host of other blues greats, including Buddy Guy, Junior Wells, Otis Rush, and Bonnie Raitt. In addition to all of that, Waterman had personally known Muddy Waters, Howlin' Wolf, and many of the rock musicians they inspired, including the Rolling Stones.

As I walked through the Chelsea Market looking at Waterman's photos, I was struck by how full of life they were. Waterman had more than just a great eye, more than just access to the musicians in his photos. He understood them intrinsically.

If I had to choose my favorite, it would be Waterman's photo of Skip James onstage at the 1964 Newport Folk Festival. It's a magnificent shot that depicts James singing the first word of "Devil Got My Woman," marking the moment of his rediscovery. The song that inspired Robert Johnson to write "Hellhound on My Trail" would now inspire a new generation, and Waterman had the foresight to capture it on film.

When we got to the last group of photos, I noticed a tall, lanky guy in a motorcycle jacket standing nearby. It was my friend Jon Paris, a great bluesman in his own right. Jon had played with lots of famous musicians, including Johnny Winter and Les Paul. And in a fairer world, Jon would be equally famous.

"Hey, you guys here for Dick's show?" Jon asked.

"Yeah, I was just telling Tom I hope I didn't get the dates mixed up. It's pretty empty. Maybe we're just too early. It's tonight, right?"

"That's what I heard. So how do you know Dick? Have you seen him yet?"

"We don't know him, but I'd like to meet him. We came for the photos and the beer. Sony and Dogfish Head are debuting Hellhound on My Ale."

"That's hilarious. Hey, do you think that's Dick over there?"

Jon pointed to an older man wearing a grey Hard Rock Café baseball jacket. The man was talking to a blond woman who seemed to be taking notes on a clipboard. I figured we had nothing to lose by introducing ourselves, so we did. Our hunch was right; it was Dick Waterman. We gave Waterman his props, and in return he gave us the rundown on the night's events: he would be giving a short speech at the end, then signing books. The blond woman nodded at this and wrote the word "books" on her clipboard. She reminded Waterman that they were scheduled to meet a friend in a nearby restaurant in ten minutes.

Before leaving, Waterman told us where the beer was, proving beyond a doubt that he's a standup guy.

Two guys were setting up tables in the middle of the market. Stacked underneath were cases of beer. We sauntered over like two stray cats who'd spotted a can of Friskies, trying to play it cool and still accomplish our mission. Tom turned on his friendly Minnesotan smile and said, "Hey guys, how's the beer? Have you tried it yet?"

"Yeah, we drank some yesterday," one of them answered. "It's good."

I noticed a few coolers beside the table and asked, "So how do I get one? I've been dealing with Sony and the Johnson estate all week, and I could use a drink."

I had his attention now. "Why were you dealing with Sony and the estate?"

"Because I found the third photo of Robert Johnson."

"You know, I read the *Vanity Fair* story," the guy said. "I thought I recognized you. You work at Umanov's, right?"

"Yeah, I do."

"Well then, you get the first beer of the night. Not because of the photo, but because I've met Matt. He's a good guy, but he can't be easy to work for. Here you go, buddy—you deserve this. And congratulations on the photo!"

I smiled as he handed me a cold 25-oz. bottle.

Tom quickly interjected, "Hey, I also work for Umanov."

"Then you get one too," the guy laughed, and handed Tom his own bottle.

Tom and I walked away with our score, pleased at having succeeded in our mission. I held up my bottle and proposed a toast: "To Matt Umanov."

"His legend looms large," Tom added.

"And to the Hellhound," I said as we clicked bottles and each took a swig.

Hellhound was a beer worthy of its name. It was as potent as Dogfish Head's 90 Minute IPA, but with a bit of lemon added. At 10 percent ABV, it was almost like drinking wine. After finishing our bottles, Tom and I were pleasantly buzzed. We walked around and ran into a few acquaintances. The place was starting to fill up. Two DJs were spinning music next to a table serving shots of Buffalo Trace bourbon, but this felt more like a beer night, so we decided to split another bottle of Hellhound and I drank most of it.

When the place was sufficiently crowded, the music stopped and everyone gathered around to hear Dick Waterman speak. He thanked everyone for coming to the opening of his first New York show, then told a few stories about the musicians in the photos and mentioned how grateful he was to have known them. Like the photos surrounding us, his words obviously came straight from the heart.

After the speech, I bought a copy of Waterman's book *Between Midnight and Day: The Last Unpublished Blues Archive*. Waterman signed it "To Deke—Dick Waterman." When I reminded him that my name was Zeke, he laughed and wrote "Zeke" above the name "Deke." "There, now you have both."

"Even better," I said. "Thanks, Dick, it was an honor to meet you."

With my book in one hand and an empty bottle of Hellhound in the other, I left the Chelsea Market with Tom, and we began making our way toward Bleecker Street.

"I don't know about you, but I'm pretty buzzed," Tom said. "That was some strong beer."

"Yeah, it was, and I haven't eaten since breakfast."

"You want to grab a bite or are you headed home?"

"No, I'll probably hit the Tiger for one more. You up for it?"

Tom declined, blaming the fact that he had to work tomorrow.

We parted ways on the corner of Bleecker and Jones Street, in front of the Blind Tiger. Tom was on his way home. I was on my way to going numb.

Chapter 21

From Four Until Late

On May 4, four days before Robert Johnson's hundredth birthday, Lonnie and I walked into B. B. King's. We said hello to my friend Karl, who was checking the mic levels onstage, then headed to the bar. Brian Kramer was already there finishing a beer. We joined him, and before too long, Guy Davis spotted us and invited us backstage.

Guy was filling in as the show's headliner because Honeyboy Edwards had unexpectedly fallen ill. I was sorry to hear that, but I knew it was going to be a good show anyway. Jon Paris was opening, followed by Roy Book Binder, then Guy. I had known the three of them for years, and they were great players.

As Guy and I were catching up, Jon and Roy came over to ask me what was happening with the photo. When I told them, they laughed. It was always the same: one step forward and then nothing, or worse yet, an attack. Needless to say, I wasn't wearing a T-shirt featuring the photo because Sony still hadn't produced one.

Despite the absence of Honeyboy Edwards, the show went off without a hitch. Jon delivered a raw, energetic set worthy of Lightnin' Hopkins. Roy followed with his own brand of city-slicker ragtime blues. He deliberately avoided playing songs from Johnson's repertoire and kept joking about it: "Robert didn't write this next number, but I'm sure he would have loved it." It was kind of weird, but funny, which also describes Roy, so it was righteous.

Guy's performance was joyous and soulful. He began by singing a cappella and blowing harmonica between verses while stomping his feet like a seasoned vaudevillian. He followed that with a flawless set of

Robert Johnson songs, including "Dust My Broom," "Sweet Home Chicago," and "Stop Breakin' Down Blues."

After the show, I thanked everyone and invited them to the show I was hosting at Caffe Vivaldi the next night. Guy and Roy were headed out of town, but Jon said he would stop by. Their performances had inspired me, but I was nervous that tomorrow's show might not go as well. I had to get the thought out of my head, and there was one sure way to do that.

So after work the next day, I drank two pints of Hellhound at the Blind Tiger before walking across the street to Caffe Vivaldi. By the time I got there, the place was packed. Although I'm terrible at making plans, things had fallen into place somehow. It was Cinco De Mayo and Bleecker Street was buzzing. I said to Cathy, "I can't believe how many people showed up, and there's more coming. How will they all fit?"

Cathy shrugged. "I guess they'll figure it out. Everyone's waiting— you should go inside and start the show."

"Yeah, let's do this." I pulled my hat down over my eyes, clapped my hands, pointed, and strolled in grinning. My friend Tommy handed me a beer and I surveyed the room. It was mostly filled with friends, some from as far away as Sweden, Germany, and Bangkok. They were here to help me channel a spirit, to bring out the ghost dance, to capture and release the electric poetry of the universe by paying tribute to a legend.

Honestly, I was buzzed the whole time. I remember the night as a series of snapshots, some more blurred than others. I see Brian Kramer setting up mics. I see friends coming onstage as I introduce them one by one: Nick, Rony, Ardell, Strider Bob and Johnny Brilliant, Katie and Dylan, John Van Rens, Jack Baker. I step outside for air and admire the poster Bob Jordan created for the show. People are smoking and jamming on the sidewalk. I see Gary Lucas and John Kruth performing a knockout version of "Special Rider Blues" as Ishrat smiles approvingly. I toss back a beer as William Nowik casts a spell with his guitar incantations. Arthur Nielsen and Hook Herrera and his girlfriend, Hanna, arrive. I tell the crowd they're in for a treat. Arthur is Shemekia Copeland's guitarist and Hook plays harmonica with the Allman Brothers. After their first song, I relax and turn the stage over to them.

I step outside and somehow end up over at the Blind Tiger with a beer in my hand. When some friends ask me how the show is going, I invite them to come and see for themselves. We squeeze into Vivaldi as Arthur and Hook finish their third song. The crowd wants more, but I have to give my friends Kristina, Ben, and Erik a chance to play. The mood shifts from wild to tame, from loud to calm, and then all is still. I see people eating and drinking. They look happy, but for me it's like breathing in secondhand smoke. I see the worry on Cathy's face as someone hands me a shot of Jameson and a beer. Nonetheless, I down the shot and introduce Jon Paris. I grab my guitar and ask Arthur, Hook, and Brian to join us. We play a short set, wrapping things up around midnight. I put my guitar in its case and hear time ticking as the music fades away. I look around the room and I see a blur of faces, smiling, living life . . . and then I see ashes.

On a scale of one to ten, my hangover the next day was a seven. At least the show had gone well and everyone had a good time. The only thing that bothered me was that I didn't get to wear a T-shirt featuring the photo. On May 8, Johnson's one hundredth birthday, I sent an e-mail to Mat Vlasic to see what was holding Sony up. Mat got back to me with a terse message: "Hi Zeke—We have not used the photo yet."

It didn't take Sherlock Holmes to see that Sony was stonewalling. In fact, they had already issued three other Johnson centennial T-shirts. It was time for me to do something about it, so I asked John Kitchens to give me a licensing deal. If Sony wasn't going to use the photo on a shirt, then I would. I guess my point hit home, because soon afterward I received an e-mail from Mat saying, "We are ready to use the photo."

Unfortunately, they didn't use Nick's design. In mid-November, after eight months of stalling, Sony finally released a T-shirt featuring the photo. Of course, they didn't send me one; I had to buy it.

The holiday season came and went, but I don't remember much about it. I'm sure the store was busy, because it always is at that time of year. As Johnson's centennial year came to a close, I had mixed feelings about how it had gone. Most of what I had tried to set in motion hadn't panned out. I took consolation in the small things I'd been able to accomplish. Still, I knew some people were bothered by the photo, and I suspected they were deliberately blocking its use.

Toward the end of February, I noticed an announcement for a show at the Apollo called Robert Johnson at 100. It was a tribute show featuring an impressive list of performers, including Shemekia Copeland, Bettye LaVette, the Roots, Elvis Costello, Todd Rundgren, Taj Mahal, Keb' Mo', and a host of others. The name that jumped out at me was Elvis Costello. I'm a fan, and I'd sold him some guitars over the years, but that wasn't why his name caught my eye. I couldn't imagine Elvis playing Robert Johnson's songs, but I knew it would be good. I also knew there were people who didn't want me at the show because I was the guy with the third photo.

Two weeks later, when Frank DiGiacomo came by the store to look at guitars for his son Antony, he asked if I planned to attend the Johnson tribute show.

"No one invited me and it's sold out."

Frank winced and shook his head. "I'm supposed to be going," he said, "but I'm waiting for LaVere to nix me. If I can get a plus-one, would you come with me?"

"Sure, Frank, I'll go. Thanks for asking."

The night before the show, Frank e-mailed to let me know his plus-one had been cancelled. I was upset, but I didn't lose sleep over it. I woke up, got dressed, drank two cups of black coffee, rode the train to West 4th Street, and then headed west on Bleecker.

As I approached the store, I noticed a dapper-looking man waiting out front. He was wearing a light grey Borsalino fedora with a matching plaid suit. The vintage Martin ukulele case in his hand was the perfect accessory. Yeah, it was Elvis Costello. I invited him to follow me in through the side door because the store wasn't open yet. We leave small halogen lights on overnight, and on the rare days when I'm the first to arrive, I don't turn the bright fluorescents on right away. We sat at the dimly lit front counter, and Elvis told me the tuning pegs on the uke I'd sold him needed tightening.

"I'll have Tom take care of it," I said. "He should be here in a few minutes. I heard you're playing at the Apollo tonight."

"Yeah, I'm playing at a Robert Johnson tribute show. Are you going?"

"I was supposed to be on the guest list, but I found out last night that I'm not. I guess some people don't want me there."

There was an awkward pause as Elvis eyed me suspiciously before asking, "Why?"

I told him about the photo, and he listened attentively. When I finished, he asked, "How can I see it?"

"It's all over the internet. We can pull it up on your phone."

Elvis handed me his phone. I typed in "Robert Johnson photo" and the image appeared on the screen. "Here," I said, "check it out."

Elvis stared at the image on his screen, then smiled. "Wow. Brilliant."

"Yeah, I thought you should see it before the show tonight."

"Thanks, I appreciate it." Elvis looked at the photo again, then gave me that look you give someone when you wish the world was a fairer place. "So you're not going tonight?"

"No, and it's OK. This might sound strange, but I've been telling everyone that the main reason that I wanted to go was to see you perform."

Elvis smiled at that. "Really? Why?"

"Well, you know I'm a longtime fan," I said, "so please don't take this the wrong way, but it's hard to imagine you playing Robert Johnson's music. What song are you going to play tonight?"

"I know what you mean. But if you think about it, I bet Robert Johnson and most other blues musicians got to see a vaudeville show at some point in their lives. So tonight I'll be playing 'From Four Until Late'—vaudeville style."

"Nice. I can picture that. Will you be using the uke?"

"No, I'll be playing my jumbo Harmony Sovereign. I asked Steve Jordan to play percussion with me."

"I'm sure it'll be great."

"Yeah, I think it sounds pretty good. Hey, you know, if you want, you can pass me a guitar and I'll play it for you now."

I handed him a 1930s Gibson L-00, and there at the front counter, dimly lit and peaceful, Elvis Costello performed "From Four Until Late" for me. It was beautiful and it's too bad no one else was there to hear it. Well that's not quite true—during the last verse, Tom let himself in and watched quietly from the doorway behind us.

Chapter 22

A Cold One Hundred

I was at the front counter of the store testing out a new slide on a beat-up yellow National Triolian. It was springtime in New York and business was good. I had recently sold guitars to Carlos Santana and Jack White, both serious blues fans. Anyway, there I was at the front counter working on Blind Willie Johnson's "Dark Was the Night, Cold Was the Ground" when two pretty young women walked in. One of them was carrying a clipboard, so I figured they were trying to sell something. They headed straight for two of the younger guys standing near the cash register and began chatting. After a few minutes, one of the guys pointed at me and said, "You should talk to Zeke."

"Hi, how can I help?" I asked the brunette with the clipboard.

"Hi, my name is Keke Regele. I work for VH1 and we're doing a new show about collectors called 'For What It's Worth.'"

"OK, are you scouting a location?"

She smiled. "No, we're looking for people with rare collectibles who would like to be on the show."

"Collectibles, huh? Like what?" I asked. "Give me an example."

"A guitar signed by a famous musician—you know, something like that."

"Sorry, we don't have any. What about a record signed by the Ramones?"

Keke perked up. "Yes, that would be great. Do you have one?"

"Yeah, they signed *Road to Ruin* for me back in the eighties. I guess it's pretty rare now because they're all gone except for Marky."

"Would you be willing to bring it to the show?" Keke asked.

"Sure, why not? It sounds like fun."

After Keke took my contact information, I said, "You know, I also own

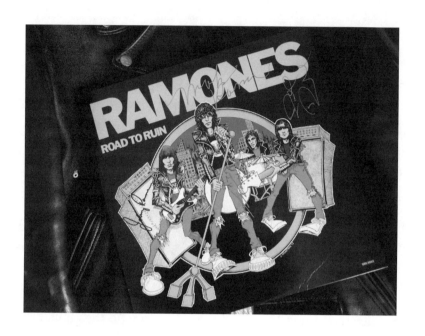

a rare photograph of Robert Johnson. It's one of just three known to exist. You might want to mention that to the producers."

"I will. Thanks, Zeke. We'll be in touch."

As much as I love the Ramones, I was really hoping the show's producers would ask me to bring the photo of Johnson and Shines. The photo had already been featured in a BBC blues documentary, and *Rolling Stone* had included it in their 100 Greatest Guitarists of All Time list. A VH1 appearance would be another great opportunity to publicize it.

On June 5, I received an e-mail from Tara Moser of Gotham Casting requesting a photo of the signed Ramones record. I sent it along with a link to the *Vanity Fair* article. Tara replied, "Hey Zeke—This is all incredible. That Robert Johnson photo is amazing. I'll be submitting all of your info at the end of the week. Thanks for your cooperation." Two weeks later, Keke e-mailed to congratulate me on being booked for the show. Things had turned out as I had hoped: the producers wanted me to bring both the Ramones record and the Johnson photo.

I don't know why, but it's never easy to deal with any situation that involves the photo. It's like playing five-card stud and knowing that you're about to be dealt a pair of jokers. Sometimes I felt as if Papa Legba were watching from the sidelines, enjoying a good laugh at my expense. And why shouldn't he? Looking back, I realize a lot of what I've been through was pretty funny.

On the night we filmed the show, it was ninety-two degrees outside and the air was sticky and unpleasant. I rode the Q train to DeKalb Avenue, and because of the heat I decided to transfer to the D train and get off at Union Street rather than walk. I'd asked Lonnie to come for moral support, and he was there waiting for me. I carried two plastic bags, one containing the photo and items relating to its provenance, the other bag holding the signed Ramones record. I asked Lonnie to hang onto the bag with the record while I went into a bodega to buy us some cold bottles of water. As I handed Lonnie his water, he dropped the bag, and it landed on the sidewalk. He froze, looking terrified. I should mention that Lonnie loves vinyl; for him, damaging a vintage album is an act of sacrilege. I took a sip of water, swallowed it, and gave him my best *I can't believe you just did that* look. Then I couldn't keep a straight face and started laughing.

When I finally caught my breath, I looked at Lonnie and said, "Nice,

Beano. You know I've owned that record for over twenty-five years."

"I know. I'm really sorry. Do you think it's OK?"

"I hope so. I'm afraid to look, but I guess we should. They might want to pull it out of its sleeve to grade it for the show. It was mint."

"And hopefully it still is," Lonnie added nervously.

Luckily, it was.

"It's fine," I said. "Let's go meet Tom. He's probably already there."

Tom was waiting for us on the corner of Fourth Avenue and President Street. I'd asked him to come because he had helped me win the photo on eBay. It bothered me that *Vanity Fair* hadn't mentioned Tom by name in the story, and I wanted him to appear with me on the show today. We walked west on President Street looking for the studio, but all we saw were empty-looking industrial buildings. Near the end of the block we spotted a small white sign that said *Film Biz Recycling*. We were in the right place.

A well-dressed man holding a briefcase was waiting outside, his sport coat draped over his arm. After a few minutes we asked if he was there for the show too. He told us he was an appraiser of rock and roll memorabilia, particularly rare records, so I told him about my Ramones album. When I mentioned that Johnny had signed it with a silver marker while the rest of the band signed their names in black, he smiled.

"I knew Johnny well," he said. "Do you know why he signed it in silver instead of black?"

"No, why? I always wondered about that."

"He did it because he hated getting black ink on his hands, and silver was easier to wash off. I'll tell you what it's worth later, when we're on camera."

He was a nice guy and it bothers me that I can't remember his name. Anyway, after our exchange, he took out his phone and called someone who let us in.

When my eyes adjusted to the dark, I was amazed by what I saw. Lights, cameras, and crew members were buzzing around a funky-looking but well-put-together set. There were also people like me, who had brought their treasured collectibles, and appraisers who would evaluate their worth—hence the show's name, *For What It's Worth*. What appeared from the outside to be an abandoned warehouse sure looked fancy inside, and it was luxuriously air-conditioned. As I took it all in, I noticed Keke walking toward me smiling, her ever-present clipboard in hand.

"Hey, Zeke, glad you made it. We're going to film your spot as soon as possible, like you asked us to do."

"Cool. I appreciate it."

"It's hot outside, huh? Can you please fill out this release while I find you some water?" Keke handed me the clipboard. I began to write, but Keke was back in a flash with three cold bottles of water. "We need to get you into makeup. You can finish filling out the form there."

I cringed at the thought of makeup and asked Keke to find out if Tom could appear on camera with me. She introduced us to the show's producer, who explained that having two presenters didn't fit in with the show's format. He was polite but insistent. Tom took it in stride, though I could see he was disappointed.

In my freshly applied makeup, looking far less glamorous than David Bowie, I was introduced to the hosts of the show. Gary Dell'Abate was the executive producer of the *Howard Stern* show, and John Hein was also affiliated with Stern as the host of the *Wrap-Up Show*. We spoke briefly about the items I'd brought and decided to film the spot featuring the Ramones record first. Within minutes, the cameras were rolling. Gary introduced me as "Zeke from Brooklyn" and had me show the record, then introduced the well-dressed record appraiser. John asked where I had gotten the record, and I told him about my friend Gene Geary. Gene is a great guitarist who played with Marky Ramone in a band called Medicine Men. In the mid-eighties, when Gene and his brother Michael owned a record store in Brooklyn, the Ramones stopped by one afternoon for a signing event. I was going to have them sign *Rocket to Russia* because I liked the cover photo, but Gene convinced me to substitute *Road to Ruin*, his personal favorite.

Upon hearing that, the appraiser smiled. "Your friend gave you good advice," he said, "because I seldom see a signed copy of *Road to Ruin*."

"Why do you think that is?" Gary asked.

"Probably because it has a cartoon drawing of the band on the cover instead of a photo." He examined the album and said, "The signatures are absolutely genuine, the cover is in great condition, and that's where the money is, but while we're at it, let's take a look at the record inside." After inspecting it, he said, "It's mint."

"So what's it worth?" John asked.

"Most signed Ramones records sell in the $200 to $300 range, but you almost never see a signed copy of *Road to Ruin*. I believe this one would easily sell for $600."

"Wow, that's a lot of money for an album," John said. "Zeke, now that you know what it's worth, would you consider selling it?"

"No. It's a piece of my past and the guys were nice enough to sign it for me. Joey, Johnny, and Dee Dee are gone. I couldn't sell it. You know what I mean."

"Yes, we understand," Gary said, "It was great to see it, Zeke. Thanks for bringing it to the show."

We took a quick break and I was escorted to a partitioned area where I was introduced to a man with a grey ponytail and a colorful Hawaiian shirt. This was Gary Sohmers, whom I recognized from *Antiques Roadshow*. Gary introduced me to Greg Holman of Heritage Auctions. I showed them the photo and we worked out a game plan on how best to present it.

The cameras began rolling and Gary Dell'Abate asked John, "Who do we have on the show today?"

"Next up is Zeke from Brooklyn."

Here we go again, I thought. I knew this wasn't going to be as easy to explain as the Ramones record, so I had brought along some props to help me. I walked onto the set carrying a pile of stuff.

"What have you brought for us today, Zeke?" John asked.

I held up a small black photo album first.

"It looks like a photo," Gary said. "What can you tell us about it?"

"It's the third known photo of Robert Johnson."

Gary explained who Robert Johnson was, and I told the story behind the photo using my props to illustrate its journey: a printout of the original eBay auction listing, issues of *Vanity Fair* and *Guitar World*, an affidavit of authenticity signed by Lois Gibson, my contract with the Johnson estate, and finally the T-shirt that Sony had produced at last.

After that, Gary introduced the two appraisers, who congratulated me on my find and commended me for the work I'd done to establish the photo's authenticity. When asked about the photo's worth, Gary Sohmers said he believed I had devalued it by publishing it in various magazines. "It's all over the internet now, so it's not the only existing copy of the photo."

Out of respect, I held my tongue.

"So what do you think it's worth, Zeke, any idea?" Gary Dell'Abate asked.

"I have no idea."

"I think it's pretty valuable. I'm going to guess that it's worth around $50,000," Gary said. "What do you think, John?"

"I think it's worth more than that. I'll say $100,000. Let's ask our experts and see what they think."

Gary Sohmers smiled broadly. "You guys must use the internet or something, because John is spot on. I would estimate the value of the photo at $100,000, based on the sale of one of the other two known photos of Robert Johnson, which recently sold at auction for that amount."

"Wow," John said for the second time that day. "That's a lot of money, Zeke. If you could get $100,000 for the photo, would you consider selling it?"

"No, I think the appraisal is too light. Maybe we should stop filming and talk off camera, because I can't believe that one of the other Johnson photos recently sold at auction. Can you show me the photo you're referring to?"

We looked at the producer, who gave us the sign to keep rolling.

Why is it that so often when you expect a fastball, life throws you a curve? Gary Sohmers showed me the photo, and I glanced around the set, half-expecting to see Papa Legba in the corner bent over with laughter. I won't go into detail about the photo I saw that day, but it was not one of the other known photos of Robert Johnson.

I explained this to Gary and pointed out that although someone had paid $100,000 for it, the photo had no provenance at all. In fact, the previous owner had first listed it on eBay for an even higher price, hoping to find someone gullible enough to buy it. Needless to say, it didn't sell at that time.

"I can't believe someone paid a hundred grand for that," I said. "No one I know believes it's Johnson. It doesn't really look like him and there's no provenance whatsoever to support it. Are you sure it sold?"

"Yes, it recently sold at auction," Gary said.

"Well," I said, pointing at the stack of goodies I'd brought, "all I can say is if that photo, with no forensic evidence, no endorsement from the Johnson estate, and no support from the media just sold for $100,000, then I think that mine is worth more."

Gary agreed with me and graciously admitted, "It just goes to show that sometimes the owner of an item knows more about it than the appraiser. When it comes to Robert Johnson, Zeke is an expert."

"OK, so let's play the game," said John. "If you wouldn't sell it for $100,000, then how much would you sell it for?"

"I would think it's worth five to ten times that amount," I answered. Although I had no intention of selling the photo yet, I didn't mind placing a monetary value on it. A photo of Billy the Kid had recently sold at auction for over $2 million. I gave my answer with that in mind.

"Well, it's wicked cool," Gary said. "Congratulations on finding it and thanks for bringing it."

When the cameras stopped rolling, a few crew members asked to see the photo up close and said they were blown away by it. Tom and Lonnie slapped me on the back and assured me that I had done a good job, but I felt sick on our walk to the subway.

"Maybe I should have just let it go and accepted the $100,000 appraisal."

"No, you did the right thing," Lonnie said.

"I agree," said Tom.

"Who knows how they'll edit it. I hope I don't come off like another moronic blues expert. I'd hate that."

"You won't. Just calm down, all right?" Lonnie said.

"Yeah, it went well," Tom assured me. "Hey, there's a Dunkin' Donuts. Let's go in and cool off."

There's nothing caffeine and air-conditioning can't fix. Well, sometimes you need a good lawyer too, but fortunately this wasn't one of those times. This was a cool-off, calm-down, trust-your-friends-it-will-be-OK time.

As it turned out, they were right. *For What It's Worth* premiered eight months later, on February 21, 2012. The first episode featured Jack White, Third Man Records, and a guy who collected Mr. T dolls. It was funny and ridiculous. The following week, episode two featured John Resnikoff and his celebrity hair collection, followed by a tour of United Record Pressing, then me and my $100,000 photo. That's right, they edited out the part where I corrected the appraiser.

Chapter 23

Long, Long Distant Land

Well I never been to England but I kinda like the Beatles.
—Hoyt Axton

I guess I'm old school, and maybe that's why I don't grasp the mechanics of modern communication. I don't own a cell phone. I know that's weird, but I just can't. My friends and family have tried to convince me to get one, but in order for it to happen I would have to become a different person—someone with ambition, a charismatic go-getter with better posture and better shoes. It's really a moot point, because I'd probably just end up losing it.

Lately it seems that everywhere I turn, I see people shouting into their phones or squinting at their tiny screens while frantically thumb-typing. In these days of Facebook, Instagram, and Twitter, news travels at lightning speed, but the process behind it continues to elude me.

Besides phones, there are lots of other things I don't know much about, like travel. I'm a native New Yorker and I like living here. Yeah, it's crowded and expensive and everyone's always in a rush, but I'm used to it and I love the cultural diversity. If you know where to go, you can enjoy food from anywhere in the world while listening to the indigenous music of that country. You don't need a car to get around; you can walk or catch a cab, and there's always the subway.

I know my city pretty well. I could navigate Greenwich Village blind-folded or blind drunk and still find my way home. Those who know me can confirm that I've done the latter. I know the rhythm of the streets, how it changes from one neighborhood to another: Chinatown,

165

Little Italy, Soho, Greenwich Village, Times Square, Hell's Kitchen, Central Park, the Upper West Side, and Harlem. Each has its own flavor, different smells and sounds, different languages, different clothing, food, and music, and even different air.

I try not to leave New York unless I have to. I don't feel like I've missed out, because if you sit at the front counter of Matt Umanov Guitars, the world comes to you. Every day I meet people from all corners of the earth. I get to know them and help them find what they're looking for. Most will bring home a souvenir from our store: a T-shirt, strings, picks, or, hopefully, a guitar.

A few have become my friends, and I don't see them as often as I would like. It's not like I have my own Learjet and can day-trip across the pond to England. Besides, I wouldn't know what to do once I arrived. All I know about England is that some of my favorite bands came from there. Maybe it's because the English respect the blues so deeply that its influence is etched into the grooves of records by everyone from the Rolling Stones to the Sex Pistols. Amy Winehouse channeled its power, and you can feel it in Adele's music as well.

So I'm not connected to a phone—or, in a larger sense, to the modern world. Pragmatic thinking is beyond me. You could say I'm a slacker, and there's some truth to that, but I believe it's best to set things in motion and let them go where they will. For me, it's about balance. If you're standing in the middle of a tightrope stretched between two skyscrapers, why not stop and enjoy the view? Why worry about getting to the other side? There's no rush. It's better to savor the moment, look around, and take it all in, because you might never be there again.

I don't know what drives the cosmic bus, but I know the wheels of the great machine are always turning, even as we sleep. On the morning of Sunday, February 3, 2013, after two cups of black coffee, I turned on my computer and a story on the *Guardian*'s website caught me completely by surprise:

Robert Johnson: rare new photograph of delta blues king authenticated after eight years

Forensic examination of old photo identifies the Mississippi guitarist said to have made a pact with the devil

Perhaps the most infamous music deal ever struck involved no contracts and no lawyers. The blues singer Robert Johnson, so the legend goes, acquired his unearthly musical talent after meeting the devil at a crossroads.

Until now, there were only two verified photographs of Johnson (1911-1938), who remains the most inspirational musician produced by the Mississippi Delta and the man Eric Clapton once anointed as "the most important blues musician who ever lived." This weekend a third, newly cleaned-up and authenticated image has been released by the Johnson estate showing him standing next to musician Johnny Shines. . . .

The story was a bit longer, detailing my discovery of the photo and Lois Gibson's role in authenticating it.

I'd be lying if I said I wasn't pleased. I leaned back in my chair, smiled, and sipped my coffee. Then I started talking to myself. I do that when I'm alone and trying to rationalize the irrational. *Who wrote this,* I asked aloud, *and why?* I reread the story to see if I'd missed something. The author's name was Vanessa Thorpe. I didn't know her, and I had no idea what had prompted her to write the article or why the *Guardian* had run it. Almost six years had passed since Lois Gibson first authenticated the photo. Nothing had changed, yet for some reason the photo had found its way into an English newspaper article that made it sound like breaking news.

And so we come full circle, back to phones whose workings are foreign to me and countries whose ways are equally unfamiliar. If I were an urbane, thumb-typing globetrotter, I might have more insight into why the *Guardian* article was shared more than sixty thousand times on Facebook. As it is, the best I can do is venture a guess that a publicist at VH1 was ordered to create a buzz about the photo just in time for its appearance on *For What It's Worth.*

The *Guardian* story made the rounds, spreading like an oil slick: first to worldwide newspapers, including Sweden's *Dagens Nyheter,* then to websites like American Blues Scene, and finally to the forums, where it once again ruffled the feathers of the sensitive birds who nested there.

I don't know exactly how many people saw the *Guardian* article, and I wonder how many of the sixty thousand who shared it on Facebook actually read it. Marshall McLuhan was right in declaring that "the medium is the message." More and more, as we try to keep up with technology, headlines eclipse stories. We scroll through news feeds on Facebook and glance at our friends' posts. If a compelling photo or a headline catches our eye, we click "Like" and move on. Occasionally we stop to read the story, but mostly we don't have the time. There are too many posts by too many friends, too many stories to like.

Chapter 24

The Crossroad

"Hey, Cat, I got this weird phone call from some guy in England today."

"What was weird about it?"

"I don't know . . . he said something about a blues documentary. He saw the *Guardian* article and wants to interview me."

"So, that's good, right?"

"Yeah, it's good, but . . ."

Cathy rolled her eyes. She knew what was coming.

"I'm not going to do it," I said.

"Why not?"

"Because I already did a TV spot for VH1 and being in front of a camera isn't my thing. Besides, it's a pain dealing with film crews and their crazy schedules."

Cathy grimaced. "OK, but I still think you should do it."

"I'll think about it," I said. But we both knew I wouldn't.

Later that night, I e-mailed Tom Woolfenden, the assistant producer at BBC Music Entertainment who had called me.

tom,

thanks for your interest in the photo. i believe that documenting the history of music is important and I'm sure that your program is worthwhile, but at this time i prefer not to participate.

best wishes,
zeke

A few days later, Tom replied.

Dear Zeke,

Many thanks for getting back to us. We'll be visiting NYC at the end of March. Could we contact you again nearer the time to see if things have changed? We would only need thirty minutes or so of your time.

All the best,
Tom

Thirty minutes? Yeah, right. I knew it would be more like an hour and a half of lights, camera, pause, and reshoot. Still, maybe Cathy was right. I left the door open, telling Tom he could contact me at the end of March.

Easy, right? Wrong! In the weeks that followed, Tom e-mailed me ten more times. First to set a date for the shoot, then to find a place, and then the date and place changed. My patience was wearing thin. When Tom told me how many people they planned to interview, I decided to step aside.

tom,

listen . . . i didn't realize that you have over 50 people to interview.

i was afraid that this was going to be the case which is why i originally declined to get involved.

the robert johnson photograph has been authenticated, but some of the blues forums have been vicious.

i don't feel comfortable being on the same film as some of the people who you will be interviewing.

please understand that for this reason i am stepping aside.

thanks and best wishes,
zeke

Tom tried to persuade me to reconsider.

Dear Zeke,

Sincere apologies for this. I appreciate your concerns. So sorry to muck you about.

Our programme is a celebration of the blues. We are speaking with musicians like James Cotton, Charlie Musselwhite, John Hammond, Taj Mahal, Bonnie Raitt, Billy Boy Arnold, Blind Boy Paxton, Jimmy Duck Holmes, Johnny Winter and others.

We're not out to debate the Robert Johnson photograph. Your interview would be a way to illustrate the mythology of Johnson and the reality of tracking him down. It's a great story. One we'd really like to include.

I do hope you can reconsider. The producers (Sam Bridger and Mick Gold) will be in NYC from March 16th to March 24th. They are more than happy to meet informally and talk about any concerns. Would that be possible for you? I hope so.

All the best,
Tom

It was a nice try, but I stood my ground. I didn't understand why they wanted me to appear on the same show as blues royalty. It made no sense. I'm just a guy who found a photo.

The following morning, Tom tried one last time to convince me.

Dear Zeke,

Sorry to hound you.

Several of our contributors have mentioned the new photo of Johnson and are thrilled there are now three images.

Sam Charters, author of *The Country Blues*, famed blues hunter and record producer, mentioned the photo when we contacted him. He is taking part in our programme. He wrote:

"Have you seen the new photo of Robert Johnson that's just surfaced? It's certainly him. The man with him is a very young Johnny Shines, whom I immediately recognized. If you remember the sleeve notes for Chicago/The Blues/Today! you might remember that Shines sang one of Robert's songs and he talked with me about "running" with Robert when they both were very young. They certainly look young in the photo."

By spotting this photo and getting it into the public domain, you have changed the history of the blues. We now have more information on

Johnson, and that insubstantial phantom of the blues has become a bit more real.

This photo has been written about around the world. We will mention it in our film. The way Johnson has grown from an unknown, marginal figure (acclaimed by John Hammond in 1938 but probably not by anyone else) to one of the most influential and iconic artists of the 20th century is pretty extraordinary. We would very much like to hear your account of how you found it.

We would be available to meet you and talk this through once we are in NYC. It goes without saying that we would still love to film with you at a time and place that works for you from March 16th to March 24th.

All the best,
Tom

In the hierarchy of blues historians, Sam Charters was the Godfather. Tom had made me an offer I couldn't refuse. On March 21, I spent the first half of the day working at the store, then took a short walk east down Bleecker Street to Terra Blues. It's amazing how different most clubs look in the daytime. Without the lipstick-red neon and the pearlescent glow of stage lights, without sweat glistening on cold glasses and warm bodies, without the electric buzz of alcohol and guitars, I was struck by how desolate Terra Blues looked as I knocked on the front door.

"Hi, my name's Zeke," I told the tall, dark-haired man who answered the door. He looked like he could have been a roadie for Motorhead.

"Yeah, hi, Zeke. I'm Sam Bridger. I'm working the camera today. Come inside and I'll introduce you to the others."

As my eyes adjusted to the darkness, I noticed two men sitting beside a large camera.

"Zeke, this is Mick Gold. He'll be interviewing you. And this is John Quinn, our soundman."

Even in the dimly lit room, I could tell these guys were the real deal, three road warriors. Mick pointed to a cooler on top of the bar. "Help yourself to a beer, Zeke. Did you bring a reproduction of your photo?"

I popped the top off a cold IPA and took a swig. "Thanks, yeah, I brought an exact copy and some other stuff too."

I showed Mick my array of magazines and a large coffee-table book called *Tragedies and Mysteries of Rock and Roll.* As the title implied, the book featured legendary musicians who had died young. The first entry was Robert Johnson, and it boasted a full-page reproduction of my photo. As Mick and Sam adjusted the lights, I helped myself to another beer.

"When you're ready, we could use you over here, Zeke."

Mick was seated at a small, round table in the middle of the room, his back to the camera. I sat across from him. My chair was well lit, while Mick's was shrouded in darkness. From my vantage point, Mick was just a silhouette. "I'll be off camera, asking questions," he explained. "In the final edit, no one will see me or hear my voice. They will only see and hear you."

I nodded as if I understood, but I didn't.

"Let's get a level on Zeke's voice, John."

After John gave the OK sign, we began filming. For the next hour, I talked about Robert Johnson's life, legend, and legacy. I began by explaining that I had bought the photo with pure intentions, not to hoard it jealously but to protect it and share it with others.

"When I decided to buy it, I knew I was biting off more than I could chew, because despite all of the research about his life, we really know very little about Robert Johnson," I told my silhouetted interviewer.

"Can you elaborate on that a bit more, Zeke?"

"OK, let's see . . . according to most historians, Johnson used different surnames while traveling. Robert Spencer, Robert Dusty, and several others. He would leave places suddenly without saying goodbye, he'd just vanish. The accounts of those who claim to have known him vary widely, and it's hard to know who to believe. The truth is that it's impossible to know someone who doesn't want to be known."

"Interesting. What can you tell us about the photo? Has any new information come to light?"

"The funny thing about the photo is that it's as enigmatic as Johnson himself. My research shows that everything about it is period correct, and yet I've been unable to conclusively prove its authenticity. After Lois Gibson authenticated the photo, I assigned the copyright to the Johnson estate and they licensed it through Getty. The photo has appeared in books, magazines, and television shows. The media has accepted it as genuine, but there are those who disagree, and they are extremely territorial when it comes to Robert Johnson."

"Why do you think that is?"

"Passion, maybe? Perhaps some of it is ego and the need to be right. The doubters have accused me of all sorts of crazy things. Some claim the photo is actually a composite of two different photos that I deliberately Photoshopped together. Some believe that I'm only in it for the money, which is ridiculous because so far it's been one of the worst-paying gigs ever. And then there are the 'blues scholars' who look down their noses at people like me. How dare someone without a doctorate unearth a lost photo of Robert Johnson. Some of these guys know me, they know that I'm as into it as they are, but I'm not a member of their club and honestly I don't want to be. They've been on the attack from day one, and they will continue to do so."

"Why?"

"It's about control. The worst of them will argue that Robert Johnson wasn't important because he was commercially unsuccessful in his time. They talk about musicians as if they were athletes: who's better, Blind Lemon Jefferson or Blind Blake, and according to them, both are better than Robert Johnson. Some say that if it wasn't for Eric Clapton, Johnson would be an unknown, which is absurd. It's incredible how they fail to recognize Johnson's main contribution to the music scene."

"Which is what?"

"Songwriting. Sure, he borrowed heavily from other musicians like Leroy Carr, Skip James, Lonnie Johnson, Peetie Wheatstraw, and Bumble Bee Slim, but Johnson's lyrics are complex, and the way he delivers them is frightening. I mean, take 'Crossroad Blues,' for example."

"What about it?"

"Let's look at the words. There's an underlying fear to them. 'I went to the crossroad, fell down on my knees / I asked the Lord above have mercy now, save poor Bob if you please.' Johnson is in a desperate situation, praying for help.

"Now, let's look at the next verse. 'Standing at the crossroad, I tried to flag a ride / Nobody seemed to know me, everybody passed me by.' He's trying to find a way out, but why? Here's the next verse. 'The sun's going down boy, dark gonna catch me here / I haven't got no lovin' sweet woman that love and feel my care.'

"OK, there's the answer. What is Johnson saying? Is he afraid of the devil, or is he afraid of something else? In Mississippi, during Johnson's lifetime, a black man alone on the outskirts of town at night ran the risk of being lynched. His vulnerability is enhanced by the fact that he has no girlfriend and therefore no place to safely spend the night.

"Now here's the final verse: 'You can run, you can run, tell my friend boy Willie Brown / That I'm standing at the crossroad, I believe I'm sinking down.' Whatever he's running from, Johnson realizes that there's no escape."

When I finished talking, Sam shot close-ups of the photo while Mick and I chatted. "You know, Zeke, it's interesting that out of everyone I've interviewed, you are the only one who brought up the topic of racism."

"How is that possible? You're shooting a documentary about the blues, right?"

"We are indeed, which is why your observations struck me as astute. I hadn't considered that 'Crossroad Blues' might have been a way for Johnson to make a statement about racism until you pointed it out."

"Mick, can you imagine what it was like for Johnson in Mississippi in the thirties? Even at his first recording session in San Antonio, he probably had to enter through the back door of the Gunter Hotel. And what I find scary is that it wasn't so long ago. It's hard to believe I'm the only one who brought it up. I guess you can edit it out if it doesn't fit your format."

"No, Zeke, it was good. Would you mind Sam shooting a few photos of us together before you head out? I've been doing that with everyone I've interviewed. It's for myself, not for the program."

After taking the photos, I gathered my things together and left. As I walked west on Bleecker Street, I mumbled to myself, "They'll never use it." As it turned out, they didn't. When the documentary *Blues America* aired months later on BBC One, Keith Richards and other celebrities sang the praises of Robert Johnson, but no one talked about the duality of Johnson's "Crossroad Blues."

Chapter 25

Play 'Em Now

Years ago, when Bob Dylan asked "Is this a good guitar?" before buying an old Gibson I'd shown him, I didn't fully understand the profundity of the question. What defines a "good" guitar? Experience has taught me that there are certain absolutes. For example, an instrument has to be structurally sound. Its braces need to be intact, and its neck needs to be straight and set at the proper angle. If a neck is back-bowed, the guitar will buzz. If it's forward-bowed with too much relief, the action will be high and the guitar will be hard to play. On acoustic guitars, a neck that's set too far back can cause the bridge to break, while one that's set off center can result in a high E string that slips off the edge of the fingerboard.

One also has to consider the issue of weight. How heavy is too heavy? That depends on personal preference and the integrity of one's spine. The average solid-body electric guitar weighs about seven and a half pounds, though some Gibson Les Paul models can weigh almost twice that. Most acoustic guitars weigh in at about four pounds. Some are a bit lighter or heavier depending on size and the type of wood they're made of. Light guitars have an airy sound that works well for finger-style players, while flat-pickers gravitate toward more heavily built instruments.

I always laugh when I hear the expression "size doesn't matter," because it's a lie. Size always matters, in all things, including guitars. If it fits right and it feels good, then you'll keep it. If not, you'll eventually end up with a different one—but that's true of all things, isn't it?

Wood is important, and "good" wood can be expensive. Rosewood, maple, mahogany, and ebony are hardwoods used in the construction of fine guitars. Rare variations like Brazilian rosewood, flamed maple, and Adirondack spruce can double the price of a guitar, but they aren't always the best choices. Sometimes less expensive, more common varieties are preferable. It depends on the sound you're looking for. Many of the early bluesmen played on mass-produced instruments with bodies of birch and necks of poplar, both inexpensive woods. These guitars have become synonymous with the artists who played them, and they are now coveted by players looking for an authentic blues sound.

Sound is subjective. No matter how terrible an instrument may sound, there's always someone who will love it, and the reverse is also true. Years ago, Matt Umanov told me that if someone likes a particular guitar, they will describe its sound as "bright" even if it sounds warm. He was right about that. Matt also pointed out that "red guitars sound red," and he was right about that too.

Looks are important. If you like the way something looks, then you're drawn to it. I always advise beginners to buy an instrument that appeals to them visually as well as sonically, because I know they'll pick it up and play it more often.

Whether it's new or old, common or rare, low-budget or high-end doesn't matter as long as you feel a connection with an instrument. When Carlos Santana decided to buy a new guitar I'd shown him, it surprised me. "Couldn't you just call artist relations and have them send you one for free?" I asked.

"Yeah, I could, but you know how it is." Carlos smiled and ran his hand across the strings. "We all like to choose our baby, and this one spoke to me."

Carlos was right. No two guitars are alike. In a side-by-side comparison of identical models made in the same factory on the same day, there's often a noticeable difference. One guitar might sustain more or play more easily than the other. I've helped to spec out lots of custom builds from renowned makers, but fine wood and craftsmanship don't guarantee magic. Buying sight unseen is a roll of the dice; they can come up lucky seven or snake eyes. It's best to try a guitar before you buy it, and find one that speaks to you.

That's the most important thing. As Carlos said, an instrument has to speak to you. It doesn't matter whether you're a collector or a player; if you feel a connection with an instrument, trust your gut and buy it. You'll be glad you did. That's how I ended up with my beloved 1962 Fender Jaguar.

When Pete Bennett sold it to me, the guitar was literally in pieces. It was missing its backplate, its nut, some screws, and most of its paint. All of the electronics were there, but they were wrapped in baggies sealed with decaying masking tape. The pickguard was badly scratched, as was all the chrome. As a final, pitiful touch, the neck was back-bowed with worn-out frets.

When I asked Pete how this classic guitar had ended up in such poor condition, he told me he'd gotten it secondhand as a teenager and had disassembled it in order to repaint it. I don't recall the exact details, but the story involved a fire in which the missing pieces of the guitar were lost. After that, the guitar sat in the attic of Pete's parents' home for decades, unplayed and forgotten. Pete rediscovered it when his mother called to let him know she was selling the house and he should come by to see if there was anything he wanted.

I could tell Pete felt bad about what had happened to the guitar. When I explained how much work would be involved in restoring it and explained that most dealers would just buy it for its parts, he seemed bummed out. I was too. We both knew it would be a shame to part out a vintage Fender.

I picked up the neck and ran my hand along it. It was C-shaped with lots of wear, my kind of neck. I lifted the body and looked underneath the pickguard. The original sunburst finish was still there, but the rest of the body was stripped bare and felt rough to the touch. Still, for some unknown reason it spoke to me, and Pete saw it.

"You can have it if you want it," he said. "I don't need the money. I just want to see it restored and know someone's playing it."

"Yeah, I respect that, but I couldn't take it for free."

"Well, how about this, then? I'm about to go for dinner. You can have the guitar for the cost of my meal."

I smiled and said, "Bon appétit. Thanks. I'll get it working again."

"I know you will. Here's my number. Let me know how it sounds when you play your first gig with it."

It took several months for me and five of my friends to get the guitar working again. After I played my first show with it, I called Pete to thank him and let him know it sang with the ferocity of Muddy Waters. It's been my go-to guitar ever since, and it still speaks to me.

I've been selling instruments for decades, and thousands of guitars pass through my hands each year. Fortunately, the number that have spoken to me is less than one might imagine, but some I'll always remember. There was a black Gibson L-5 from 1929 that was custom-made for a woman named Veda Santos. I can still picture the truss rod cover with her name on it and the beautiful flamed maple peeking through the worn finish on the back of the guitar's neck and body. It had obviously been played and loved, and that might be part of the reason why it sounded so good. Veda's L-5 could handle any style of music: blues, jazz, country, even classical. Everyone who tried it fell in love, including me, but I couldn't afford to buy it and eventually it sold.

Another guitar that called out to me was a hundred-year-old, jumbo-bodied twelve-string made by Holzapfel and Beitel. It looked like Lead Belly's Stella, with a beautifully worn patina, and it sounded as ghostly as an old calliope or Blind Willie McTell's voice echoing through the streets of Augusta. I don't usually go for twelve-strings—they're harder to tune and they feel a bit awkward to play—but this one was special. We strung it with heavy-gauge strings and tuned it to C, which is two steps lower than usual. My friend Pete Francis bought the guitar and used it on one of his records. It's currently owned by Steve Earle, and I'm glad it's in good hands.

Generally speaking, I like guitars that growl. There has to be some dirt in the sound. I've flirted with several small-bodied Gibsons, especially L-1 and L-00 models. They're lightly built and sound great for blues, but when it comes to playing slide, I prefer National resonator guitars, particularly steel-bodied Duolian and Triolian models. I've played hundreds of them, new and old, and it's hard to pick a favorite. Most of them sound like Tom Waits singing in the shower, and some look like rusted engine blocks that would be more at home in a scrapyard than a high-end guitar shop. What I'm saying is that in my eyes, they're perfect.

The most perfect example I've ever seen was a 1931 Duolian I sold to Jeff Tweedy. I hadn't seen Jeff in years. I was out of town when he stopped by the shop and bought a blonde Gibson J-200 Matt and I had brought back from one of our guitar expeditions. The guitar sounded great and the original owner's name, "Bob," was engraved into one of its two pickguards. We thought that was cool, and so did Jeff, because his dad's name is Bob.

When I finally caught up with Jeff, he told me he was looking for a National guitar to use on a record he was doing with Mavis Staples.

"Wow, you're recording with Mavis? Very cool."

"Yeah, we're working on a blues/gospel record."

"I love that stuff, and this is the right tool for the job," I said as I passed the 1931 Duolian across the counter to Jeff. The guitar was an anomaly in that it appeared never to have been repaired or even played. Its grey crystalline finish was flawless and it sounded like Mahalia Jackson singing "Move on up a Little Higher." I knew Jeff would buy it, and he did.

As I was writing the receipt, I asked, "So when we first met and you told me you were forming a new band called Wilco, what guitar did I sell you? Was it a J-45 or a J-200?"

"You sold me a J-200. It was my first really nice guitar."

"Yeah, I remember telling you that I thought you had a nice voice, too," I said, and it made Jeff laugh.

"I hear you've bought a few more since then," I joked, knowing full well that Jeff had amassed an extensive guitar collection.

Jeff smiled. "Yeah, quite a few more."

"How many?"

"This one makes it three hundred."

"Oh wow. Well, it's a great one and I hope you make a great record with it."

As it turned out, he did. Jeff played that guitar on Mavis Staples' *You Are Not Alone*, which won a Grammy Award for Best Americana Album in 2011.

Along with Gibsons and Nationals, I like vintage Oscar Schmidt guitars. They're not as well made as their Gibson counterparts, so they usually require major restoration in order to play properly. Schmidt was founded in Jersey City in 1871. During their heyday, 1920 through

1930, Schmidt produced all types of stringed instruments, including mandolins, banjos, ukuleles, and zithers. Schmidt supplied several jobbers and retailers who used various brand names, such as Stella, Sovereign, Victoria, and La Scala, which can be confusing to collectors.

Like many blues enthusiasts, I became aware of Oscar Schmidt guitars because Lead Belly played a jumbo twelve-string Stella. They're rare and also pricey, so I set my sights on a less expensive six-string model. My first opportunity to try one came when Jimmy Vivino brought his to the shop for restoration. I liked it and eventually bought a similar one for myself. This was the one I sold in order to buy the Robert Johnson photo. I still own a Stella "Decalomania" model Matt gave me. It's decorated with decals of vines and flowers, and it has a vibe, but it doesn't compare to the one I sold.

I've played lots of guitars made by Schmidt since then, and some were good, but they didn't speak to me in the same way. The one that came closest was a Victoria I sold to Jack White. He came to the store with Fats Kaplin, a talented musician I'd known for years. Fats was now a member of Jack's band.

"Maybe you can give me some advice," Jack said to me. He was carrying an old parlor-sized guitar case. "I just bought this and it sounds kind of dull."

I opened the case. The guitar inside was a Celebrated Benary flat top from the late 1800s with a metal disc in the sound hole that said "Tilton's Improvement." I probably smiled when I saw it, because although Benary guitars are relatively obscure, I knew all about them. "Here's the deal," I said. "This was made in New York around the turn of the century. It's cool and kind of collectible, but this silver disc in the sound hole isn't just there for decoration. It refers to a patented structural design by a man named William Tilton. Basically, there's a wooden bar inside to help support the top. And check this out," I said, pointing to the metal tailpiece. "It's screwed down into the top. It's an interesting design, but it mutes the sound."

"Wow, do you think different strings might help to liven it up?" Jack asked.

"They might help a bit, but that bar inside is a tone-killer. Hey, you know, LaBella just sent me some sample sets of a new type of string that might work well for this guitar. I'll give you a set and you can try them, but you know, I have a guitar here that you'll like way more than this one."

I passed the Victoria guitar to Jack.

"This was made by Oscar Schmidt in the twenties. It's the same size as Barbecue Bob's twelve-string, but with six strings, and it's long scale, really long, probably twenty-six and a half inches, so you need big hands to play it. But that's not a problem for you."

Jack laughed. "No it's not." He strummed a few chords, and I could see that he had connected with the Victoria.

"Is it for sale?" he asked.

"Yeah."

"OK, I'll take it." Jack handed me his credit card. When I gave him his receipt, he asked, "So who's the guy with the Robert Johnson photo?"

"That's me."

"That figures. You know, I think it's him. It's not just the face and the hands—you can tell by the body language. It's a great photo," Jack said. "Thanks for finding it for the rest of us."

Chapter 26

Tell Me All About It

The phone kept ringing. I hate talking on the phone, but I hate repetitive ringing even more, so I answered it.

"Hi, Zeke, this is Caine O'Rear from *American Songwriter*. I was wondering if you could answer some questions for me about the Robert Johnson photo you found."

"Sure, what do you want to know?"

"Has any new information come to light in recent years about the photo?"

"Well, I've done a lot of research on the image and the guitarists' clothing. Lois Gibson weighed in again, and I thought the clothing couldn't have existed before a certain point, but it turns out I was wrong."

If you look at the film footage of Cab Calloway from 1933, his band is wearing very similar clothing to Johnny Shines in the photo—a particular white suit looks almost identical. Not Cab's, he always wears a tuxedo, but his band has these big white suits. Robert Johnson's tie in the photo dates from earlier than I'd thought, and his suit could be from any time between the early thirties to . . . well, men's suits didn't change much until the late thirties, when they started getting way wider lapels and shoulder pads. Not zoot suits, but earlier. So it was hard to put a date on the photo that way. The estate was dating it circa 1935, and I agreed. After living with it for a while and doing more research, I now thought it was taken right around the same time as the Johnson cigarette photo.

Johnny Shines' daughter, Caroline Shines Edwards, had recently mentioned the photo on her Facebook page; she believed it was a photo of her father. (Later, Edwards also told *American Songwriter*, "Yeah, that's dad.")

Frank DiGiacomo had recently interviewed Steve Earle for *Billboard*, and Earle said he believed my photo was the third known image of Robert Johnson. The late blues writer and historian Sam Charters had also agreed that the photo depicted Johnson and Shines (which I had found about in one of the e-mails from Tom Woolfenden of the BBC). Charters had been responsible for Shines' inclusion on *Chicago/The Blues/Today!*, the seminal three-disc set released by Vanguard Records in 1966. I explained all this to the editor of *American Songwriter*.

"So you've still got the actual photo?"

"I still own the photo, but I assigned copyright to the estate, so they control use. It's their family, so I thought it was the right thing to do."

"What's your general take on Robert Johnson in terms of his influence?"

"In my opinion, he was the Jimi Hendrix of his time. He took styles that already existed and sort of combined them in ways no one else had done. Just like Hendrix coming out of the Chitlin' Circuit and the Ike Turner school of guitar playing, Robert Johnson borrowed heavily from people who came before him, but he put it out in a way that was his own unique voice. It sounds more like Chuck Berry and people who were recording at Chess Studios—Muddy Waters and Howlin' Wolf. I think it was the origin of what we came to accept as rock music. I think it was very important, as important as Hendrix was in the sixties for guitar."

"Regarding the guitar in the photo, do you still believe that to be a Harmony from the mid-thirties?"

"I believe it's a Chicago-made guitar. When they were doing solid peg heads in Chicago, usually they were slot heads up until '32. So it's post-1932. They went to fourteen frets later on, but it's really hard to identify. The tailpiece, you see, you don't have a logo on the guitar. What I thought was a logo was just a tear in the photo's emulsion. I've looked at it much closer now, and there is no logo. Half of the tuners are broken, so there is a set of stripped tuners hanging off of the guitar.

"There's no nut, so we can't identify how it was strung; we don't even know if it's being held upside down. No logo, no nut, no strings. In terms of it being a twelve-fret Chicago-made guitar, absolutely it is. The headstock is the Harmony headstock. It's what you'd see coming out from Harmony. It's different from Kay, it's different from Regal. Harmony was making guitars for a lot of different stores, and it could have had any brand name on it. It could have been Bluebird, it could have been Harmony—there were hundreds of them."

"Interesting, can I quote you on some of this? We're doing a blues issue in May."

"Cool, but if you use the photo, be prepared for an attack by the blues police."

"I know, and I don't understand why."

"Me neither. I'm just warning you to tread carefully."

"I'm not worried about it."

"OK, thanks, Caine. Be good."

I shook my head as I hung up the phone. I liked that the photo was going to appear in *American Songwriter*, but I knew it would stir up controversy and cause me more aggravation. It always seemed to go that way with the photo, but maybe this time it would turn out differently.

Good things were underway. The exclusive contract between the Johnson estate and Sony had expired, leaving the estate free to pursue other options, so I reached out to Ben Blackwell at Third Man Records. Ben was interested, and I put him in touch with John Kitchens, hoping it might lead to a vinyl reissue of the Johnson catalog reimagined by Jack White, Ben Blackwell, and the other good people at Third Man. I liked what they had done with previous reissues of Charley Patton, Blind Willie McTell, and the Mississippi Sheiks. It was creative. By using new cover art and colored vinyl, Third Man's reissue series appealed to younger record buyers as well as established collectors. I was confident that they would do something special with Robert Johnson, and I hoped they might want to use my photo of Johnson for the album cover.

Emotionally, I was in a bad place. I had lost too many people in the years since buying the photo, including friends like Chris Whitley, Willy DeVille, Suze Rotolo, and Lou Reed. And also family: my parents, my brother, and my cousin Brad, who was like a younger brother to me.

For whatever reason, I started writing. Maybe it was an outlet, or a way to keep those I'd lost alive. It seemed to help a bit, and Cat encouraged me to keep at it, as did my friend Sara White. In addition to bartending, Sara wrote for the hipster-oriented *Off Track Planet's Travel Guide,* and she had also written a play called *Victim.* She was good at her craft and she believed in me. I began carrying a notebook with me everywhere I went, even into bars. Tom had left Matt Umanov Guitars to open his own store, and we lost touch. I was flying solo, trying to catch a buzz, trying to resurrect the dead, and trying my best not to fall.

It wasn't pretty and I knew it, so I started going places where no one knew me. I didn't want to talk. I wanted to be alone with my thoughts, surrounded by my ghosts, writing—sometimes in my head, sometimes in my tattered notebook—trying to find the right words to keep those I'd lost alive.

I was looking for something, but I didn't know what it was. One night after work, for no particular reason, I began walking east instead of west. I had no idea where I was going, and it didn't matter; I just kept walking. On East 7th Street between 3rd and 2nd Avenue, I found myself standing in front of two bars I'd never noticed before. I was trying to decide which one to enter when I heard a voice behind me ask, "Are you from around here? You look lost."

I turned to see a guy leaning against a parking sign. He was smiling, and something about him reminded me of Ray Bolger. Maybe in my world, at this moment, this guy was the Scarecrow and I was following the Yellow Brick Road. If I talked to him, he might be able to tell me where the Wizard was hanging out.

I tipped my hat, then grinned and answered his question.

"Yeah, I work at a guitar shop on Bleecker Street. My name's Zeke."

"Nice to meet you, Zeke. I'm Steve. What brings you around here tonight?"

"I don't know, I just starting walking and this is where I ended up. I guess I'll get a drink."

"What are you drinking?"

"Probably beer. Which of these bars do you recommend?

Steve pointed to the bar on the left. "That one has craft beers. The other one is a sports bar. I'm hanging out watching the game with a few of my friends, and one of them is a music agent. You guys probably know some of the same people. I bet you could tell some stories I'd enjoy hearing. If you want to come inside and meet him, I'll buy you a beer."

In the sports bar, Steve introduced me to Justin Bridgewater, a music agent who worked for the Agency Group. Steve was right: Justin and I spent the next hour swapping stories about musicians we both knew. When Justin asked me if I was working on any projects, I told him about the photo and mentioned that I had started writing a book about it.

Upon hearing that, Justin grinned. "You have some good stories, Zeke. You should meet my friend Marc Gerald. He heads our literary division."

It was late, and I figured this was just bar talk. "Sure, I'd like to meet Marc. Here, take this." I gave Justin a Matt Umanov guitar pick with the store's telephone number printed on it. "You can reach me there any time."

"We'll be in touch," Justin said.

I thanked Steve the Scarecrow and headed west, toward home.

Five weeks later, Justin called to set up a meeting with Marc Gerald. We met at the store, just before closing, then headed to a place nearby for beers. I liked Marc right away; he had held all sorts of interesting positions, such as editor at *True Detective Magazine*, writer/producer for *America's Most Wanted*, and head of Old School Books, a W. W. Norton publishing imprint credited with starting a resurgence in urban black literature. I told him my story and handed over the pages I had written. He said he would call me after reading them. We finished our beer and went our separate ways. I had no idea if Marc would like what I had written. If he didn't, I hoped he would want to work with me anyway.

A week after our meeting, Marc called to let me know he thought I had some raw talent, but he didn't like what I had written. He believed my story was worth telling, and he offered to help me if I was willing to start from the beginning. It was a generous offer and I accepted.

Marc took me under his wing, and I listened and learned. I spent most of my spare time writing. After three months, I handed Marc ninety pages and crossed my fingers. He thought it was good, but not good enough. At that point, Marc could have wished me well and said goodbye. I'm not sure why he didn't. Instead, he suggested I find an editor and told me to contact him when I had a rewrite to submit.

The whole thing had started to seem exhausting. I was about ready to call it a day when my daughter Caitlin asked, "If you had your choice of anyone in the world to edit your book, who would it be?"

"Poppy Z. Brite," I answered. I'd read Brite's horror novels and other work and liked the style.

"Good choice, Dad. Just so you know, these days Poppy goes by the name Billy Martin. He's a guy. You should reach out to him. Maybe he'll do it."

"Oh wow, Billy Martin, huh? OK, I might as well try," I said.

And so I reached out to Billy, who offered freelance editing services, and he agreed to help me. Yeah, the dots were connecting.

Chapter 27

Boys, Please Don't Block My Road

It was a perfect spring day in Brooklyn, the kind of day where you don't care where you're going as long as you're outside. As Cathy and I strolled along 7th Avenue, casually making our way toward Prospect Park, we paused in front of the Barnes & Noble on the corner of 6th Street.

"Hey, you should see if they have the magazine," Cathy said, meaning the issue of *American Songwriter* I'd been interviewed for.

"Yeah, I guess I should. It's Robert Johnson's birthday. He would have been 104 years old today."

"That's funny. I bet they'll have it then," Cathy said with a smile.

Cathy headed downstairs to look at the latest mystery novels while I perused the music magazines. I didn't see *American Songwriter* and instead ended up leafing through the latest issue of *Guitar World*. Joan Jett was on the cover. Having satisfied my inner gearhead, I turned to walk away and noticed a small cart behind me. There was a stack of magazines on the cart's bottom shelf, and I laughed when I spotted *American Songwriter*. Caine had told me the photo of Johnson and Shines was going to appear in the magazine, but I hadn't expected to see it featured on the cover.

I bought a copy, and Cathy and I walked over to the park.

"It looks great on the cover. Are you happy?" she asked.

"Yeah, I am, but . . ."

Cathy shook her head knowingly, waiting for the inevitable.

". . . they're going to try their best to kill it this time," I said.

"You're probably right, but maybe they'll leave it alone."

"They won't. It looks too good. Check it out," I said as I opened the magazine and began flipping through the pages. "It's a great issue. They've covered all the bases, everyone from Son House to Lightnin' Hopkins. There's even a piece about female blues singers by Alynda Segarra from that band that I like, Hurray for the Riff Raff."

In the shade of an old elm tree, Cathy took a photo of me holding the copy of *American Songwriter*. I looked happy in the photo, and why not? It was a perfect day, just like the one Lou Reed sang about. I decided to relax and enjoy it, knowing it wouldn't last.

And it didn't. As I had anticipated, an attack soon followed. Within a week of the magazine's release, this Facebook post appeared on the Johnson estate's homepage, apparently written by the estate: "That's not Robert Johnson and an article debunking the photograph is about to come out signed by dozens of major blues scholars, historians, authors, academics, and performers. The 'forensic expert' who wrongly authenticated this photo also 'authenticated' another photo supposedly of Johnson and Robert Lockwood that, upon careful investigation, couldn't be any earlier than post WWII. Apparently she'll do anything for money. This 'expert' missed some very glaring errors in this photo. It is NOT Robert Johnson."

It didn't make sense. Why would the estate backhand the photo when they owned the copyright? Something was wrong. Maybe their page had been hacked. But who would do that, and why? A few names came to mind, so I surfed Facebook and I found this on Bruce Conforth's page: "Michael and everyone else, on the Real Blues Forum is a first draft of part 1 of a report I'm writing (to be signed by many others, anyone who wants to join in) debunking this stupid 3rd photo. I cite you Michael and Honeyboy, as well as many other things. I invite you all to take a look."

"Wow, really, Bruce?" I muttered. I took a sip of coffee and stared at the computer screen, weighing my options. I could fire back and battle it out online, or I could take a more diplomatic approach and send Bruce a private message. A mutual friend had told me Bruce was having health issues, and I was genuinely sorry to hear it. I reached out to Bruce by e-mail and ended my message by saying, "I hope that you heal up soon."

Bruce got back to me the next day. He said that as a member of the executive board of the Robert Johnson Blues Foundation, he had administrative rights to post on their Facebook page. It bothered me that Bruce wasn't using his own identity and that his posts looked as if they had been written by the Johnson estate. Morally it was questionable, and legally it violated my contract with the estate.

Bruce went on to explain that he was "put in charge of assembling the evidence by a large group of blues scholars who were tired of seeing what they believed to be not a photo of Johnson or Shines continuing to be presented as such." According to Bruce, "the fact that non-experts like Getty Images and Sony who just want to make a buck off the photo had accepted it" carried no weight. A report detailing all that he believed to be wrong with the photo was forthcoming, he assured me. In closing, Bruce thanked me for my concerns about his health and wished me the best.

So once again I had offended the blues police, and this time they were shooting to kill. A few days later, on May 16, Bruce posted his report on the Johnson estate's Facebook page. It was a laundry list of grievances that began with this:

A NEW ANALYSIS OF THE TWO ACCEPTED PHOTOS OF ROBERT JOHNSON AND THE ALLEGED NEW 3RD PHOTO

Does this photo show a young Robert Johnson with an equally young Johnny Shines? Much controversy has surrounded the picture since it was bought on eBay by Zeke Schein who believed it to be the legendary blues musician. Since its "discovery" the photo has been "authenticated," purchased by Getty Images for global use, accepted by the Johnson estate as legitimately depicting their ancestor, and even graces the current (May 2015) issue of the magazine American Songwriter. But is it really Robert Johnson? This collection of blues experts say "No, it isn't."

Bruce and his "experts" believed their opinion outweighed that of Robert Johnson's family and that of Caroline Shines Edwards, Johnny Shines' daughter. It seemed that nothing short of a resurrection would appease them.

In an attempt to debunk the photo, Bruce questioned its provenance. He raised doubts about whether the clothing was period correct and dwelled on the possibility that the photo had been reversed. Although

Bruce wasn't there on the night when I showed the photo to Robert Lockwood Jr. and David "Honeyboy" Edwards, he wrote definitively about their impressions of it. Bruce not only questioned the photo's authenticity; he questioned my integrity as well as the Johnson family's and Lois Gibson's.

Bruce was a contributor to *Living Blues,* so naturally many of his colleagues from the magazine cosigned the report. Among the other cosigners were an assortment of PhDs, blues writers, disc jockeys, and various others who were involved in the music business. Like me, all of them were longtime blues fans. I knew some of them personally, and I appreciated their work, but let's face it—none of their opinions was worth any more than mine.

Some of the heaviest hitters in the music world believed in the photo's authenticity. In addition, I had the Johnson and Shines families on my side, as well as the world's most successful forensic artist. I didn't want to argue publically or embarrass anyone, so I withdrew. The way I saw it, Bruce's report was based on speculation and opinion. He had failed to fire the fatal shot, so there was no reason to fight. Still, there were things I could do quietly.

I e-mailed Steven Johnson and John Kitchens, asking them to please remove Bruce's posts from the family's Facebook page. When they did, Bruce reacted by going to the media. On Saturday, May 23, 2015 a story by Alan Yuhas appeared in the *Guardian.* The headline read, "Robert Johnson photo does not show the blues legend, music experts say."

The story was an abridged rehashing of Bruce's report, but it included some tasty quotes from the "experts." In attempting to justify his actions, Bruce called the photo a joke:

> "Within the blues community the photo just got to be kind of like a joke in a sense," said Bruce Conforth, a professor of American culture at the University of Michigan. "But all these signatories, we finally all got together and said, 'Well, you know it's time for this to no longer be a joke. It's time to really put an end to this.'"

Elijah Wald accused me and the Johnson family of being motivated by greed:

"It's not about history and it's not about music," Wald said. "It's about money. I understand that everyone who finds an old painting in their attic wants to think it's a Da Vinci, but we don't tend to say, 'Yeah, you could be right!' If it's a fact that that is a picture of Robert Johnson, then it's worth a fortune."

Two unnamed forensic anthropologists from North Carolina and Italy were cited as having concerns about the shape of Johnson's earlobe. If they were so certain, why did they choose to remain anonymous? Maybe they didn't want to publicly challenge Lois Gibson, or perhaps the conclusiveness of their findings was exaggerated.

I was pleased to see a quote by John Kitchens in support of the photo's authenticity: "We thank those of you who recognize this as Robert Johnson and hope you realize the months-long process involved in authenticating the photo." This was followed by the line, "Kitchens did not immediately respond to a request for comment." I wasn't surprised by that, or by this: "Asked about the photo criticisms, Michael Johnson, grandson of Robert and a member of the Robert Johnson Foundation, said 'Oh, I have a comment,' but declined to elaborate on the record and referred an official statement to Kitchens."

I decided to follow Michael's lead and remain silent. It was best to allow John to speak for all of us.

Three days later, a story appeared on the Consequence of Sound website. It was basically a rewording of the *Guardian* article with a nastier headline: "Experts say purported photo of blues legend Robert Johnson is fake." Fake, huh? I knew from experience that when a headline like that appears on a busy website, it will soon be bouncing all over the internet. I e-mailed the story to John and waited for his reply.

A few days passed with no word from him, and another story surfaced, this time on the Texas Monthly website. It wasn't meant to be funny, but the headline made me laugh: "49 Experts Agree: That Third Photo of Robert Johnson Is Not Authentic." Cathy heard me and came over to see what was so funny.

I pointed at the computer screen.

"It's not funny," she said. "Why are you laughing?"

"Now we know how many experts it takes to change a light bulb," I replied. "One to screw it in, and forty-nine others to say it's not real."

I didn't mind being disagreed with; everyone is entitled to their opinion. What bothered me was the grandstanding and the increasing contempt that accompanied each new article. In the latest one, Elijah Wald proclaimed, "I would have thought this whole thing was kind of silly were it not the case that this really is starting to surface as a picture of Robert Johnson . . . nobody thinks the photo is [real], which is what's so funny about it." When the article's author, John Nova Lomax, pointed out that Elijah's statement wasn't exactly true and that Steve Earle, Jack White, and Johnny Depp believed the photo was real, Elijah replied, "Hogwash. Why would any of these people, none of whom ever met Johnson, be in any position to positively ID the man?"

Statements like that were getting under my skin. By Elijah's logic, he himself had no right to weigh in. Neither did Bruce Conforth, or anyone else who hadn't personally met Robert Johnson.

Elijah had plenty more to say, but what annoyed me most was this: "Wald thinks the man on the left looks more like B. B. King than Johnson. Maybe it is, maybe not." I was tired of hearing this, because I knew for a fact that it wasn't a photo of B. B. King. Frank DiGiacomo had shown the photo to B. B. King himself, who laughed when asked if he was the man in the photo. "No, it's not me," King replied. "I'm not that old."

King's response supported my research showing that the suits in the photo predated styles he had worn. King was born in 1925, fourteen years after Johnson. His suits were a later style than Johnson's, and to my eye the two men had completely different features and body types.

Over the next few days, the domino effect continued as the story spread to various music websites. On June 1, John Kitchens e-mailed to let me know why he hadn't gotten back to me. He had been away, working at a summer camp for pediatric cancer patients. "I got back today and everything seems to have blown up," John wrote. "I have messages from reporters, you, Lois Gibson, the Johnsons, etc." John's gut reaction was to ignore the naysayers and hope they would go away, but he was also working on a response in case they didn't.

Although it was easy enough to punch holes in Bruce's report, an online shootout over old hats and ties seemed like a waste of time. I suggested to John that one well-placed bullet in the form of a brief statement from the Johnson estate would suffice. By the end of June, John still hadn't released his response, and on July 1, I discovered why when I saw the Associated Press headline: "Claud Johnson, Son of Blues Singer, Dies at 83."

I was saddened by the news and I offered my condolences, knowing all too well the pain of losing a loved one.

Chapter 28

Two and Two Is Four

And then there was a period of silence. Perhaps it was out of respect for Mr. Claud, or maybe the naysayers believed they had finally killed the photo. It lasted for about six weeks, until the middle of August, when *Rolling Stone* published its list of the 100 Greatest Songwriters of All Time. Robert Johnson was included at number twenty-three, and I was glad to see they had used the third photo. A few days later, a newly expanded version of Bruce Conforth's report appeared on the website academia.edu.

I began reading it and got sucked into a black hole of academic foofaraw. It was like peeling back the layers of an overgrown Vidalia; at its core there was nothing. Bruce had created a fictitious narrative around the photo. It reminded me of a quote from one of my favorite photographers, Garry Winogrand: "There isn't a photograph in the world that has any narrative ability, any of them. They do not tell stories. They show you what something looks like to a camera. The minute you relate this thing to what was photographed, it's a lie."

That was exactly what Bruce and the others had done. They had looked at the photo and asked it to tell a story. When was it taken, and by whom? Could it have been printed in reverse? Why was the man in the photo holding a broken guitar? Upon realizing no answers could be found, they created stories about the photo, and that was the underlying problem with the report. Like most things pertaining to Robert Johnson, it was based on narrative and speculation instead of fact. While I couldn't conclusively prove the photo's authenticity, the naysayers had failed to debunk it.

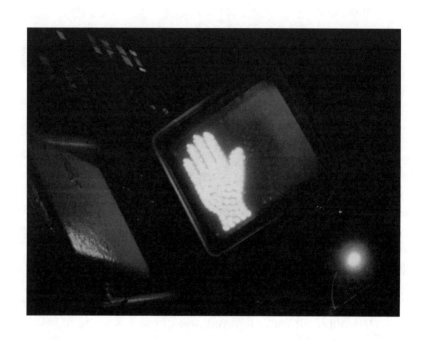

When I first spotted the photo on eBay, I had mixed feelings about bidding on it. I knew that if I won, I would soon be tilting at windmills. Some would think I was crazy, some would try to mess with me, but I saw myself as Quixote at the Crossroad. I set out on my mission with the purest of hearts and the noblest of intentions. Ten years later I was still suffering the consequences of that decision.

I have to admit it: the attacks hurt my feelings. I knew some of the report's cosigners personally, and we had friends in common. They could have reached out to me before going to the press, but they didn't even try. I mean, they all knew where I worked. They also knew I was heavily into the blues, and yet they accused me of only being in it to make a buck. After reading Bruce's report, a journalist friend of mine said, "Wow, the blues scholars really did a drive-by on you, huh?" I laughed as I imagined a sleek 1936 Terraplane screeching around the corner of 7th Avenue and Bleecker, filled with middle-aged professors yielding tommy guns. I pictured them leering at me as I swept the sidewalk outside the store. "Eat lead, blues boy" and the sputtering of gunshots would be the last sounds I'd ever hear.

Well, those and maybe a little self-satisfied snorting as they watched my blood run into the gutter.

As the summer faded to fall, the hoopla over the photo also began to fade. Six months had passed since Bruce released his report, and the Johnson estate still hadn't issued a formal statement. By December of 2015, I had given up trying to convince John Kitchens that a response was necessary. I had other things on my mind. Marc Gerald was in the process of negotiating a book deal for me and Billy. Documenting the photo's story was important to me, and I was grateful for the opportunity. It was a better use of my time than arguing about earlobes and zoot suits with blues scholars.

At the shop, the Christmas season was busy, frenetic, and kind of merry. It was also exhausting. Between working all day and writing at night, my plate was full. Occasionally I'd take a break and surf the web to see what was happening in the outside world. On December 17, a *Houston Chronicle* headline caught me by surprise: "New photo of bluesman Robert Johnson unearthed; only third photo in existence." According to Dylan Baddour, who wrote the story, "a newly analyzed photo" said to include Robert Johnson had "turned up in an antique Winthrop desk, filled with odds and ends, bought in a 2013 auction by Donald Roark, a 64-year-old retired lawyer and professor in Pensacola, Florida." The photo showed two men and two women sitting around a table. Below the photo were the names "Robert Johnson," "Caletta Craft, wife of Robert Johnson," "Estella Coleman," and "Robert Lockwood Jr."

That was pretty wild, but what really blew my mind was the next line of the story: "The identification comes from Lois Gibson, award-winning forensic artist for the Houston Police Department and professional analyst of historical photographs. She also announced identification of a Johnson photo in 2008; that one was accepted by the Johnson estate but widely contested by blues historians."

Holy Michael Corleone, Batman! I thought. *Just when I thought I was out . . . they pull me back in.* And that's what happened. By the following day, the story had spread to several websites, including American Blues Scene, Guitar Player, Inweekly, and History Buff. As expected, friends were stopping by and e-mailing to get my take on the latest photo.

To be honest, if I had found the photo in an old desk drawer, it wouldn't have occurred to me that one of the men might be Johnson. The man in question was drinking from a glass that obscured the lower half of his face. Still, Lois had given it her nod of approval, so I decided to take a closer look. The eyes and ears looked similar to Johnson's, as did the hands; however, the bridge of the nose appeared to be narrower. The man in the photo was more casually dressed than Johnson was in the other photos. His loose-fitting white shirt and pants didn't pair well with his black fedora and wingtip shoes, but the hat looked identical to the one Johnson wore in the Hooks Brothers photo, as did the shoes.

As for the identities of the other subjects, it was hard to tell. I had seen just one photo of Caletta Craft, the one from the booklet that came with the Johnson box set, and to my eye the woman in that photo bore only a vague resemblance to the woman identified as Craft in this new photo. I couldn't weigh in on the woman identified as Estella Coleman, since I had never seen a photo of her. In fact, Lois had identified the woman based on the assumption that the young man sitting next to her was Coleman's son, Robert Lockwood Jr. Oddly enough, it wasn't that big of a stretch to imagine that it might be Lockwood. To my eye, the face was a close match, but what did I know? I wasn't a forensic expert and it wasn't my place to offer an opinion. The thought made me laugh. I pictured Bruce Conforth frantically typing away at his desk, enraged by the latest offering. It was fresh meat and there was no doubt that he would soon pounce on it.

Within days, the forum dwellers had taken the bait. I watched from the sidelines as they tore into it like piranhas on a pork loin, furiously attacking Donald Roark for unearthing the cursed relic and Lois Gibson for authenticating it. Spurred on by their actions, Bruce appeared in full riot gear, firing every weapon in his arsenal of academia. The first bloodshed was at the website History Buff, where I noticed a barbarous headline: "That New 'Robert Johnson' Photo that Went Viral? It's a Total Hoax." The subheading below read, "We spoke with a blues scholar about how so many people—including us—fell for the false identification."

Bruce enumerated his problems with Roark's photo:

First, the lower half of the alleged Johnson figure's face is obscured by his hand and the glass he's holding, making his entire face unidentifiable. There's no way of knowing whether he had a cleft chin, buck teeth, or a beard. The woman identified as Craft looks nothing like the only known photo of her. And Craft died in 1932, meaning that the photo had to be taken in 1931. That would make "Johnson" 20 and "Lockwood" 16, while the two men in the photo appear older than that. Johnson didn't meet Coleman and Lockwood until some time after 1932. Further, the quartet is sitting around a table and chairs of bent-chrome design that didn't become commonly popular until after WWII. The women's clothing and strapped shoes are not 1931 vintage, nor are their eyeglasses or hairstyles, and even the Coca Cola bottle on the table is of a size that wasn't used until 1950. Finally, the photo appears to be a faded color print, not a black and white photo, and color film was not available in 1931. Kodak didn't start producing color film for cameras until 1936. There is simply no way this photo could be from 1931 or even 1932 and it clearly is not the people Gibson claims it to be.

Bruce raised some interesting points. I wasn't an expert on Coke bottles or furniture, but I knew enough about old cameras and film to see that he was wrong in his assessment of the photo itself. It was clearly a black and white print that had faded, not color as he believed.

Attached to the article was a link to a YouTube video. With the help of professor Mark Nixon and a computer facial recognition program, Bruce compared the face of the man in the newest photo to Johnson's face in the Hooks Brothers photo. I watched it, and all I can say is that it came off as an amateur effort. If this were a murder case and I was sitting on the jury, I'd trust Lois's eye on this one.

The article also mentioned that Bruce had recently debunked a guitar allegedly owned by Johnson. It didn't take a guitar expert to do that; all one had to do was compare the logos on the two headstocks. The word "Gibson" was slanted on Johnson's own 1929 L-1 and straight on the latest find. Clearly no match there. Too bad—I would have loved it to be the real deal, and I felt the same way about Donald Roark's photo. If genuine, these items were a window into Johnson's world. They could provide us with a glimpse of the man behind the myth. I suppose that's where Bruce and I differed most. As a fan of Johnson and his music, I hoped each new discovery might turn out to be real, and so I saw value in their existence where Bruce did not. At the end of the *History Buff* article, Bruce said, "No matter what we publish, there will always be mythology. There will always be people who want to believe that Robert Johnson sold his soul to the devil at the crossroads. But I think [the biography that Bruce had cowritten] will go a long way toward dispelling a lot of things. So the fact that we don't have more photographs or we don't have his guitar—I mean, those would be nice things, but what do those things themselves actually tell us? Virtually nothing."

Surprising words from a former curator of the Rock and Roll Hall of Fame.

The debate over the new photo spilled over to various websites. Bruce Conforth and Frank Matheis coauthored a particularly nasty piece called "Another Robert Johnson Photo Debunked" and posted it online at thecountryblues.com. The subheading read, "It seems like they want to make any black guy in a hat out to be Robert Johnson!" Before ripping into the latest photo, they took a few shots at the one

I'd found, claiming that it had been "thoroughly debunked" and was "now merely the subject of ridicule." If that were true, then why were they still attacking it?

I was tired of their self-congratulatory posturing, and apparently so was Donald Roark. He posted a personal response to Bruce online titled "Why the hate, Bruce?" It began: "Why the hate, Bruce? It's only a photograph. May I call you Bruce? It seems with the personal nature of your attacks on me, on Lois Gibson, on this poor photograph, that we should be on a personal basis. Even though you have never tried to contact me, never asked to see the photograph, never bothered to see what you are calling a 'total hoax.'" Roark continued:

> I am interested in the difference between a "hoax" and a "total hoax." What is that difference, if you don't mind? I suppose a "total hoax" is worse than a "hoax"? More complete, perhaps? Either would imply a deliberate fraud. Strong words, especially from someone who has never even seen what he is so lathered up about.
>
> And why the anger? You appear to be an angry and unhappy soul. Sending letters to the editor on Christmas Eve? Really? Don't you have a life of some sort? It's just a poor photograph, Bruce. Get a grip.
>
> What I am talking about, of course, is Bruce Conforth's jihad to vilify the photograph which I believe is a 1930s photograph of Robert Johnson, Robert Lockwood, Jr., Caletta Craft, and Estella Coleman. He has saturated the web with a number of allegations, which I believe need to be addressed and the real truth told.

In the body of his response, Roark went on to defend the authenticity of his photo and Lois Gibson's reputation. I found his approach funny and over the top, but he had spoken up and defended his position. I had never publicly responded to Bruce and his cohorts, because I believed that it was the Johnson estate's place to do so, not mine.

By the end of January 2016, John Kitchens still hadn't released a statement in support of the photo. Maybe he believed Bruce would eventually stop and go away. Most people would have, but not Bruce. He kept going.

In February of 2016, *Living Blues* published an article by Bruce called "The Business of Robert Johnson Fakery." It was a proclamation of Bruce's service to humanity through his vigilant efforts to debunk all things Johnson. As far as I was concerned, he had finally crossed a line. I forwarded the article to John and urged him to release a formal response. He did:

Formal Response of the Robert Johnson Estate to the 'Report' Regarding the Legitimacy of the Third Photograph

February 29, 2016, 06:17 pm

Last year, Bruce Conforth published a report which he claimed provided evidence that debunked the authenticity of the third photograph of blues legend Robert Johnson, which was discovered by Mr. Zeke Schein in 2005. There are dozens of co-producers of this report, none of whom have the credentials to make the assertions outlined in the report. They include musicians, authors, historians, a sociology professor and one forensic psychologist. The forensic psychologist, Ian McKenzie, Ph.D., may arguably have some credibility; I do not know him. I do know that all I have been able to find online about him is that he is a long-time blues enthusiast, a Big Bill Broonzy fanatic and an occasional blues musician.

Another of the "blues experts" who co-produced the report is John Tefteller, a record collector. I do not know Mr. Tefteller personally, but do question his motivation for coproducing the report. Before joining with Conforth to dispute the authenticity of the photograph, Mr. Tefteller attempted to license the photograph from Mr. Schein to use on the cover of his 2009 Blues Calendar. Mr. Schein wisely decided to work with *Vanity Fair* instead.

Additionally, Conforth references "two of the world's foremost forensic anthropological labs" as having examined the photograph and cited them as saying "there was not enough data to conclude that the photos were or were not Johnson." (Conforth Report, p. 3.) Conforth does not name the labs to which he referred and does not identify the forensic experts who came to this conclusion.

The Johnson estate did not consult with historians or musicians—it wasn't writing a book or composing a song. Instead, the estate sought out and retained Mrs. Lois Gibson, who is identified in the Conforth report as a sketch artist. Conforth fails to mention, however, that Mrs. Gibson literally wrote the book on forensic art (*Forensic Art Essentials*), that she is also "The World's Most Successful Forensic Artist" (*The Guinness Book of World Records*) and that she is a professor of forensic art at Northwestern University and the Institute of Forensic Art (Houston, TX). Mrs. Gibson is what the law refers to as a forensic expert, which is why she was hired by the Johnson estate.

With the foregoing in mind, Conforth expects his readers to disregard one of the world's leading forensic experts and to simply accept his report because he, an American Culture professor, says so. The Johnson estate stands by the only legally admissible expert evidence produced on this issue.

I do not know Bruce Conforth, nor do I personally know any of the other co-producers of the report. I wish, however, that Conforth had contacted me as he was preparing his report so that he and I could have had a meaningful discussion regarding the claims he was making. That did not happen. In April 2015, before the release of the final report, I was alerted to an online article dated March 12, 2013. The comment section was still open and had been recently active. I read the article and commented on behalf of the estate. Conforth correctly quotes me in his report, but then takes herculean leaps in his analysis of my response. For example, in his attempt to establish the Johnson family's "less-than-pure" intentions in authenticating the photograph he states: "[t]his reliance on a process that [estate attorney John] Kitchens even admitted the estate wanted to succeed ('I will not pretend that the estate did not want this photo authenticated' April 21, 2015) seems questionable." Conforth Report, p. 3. What would Conforth have expected? Perhaps he would have imagined that my conversation with Mr. Schein would have been more like the following:

Schein: My name is Zeke Schein and I have identified what I believe to be a photograph of Robert Johnson.

Kitchens: I appreciate you calling me about this. I'll send the photograph to an expert to be examined. I must tell you, though, we sure hope that it's not Robert Johnson. It would be a nightmare to find out that another photograph of one of the most influential blues and rock musicians of the 20th century has been discovered. After all, there are already two photographs out there. A third would simply be too many.

Such an approach would have been ludicrous. Yes, the Johnson estate wanted the photograph to be authenticated. It did not, however, simply rely on Mr. Schein's belief that the man in the photograph was Johnson. Doing so would have certainly been the easier route. The estate wanted to *know* whether the man was Johnson and all of its actions were geared towards acquiring that knowledge.

It was the estate's desire that the allegations leveled in Conforth's report would fade into the background. Unfortunately, that has not happened and, most recently, Conforth was published in the February 2016 edition of *Living Blues* magazine, a publication to which he is a regular contributor. Because he has not and apparently will not go away, this formal response was required.

In addition to the lack of expert support for his position, there are plenty of holes in Conforth's report. For example, Conforth cites as "evidence" his argument that Johnson wouldn't wear or even have available to him the zoot suit he is wearing in the photo discovered by Mr. Schein, especially considering the "very conventional suit [he wore] in the genuine Hooks Brothers' photo." (Conforth Report, p. 6.) Had Conforth called me before publishing his report, I would have told him that Johnson did not buy the "very conventional suit" worn in the Hooks Brothers photo. That suit had belonged to his nephew, Lewis. Lewis gave Johnson the suit just before he (Lewis) was shipped off by the Navy. This information was given to Mr. Stephen LaVere by Johnson's half-sister Carrie Thompson and testified to under oath by Mr. LaVere during a deposition in 2009. I would have also told Conforth that Johnson's second-hand suit was tailored by a Jewish man on Beale Street in Memphis; this tailor also made zoot suits. This information was given to me by Annye Anderson, Carrie Thompson's half-sister, during her deposition in 2009.

Finally, Conforth, when providing his "credentials" at the conclusion of his report, states that he is an Executive Board Member of the Robert Johnson Blues Foundation. A similar claim is made at the end of his article in this month's *Living Blues* article, except he says he sits on the executive board of the Robert Johnson Foundation (he excludes "blues"). Although the Estate of Robert Johnson and the Robert Johnson Blues Foundation are separate entities, I represent both of them. **Bruce Conforth is not, nor has he ever been, a member of the executive board of the Robert Johnson Blues Foundation.**

Chapter 29
Deep Down in This Connection

"So what's going on with the book?"

"I'm writing the last chapter now."

I was talking to Todd Lefkovic, who owns Foods of New York Tours, a business he started in 1999 to help tourists learn about our city's history while sampling the best of the local cuisine. Besides food, Todd's really into music. He's a friend and when we bump into each other, we usually stop and talk.

"Wow, so you're almost finished. I remember when you first told me you were thinking about writing a book. How long ago was that? Almost three years ago, right?"

"Right."

"And when I asked where you were even going to start, you told me a story about Patti Smith and I said, yes! And to find out now that you're almost finished is super cool."

"Thanks, I hope people will like it. I really tried to capture the feel of the neighborhood, but it was hard because so many of the old places are gone."

"I know, it's changing. The only new stores coming to Bleecker Street are places that serve food and drinks. They're the only ones who think they can make it. Even Bleecker Street Records is gone, and they'd been in that space for decades."

"Yeah, I know," I said. "I can't believe it's a Starbucks now."

It was sad how much the Village had changed since I first started working at the store. The magic was fading, but there was still music to be heard.

"What's going on in the clubs?" I asked Todd. "Anything good?"

"The only places I go to are Caffe Vivaldi, Terra Blues, City Winery,

and 55 Bar. All the other good ones are gone—CBGB, Mondo Cane, Mondo Perso, Manny's Car Wash, Chicago Blues. I remember seeing some great shows at the Bottom Line years ago."

I shook my head in commiseration. "Yeah, me too."

"It's funny how Vivaldi hasn't changed at all," Todd said with a laugh, "except did you notice they moved the piano to the other side of the room for a while? And then they moved it back."

"Yeah, I saw that. I don't think I could perform there with the piano on the other side. I'd feel like I was in California or something, with the ocean on the wrong side. It would mess with my sense of gravity."

"Only you would say that." Todd smiled at me. "You know, what I love most about Vivaldi is that singer/songwriters go there to perform, and whether they're great or not, they feel appreciated. And Ishrat is a guy who's trying to keep it all together. He's fighting with his landlord, and it's been a struggle. He's trying to keep it so people don't have to pay to get in, and personally I think he should charge admission, because he's not making enough money. It would change the feel, but it's either charge a cover and stay in business or don't and go under. But I think Ishrat's doing a good job."

"Yeah, me too," I said. "I used to run into Dave Van Ronk there all the time. He'd be drinking coffee with Chris Lowe, reading the paper, and talking politics. Dave would have a field day with what's going on right now."

"I bet he would. So what about you—seen any good shows lately?"

"I haven't been going out much. I stopped drinking about a year and a half ago, and right around that time, Ronnie Earl came by the store. I'd met Ronnie ages ago through John Campbell. He was cool then, but he seemed way more together now. When I mentioned that, he said, 'It's probably because I've been sober for the past twenty-six years.' After hearing that, I remember looking down at my feet and saying, 'It's been four months for me.' And then Ronnie looked me in the eye and asked me for my phone number. 'I'm going to call you. Let's keep in touch.' We connected, and he still calls to check up on me."

"Wow, that's great."

"Yeah, it helps. So the last show I saw was when Ronnie invited me and Cathy to see him play at B. B. King's. He told me to bring my guitar if I wanted to sit in with the band."

"Did you do it?"

"I didn't bring my guitar, but I did end up playing. During the show, Ronnie came to our table and played for us, and then he handed me his white Strat and asked me to join him onstage. I love Ronnie, so I got up and played a song with him. At the end of the set, he and Diane Blue played Robert Johnson's 'Malted Milk' and dedicated it to me and Cathy. It was sweet."

"So you played onstage at B. B. King's with Ronnie Earl." Todd grinned approvingly. "Were you nervous at all?"

"Yeah, at first, but what freaked me out the most was playing a white Strat."

"Really? Why's that?"

"When you see a white Strat, who's the first person that comes to mind?"

"Jimi Hendrix . . . at Woodstock."

"Right, so that's the first reason. I can't play like Hendrix. Nobody can."

"I see your point. What's the second reason?"

"OK, there was a guy who came to the store one Christmas Eve, just before closing. A quiet, normal-looking guy who said he wanted to buy a guitar for Jesus. What guitar do you think he bought?"

"Let me guess, a white Strat. Was it made in America?"

"No, Mexico. And now every time I see a white Strat, I picture that guy giving it to Jesus . . . and I can't play like Jesus."

"Nobody can," Todd laughed.

"Nobody except Jimi Hendrix."

"You know, I have a crazy story too. These days I'm always in the office, but back when I used to conduct food tours, this girl from Germany asked me if I wanted to hook up with her after the tour."

"Yeah, and . . ."

"And she asked me if I was into feet."

"OK."

"And her feet were filthy!"

Todd started laughing, and so did I. People walking by probably wondered what was so funny. If they had asked I would have told them: a Fraulein with filthy feet and a foot fetish.

When we stopped laughing, I said, "Yeah, dealing with the public is a trip. Do you ever miss it?"

"Some days I miss it. When I was out doing tours, I met cool people from all over the world. I liked talking to them."

"Sometimes I wonder what I'll do when I'm not right in the middle of it."

"When you're not here, you'll be bored out of your mind."

I nodded. "You might be right."

"You need the human interaction, man."

"I guess we both do."

"Oh yeah. Honestly, Zeke, I went to California for two weeks while my apartment was being renovated. I stayed at my friend's house on top of a mountain in Big Sur. After a week, I missed New York. I couldn't take a walk and just go out to a coffee shop. If we needed something, we had to get into a car and drive. I couldn't live like that."

"You know, I feel the same way. When I travel, I don't like being away for too long. I miss the energy of New York."

"I understand. When I came home from Big Sur, as soon as I hit the West 4th Street subway station, I felt rejuvenated. And when I got back onto that sidewalk and saw the IFC movie theater, it was like, Daddy, I'm home."

"I can relate. That's partly how I've remained working in the same spot for so long. I sat at the front counter of Matt Umanov Guitars, and the world walked through that door."

"That's not a bad line. You should put it in the book."

"Maybe I will."

"So you're almost finished. Do you know how it ends?"

"Yeah, I've been thinking about it for a long time. We don't really know much about Robert Johnson. I feel like I spent the last ten years of my life chasing a phantom. The more research I did, the less I knew, because it's hard to prove anything about Johnson. It's a series of dead ends. We have his music and a few photos, and there are those who argue that none of the photos show the man who made the recordings."

"Wow, that's crazy."

"It is. A researcher named Mack McCormack died last November. Years ago, he began writing a book called *Biography of a Phantom*. It was going to be the definitive account of Johnson's life, but Mack aborted it.

"How come?"

"He began to have doubts about his own evidence."

"So your book doesn't end with you proving the photo is authentic."
I shook my head.

"So what did you come up with instead?"

"Well, over a million people saw the photo online, and it created controversy because people still care about Robert Johnson. He may not have been popular in his own time, but he affected so many creative people I've known. I've been lucky to witness it firsthand when they bought guitars from me. They all saw a piece of themselves in Johnson. Bob Dylan and Steve Earle saw a brilliant songwriter. Jack White and Johnny Depp saw a handsome, charismatic performer. Patti Smith saw a masterful poet. Elvis Costello saw a skilled vaudevillian. David Blaine saw a sure-handed magician. Sam Shepard and Billy Gibbons saw mojo incarnate. John Hammond, Marc Ribot, and Bill Frisell saw a guitar virtuoso. You get my point, right?"

"Sure, and I have to ask, what did you see?"

"I saw a man who believed in possibility, like I do. Last week, after a rainstorm, Cathy and I came across a tiger swallowtail resting on a flower. It was ethereal and Cathy wanted to take its photo but she was afraid that if she got too close, the butterfly might fly away. I asked her to hand me her camera and I carefully approached the butterfly. When I got within inches of it, I shot its photo. After that, Cathy did the same and both of our photos turned out beautifully. It's all about suspending your disbelief and seeing possibility. I learned that from Robert Johnson."

As I parted ways with Todd and walked back toward the store, I thought more about our photographs of the swallowtail. A butterfly lives for only a few days, delicate and fragile. Winging through our lives for a few moments, it seems little more than a colorful phantom. A photo can freeze those moments for us, but the creature itself is still gone from this world in a heartbeat. If it has the chance to reproduce, though, the spots on its wings may live on for generations. Insects can only reproduce themselves, but people can reproduce ideas and communicate them to others through art: painting, music, words. Robert Johnson may seem a phantom to us now, but in his time he was a man who breathed and drank and sang. As well, he communicated ideas that continue to live and enrich music across its genres. The spots on his wings are still visible. For those who care to see it, I hope I have managed to offer one more glimpse of the phantom.

Acknowledgments

Thanks to Marc Gerald, Poppy Z. Brite, Nina Kooij, Cathy and Caitlin Schein, Desmond Beirne, Erin Classen, Antoinette de Alteriis, Dion DiMucci, Patti Smith, Steve Earle, John Hammond, Citizen Cope, and all who helped me. Heaven knows I needed it.

—Z. S.

Thanks to Grey Cross, who kept me marginally sane, Etsy and candlework clients, who kept me marginally afloat, and Zeke, who hoodoo'd me into this project.

—P. Z. B.

Notes

Chapter 1: Down by the Highway Side

"Man don't never knock . . .": LaVere, Stephen. Liner notes to *Robert Johnson: The Complete Recordings*, Columbia, 1990.

Chapter 3: Return Again

"It was in Friar's Point . . .": Palmer, Robert. *Deep Blues*. New York: Viking, 1981. Print.

"It was a totally different way . . .": Richards, Keith and James Fox. *Life*, Little, Brown and Company, 2010.

"Well, hell let's name . . .": Altschuler, Glenn C. *All Shook Up: How Rock 'n' Roll Changed America*. Oxford: Oxford University Press, 2003. Print.

"If I hadn't heard . . .": Dylan, Bob. *Chronicles: Volume One*. New York: Simon & Schuster, 2004. Print.

"Brian Jones had . . .": LaVere, Stephen. Liner notes to *Robert Johnson: The Complete Recordings*, Columbia, 1990.

"He had gotten fired . . .": "John Hammond Speaks about Jimi Hendrix." Private YouTube video. Posted by Fret12Admin, 2009. Accessed October 1, 2016.

"The next day Eric Clapton . . .": Ibid.

"*Led Zep II* was . . .": Williamson, Nigel. "Good Times . . . Bad Times," *Uncut*, May 2005.

Chapter 4: Mojo

"Take a scorpion . . .": Haskins, James. *Voodoo & Hoodoo: Their Tradition and Craft as Revealed by Actual Practitioners*. New York: Stein and Day, 1978. Print.

Chapter 5: The Stuff I Got

"From courtly musicians serenading . . .": Museum of Musical Instruments. "The MoMI.org Presents Dangerous Curves: The Art of the Guitar—Exhibition

Road Map." Accessed March 13, 2017. http://themomi.org/museum/mfa/index.html.

"My goal always has been . . .": Gruhn, George. "Chinery's Guitars: America's Foremost Vintage Collection." http://www.marksimonguitars.com/vgm95.html. The original article appeared in *Vintage Guitar* magazine, January 1995.

Chapter 6: Played It on the Sofa

"If you want to learn . . .": Evans, David. *Tommy Johnson*. London: Studio Vista, 1971. Print.

"So when we'd get a rest . . .": Conforth, Bruce. "Ike Zimmerman: The X in Robert Johnson's Crossroads," *Living Blues*, February 2008.

"He came there and lived . . .": Ibid.

"They would leave and go . . .": Ibid.

"Me and Willie, we was playing . . .": Ibid.

Chapter 8: Kind-Hearted Woman

"The silence of a falling star . . .": Williams, Hank. Sony/ATV Music Publishing LLC, Warner/Chappell Music, Inc., Universal Music Publishing Group, 1949.

Chapter 10: Ramblin'

"The first time I came to Helena . . .": Shines, Johnny. Interview, "The Search for Robert Johnson," Sony, 1992.

"I tagged along with him . . .": Obrecht, Jas. "Johnny Shines: The Complete 1989 Living Blues Interview." http://jasobrecht.com/johnny-shines-complete-living-blues-interview/.

"It was pretty rough . . .": Neff, Robert, and Anthony Connor. *The Blues: In Images and Interviews*. New York: Cooper Square, 1999. Print.

"He'd hear something . . .": Shines, Johnny. Interview, "The Search for Robert Johnson," Sony 1992.

"A very nice guy . . .": Ibid.

"No, no, no . . .": Obrecht, Jas. "Johnny Shines: The Complete 1989 Living Blues Interview." http://jasobrecht.com/johnny-shines-complete-living-blues-interview/.

"I had to be at that there crossroads . . .": Coen, Joel and Ethan. *O Brother, Where Art Thou?* Touchstone Pictures, 2000.

Chapter 13: What Evil Has the Poor Girl Heard?

"Her near-death experience . . .": Gibson, Lois, and Deanie Francis Mills. *Faces of Evil: Kidnappers, Murderers, Rapists and the Forensic Artist Who Puts Them Behind Bars*. Liberty Corner, NJ: New Horizon, 2005. Print.

"He was fighting . . .": Ibid.

"That feeling . . .": Ibid.

Chapter 15: Last Fair Deal Gone Down
"If you cry about a nickel . . .": Johnson, Robert. "Last Fair Deal Gone Down." King of Spades Music, 1990.

"Listen, this jass thing . . .": Maistros, Louis. *The Sound of Building Coffins.* New Milford, CT: Toby, 2009. Print.

Chapter 16: Come on in My Kitchen
"A medium height, wiry . . .": Driggs, Frank. Liner notes to *Robert Johnson: King of the Delta Blues*, Columbia, 1961.

"Mr. Law, I'm lonesome": Ibid.

Chapter 17: They're Red Hot
"Show almost identical feature placement": DiGiacomo, Frank. "A Disputed Robert Johnson Photo Gets the *C.S.I.* Treatment." *Vanity Fair.* October 27, 2008. http://www.vanityfair.com/culture/2008/10/a-disputed-robert-johnson-photo-gets-the-csi-treatment.

Chapter 19: Like Consumption
"How about Robert Johnson . . .": Des Barres, Pamela. "An Hour with Jack White." http://pameladesbarres.net/archive/an-hour-with-jack-white/.

Chapter 23: Long, Long Distant Land
"Well I never been to England . . .": Axton, Hoyt. "Never Been to Spain." Universal Music Publishing Group, 1971.

"Robert Johnson: rare new photograph . . .": Thorpe, Vanessa. "Robert Johnson: rare new photograph of delta blues king authenticated after eight years." *Guardian.* February 2, 2013. https://www.theguardian.com/music/2013/feb/03/robert-johnson-photograph-identified.

"The medium is the message": McLuhan, Marshall. *Understanding Media: The Extensions of Man.* New York: New American Library, 1964. Print.

Chapter 24: The Crossroad
"I went to the crossroad . . .": Johnson, Robert. "Crossroad Blues." King of Spades Music, 1990.

Chapter 26: Tell Me All About It
"Has any new information . . .": O'Rear, Caine. "The Story Behind the Robert Johnson and Johnny Shines Cover Photo." *American Songwriter.* April 16, 2015. http://americansongwriter.com/2015/04/story-behind-robert-johnson-cover-photo/.

Chapter 27: Boys, Please Don't Block My Road
"A New Analysis . . .": Conforth, Bruce. "A New Analysis of the Two Accepted Photos of Robert Johnson and the Alleged 3rd Photo." http://www.academia.

edu/13591934/A_NEW_ANALYSIS_OF_THE_TWO_ACCEPTED_PHOTOS_ OF_ROBERT_JOHNSON_AND_THE_ALLEGED_3RD_PHOTO.

"Robert Johnson photo does not show . . .": Yuhas, Alan. "Robert Johnson photo does not show the blues legend, music experts say." *Guardian.* May 23, 2015. https://www.theguardian.com/music/2015/may/23/robert-johnson-photo-does-not-show-blues-legend-music-experts-say.

"Experts say purported photo . . ." Kaye, Ben. "Experts say purported photo of blues legend Robert Johnson is fake." Consequence of Sound. May 26, 2015. http://consequenceofsound.net/2015/05/experts-say-purported-photo-of-blues-legend-robert-johnson-is-fake/.

"49 Experts Agree . . .": Lomax, John Nova. "49 Experts Agree: That Third Photo of Robert Johnson Is Not Authentic." *Texas Monthly.* May 29, 2015. http://www.texasmonthly.com/the-daily-post/49-experts-agree-that-third-photo-of-robert-johnson-is-not-authentic/.

Chapter 28: Two and Two Is Four
"There isn't a photograph in the world . . .": "Garry Winogrand." YouTube video. Posted by da Beat, March 5, 2011. Accessed October 2, 2016. https://www.youtube.com/watch?v=YQhZcKzbM9s.

"New photo of bluesman . . .": Baddour, Dylan. "New photo of bluesman Robert Johnson unearthed; only third photo in existence." *Houston Chronicle.* December 17, 2015. http://www.chron.com/entertainment/music/article/New-photo-of-bluesman-Robert-Johnson-unearthed-6703035.php.

"That New 'Robert Johnson' Photo . . .": Wazer, Caroline. "That New 'Robert Johnson' Photo that Went Viral? It's a Total Hoax." History Buff. January 5, 2016. http://historybuff.com/that-new-robert-johnson-photo-we-shared-last-month-its-a-total-hoax-ZrYRD6KNqmp9.

"Another Robert Johnson Photo Debunked": Matheis, Frank and Conforth, Bruce. "Another Robert Johnson Photo Debunked." The Country Blues. http://www.thecountryblues.com/op-ed/another-robert-johnson-photo-debunked/.

"Why the hate, Bruce?": Roark, Donald. "Why the hate, Bruce?" http://inweekly.net/wordpress/wp-content/uploads/2016/01/Why-the-hate.pdf.

"Formal Response of the Robert Johnson Estate . . .": Kitchens, John. "Formal Response of the Robert Johnson Estate to the 'Report' Regarding the Legitimacy of the Third Photograph." Robert Johnson Blues Foundation. February 29, 2016. http://www.robertjohnsonbluesfoundation.org/news/formal-response-of-the-robert-johnson-estate-to-the-report-regarding-the-legitimacy-of-the-third-photograph/.

Bibliography

Altschuler, Glenn C. *All Shook Up: How Rock 'n' Roll Changed America*. Oxford: Oxford University Press, 2003. Print.

Axton, Hoyt. "Never Been to Spain." Universal Music Publishing Group, 1971.

Baddour, Dylan. "New photo of bluesman Robert Johnson unearthed; only third photo in existence." *Houston Chronicle*. December 17, 2015. http://www.chron.com/entertainment/music/article/New-photo-of-bluesman-Robert-Johnson-unearthed-6703035.php.

Billman, Pete, and Dave Rubin. *Robert Johnson: The New Transcriptions*. Milwaukee: Hal Leonard, 1998. Print

Charters, Samuel. *The Country Blues*. New York: Da Capo, 1975. Print.

Coen, Joel and Ethan Coen. *O Brother, Where Art Thou?* Touchstone Pictures, 2000.

Conforth, Bruce. "A New Analysis of the Two Accepted Photos of Robert Johnson and the Alleged 3rd Photo." http://www.academia.edu/13591934/A_NEW_ANALYSIS_OF_THE_TWO_ACCEPTED_PHOTOS_OF_ROBERT_JOHNSON_AND_THE_ALLEGED_3RD_PHOTO.

Conforth, Bruce. "Ike Zimmerman: The X in Robert Johnson's Crossroads." *Living Blues*, February 2008.

Des Barres, Pamela. "An Hour with Jack White." http://pameladesbarres.net/archive/an-hour-with-jack-white/.

DiGiacomo, Frank. "A Disputed Robert Johnson Photo Gets the *C.S.I.* Treatment." *Vanity Fair*, October 27, 2008. http://www.vanityfair.com/culture/2008/10/a-disputed-robert-johnson-photo-gets-the-csi-treatment.

Driggs, Frank. Liner notes to *Robert Johnson: King of the Delta Blues*. Columbia, 1961.

Dylan, Bob. *Chronicles: Volume One*. New York: Simon & Schuster, 2004. Print.

Evans, David. *Tommy Johnson*. London: Studio Vista, 1971. Print.

"Garry Winogrand." YouTube video. Posted by da Beat, March 5, 2011. Accessed

October 2, 2016. https://www.youtube.com/watch?v = YQhZcKzbM9s.

Gibson, Lois, and Deanie Francis Mills. *Faces of Evil: Kidnappers, Murderers, Rapists and the Forensic Artist Who Puts Them Behind Bars*. Liberty Corner, NJ: New Horizon, 2005. Print.

Greenberg, Alan. *Love in Vain: A Vision of Robert Johnson*. New York: Da Capo, 1994. Print.

Guralnick, Peter. *Searching for Robert Johnson*. New York: Dutton, 1989. Print.

Haskins, James. *Voodoo & Hoodoo: Their Tradition and Craft as Revealed by Actual Practitioners*. New York: Stein and Day, 1978. Print.

"John Hammond Speaks about Jimi Hendrix." Private YouTube video. Posted by Fret12Admin, 2009. Accessed October 1, 2016.

Johnson, Robert. "Crossroad Blues." King of Spades Music, 1990.

Johnson, Robert. "Last Fair Deal Gone Down." King of Spades Music, 1990.

Kaye, Ben. "Experts say purported photo of blues legend Robert Johnson is fake." Consequence of Sound, May 26, 2015. http://consequenceofsound. net/2015/05/experts-say-purported-photo-of-blues-legend-robert-johnson-is-fake/.

Kitchens, John. "Formal Response of the Robert Johnson Estate to the 'Report' Regarding the Legitimacy of the Third Photograph." Robert Johnson Blues Foundation. February 29, 2016. http://www.robertjohnsonbluesfoundation. org/news/formal-response-of-the-robert-johnson-estate-to-the-report-regarding-the-legitimacy-of-the-third-photograph/.

Komara, Edward M. *The Road to Robert Johnson: The Genesis and Evolution of Blues in the Delta from the Late 1800s through 1938*. Milwaukee: Hal Leonard, 2007. Print.

LaVere, Stephen. Liner notes to *Robert Johnson: The Complete Recordings*. Columbia, 1990.

Lomax, John Nova. "49 Experts Agree: That Third Photo of Robert Johnson Is Not Authentic." *Texas Monthly*. May 29, 2015. http://www.texasmonthly. com/the-daily-post/49-experts-agree-that-third-photo-of-robert-johnson-is-not-authentic/.

Maistros, Louis. *The Sound of Building Coffins*. New Milford, CT: Toby, 2009. Print.

Marcus, Greil. *Mystery Train: Images of America in Rock 'n' Roll Music*. New York: E.P. Dutton, 1975. Print.

Marquis, Donald M. *In Search of Buddy Bolden: First Man of Jazz*. Baton Rouge: Louisiana State University Press, 1998. Print.

Matheis, Frank and Bruce Conforth. "Another Robert Johnson Photo Debunked." The Country Blues. http://www.thecountryblues.com/op-ed/another-robert-johnson-photo-debunked/.

McLuhan, Marshall. *Understanding Media: The Extensions of Man*. New York: New American Library, 1964. Print.

Milward, John. *Crossroads: How the Blues Shaped Rock 'n' Roll (and Rock Saved the Blues)*. Boston: Northeastern University Press, 2013. Print.

Neff, Robert, and Anthony Connor. *The Blues: In Images and Interviews*. New York: Cooper Square, 1999. Print.

Obrecht, Jas. "Johnny Shines: The Complete 1989 Living Blues Interview." http://jasobrecht.com/johnny-shines-complete-living-blues-interview/.

Ondaatje, Michael. *Coming Through Slaughter*. New York: Norton, 1976. Print.

O'Rear, Caine. "The Story Behind the Robert Johnson and Johnny Shines Cover Photo." *American Songwriter*, April 16, 2015. http://americansongwriter.com/2015/04/story-behind-robert-johnson-cover-photo/.

Palmer, Robert. *Deep Blues*. New York: Viking, 1981. Print.

Pearson, Barry Lee and Bill McCulloch. *Robert Johnson: Lost and Found*. Urbana: University of Illinois Press, 2003. Print.

Richards, Keith, and James Fox. *Life*. New York: Little, Brown and Company, 2010. Print.

Roark, Donald. "Why the hate, Bruce?" http://inweekly.net/wordpress/wp-content/uploads/2016/01/Why-the-hate.pdf.

Schroeder, Patricia R. *Robert Johnson, Mythmaking, and Contemporary American Culture*. N.p., n.d. Print.

Shines, Johnny. Interview, "The Search for Robert Johnson." Sony, 1992.

Thorpe, Vanessa. "Robert Johnson: rare new photograph of delta blues king authenticated after eight years." *Guardian*, February 2, 2013. https://www.theguardian.com/music/2013/feb/03/robert-johnson-photograph-identified.

Waterman, Dick. *Between Midnight and Day: The Last Unpublished Blues Archive*. New York: Thunder's Mouth, 2003. Print.

Wazer, Caroline. "That New 'Robert Johnson' Photo that Went Viral? It's a Total Hoax." History Buff, January 5, 2016. http://historybuff.com/that-new-robert-johnson-photo-we-shared-last-month-its-a-total-hoax-ZrYRD6KNqmp9.

Williams, Hank. Sony/ATV Music Publishing LLC, Warner/Chappell Music, Inc., Universal Music Publishing Group, 1949.

Williamson, Nigel. "Good Times . . . Bad Times." *Uncut*, May 2005.

Yuhas, Alan. "Robert Johnson photo does not show the blues legend, music experts say." *Guardian*, May 23, 2015. https://www.theguardian.com/music/2015/may/23/robert-johnson-photo-does-not-show-blues-legend-music-experts-say.